IF WISHES WERE
HORSES

IF WISHES WERE HORSES

W.P. KINSELLA

HarperPerennial
HarperCollins*Publishers*Ltd

http://www.harpercollins.com/canada

First published in hardcover by HarperCollins Publishers Ltd: 1996
First HarperPerennial edition: 1997

Canadian Cataloguing in Publication Data

Kinsella, W.P.
    If wishes were horses

1st HarperPerennial ed.
ISBN 0-00-648114-0

I Title.

PS8571.I57I35 1997   C813'.54   C97-930344-3
PR9199.3.K56I35 1997

97 98 99 ❖ HC 10 9 8 7 6 5 4 3 2 1

Printed and bound in the United States

For Barbara Turner

SECTION ONE

HEARTLAND

They say it can't be done,
but sometimes it doesn't always work.

— Casey Stengel

ONE

RAY KINSELLA

THIS MORNING I RECEIVED A TELEPHONE CALL from a man on the FBI's 10 Most Wanted List. Annie handed me the phone as I walked in the back door of our farmhouse, my shoes covered in early morning dew. The odors of morning trailed me into the kitchen, which is warm as a comforter and exudes its own odors: coffee, toast, cinnamon, frying bacon.

"This is Joe McCoy," the thin, rather nervous voice said. "Do you know who I am?"

"Everyone with a television set knows who you are," I replied.

"I'm not far away," McCoy said.

"I'm not sure I want to hear this . . ."

"Listen, don't believe everything you see on television or read in the newspapers. Events don't always happen the way they're reported. Especially not the way they're reported."

"I understand that. But what do you want from me?"

"I've heard rumors about unusual goings-on at your farm, that you have a complete baseball field in your back yard, that all kinds of people from all over the world visit your farm every summer. I've heard that weird things happen out there at night, that there are long-dead ballplayers . . ."

"Mostly true," I said. "It's no secret from anyone who wants to know. I didn't know you'd kept in touch with events in this part of the world."

"I'm calling you as a sort of last resort. I was hoping we might have something in common."

"If you want to know the truth," I said, choosing my words carefully, "though I know you only by reputation, I've always thought you were . . ." and I fumble for the exact words I want, "kind of irresponsible. And in light of your recent exploits I honestly can't see any reason to change my opinion."

"Then you don't know anything about my other life?"

There was a note of desperation in his voice.

"Other life?"

"My other life is one of the things I was hoping I could discuss with you. I know this sounds weird, but I think I may never have left this part of the world. I haven't had a byline in the *Iowa City Press Citizen* recently, have I?"

I could sense his confusion. I could see him tucked into an aluminum-and-glass telephone booth at a truck stop out on I-80. He would have had to get my number from Information, for there isn't a phone booth in America that has a phone book in it.

I laughed off his question, though I could tell it was asked seriously. I was slightly taken aback to find that Joe McCoy had, in a very few seconds, made me identify with him. Though it's been several years, it seems like only moments since I was going through some very mystifying times myself. I have a long memory where mystifying events are concerned.

"Some people who visit my baseball field see more than others," I said. "But I have nothing to do with bringing people here. Those who come are like pilgrims, they've been drawn by something within themselves."

"I see. Look, if you'll give me a minute, I'm going to try to explain a couple of things, because you're the only person who might not think I'm crazy. Have you ever heard the expression, 'Things are out of kilter in Johnson County'? It's something my mother used to say."

"My wife uses it, her family have been here for generations. I actually looked it up once, *kilter* means *in good condition*. So *out of kilter* means that things are not in good condition, though there are more sinister interpretations having to do with death and otherworldliness."

He took a deep breath. I could hear a rumbling behind him, like eighteen-wheelers groaning into traffic.

"I think someone—something—is playing a really nasty trick on me. I believe things are out of kilter in Johnson County, and, for whatever reasons, that out-of-kilterness has followed me like tin cans behind a wedding car."

Across the room, Annie used one hand to pass our daughter Karin a brown-bagged lunch, while she poured coffee for us with the other. I could hear the twins, smaller versions of Karin and Annie, rattling about in the dining room. I stretched the cord from the wall phone, pulling its whiteness taut as a baseline, until I was able able to sit at the kitchen table. If I let go of the receiver it would slam against the wall as if propelled from a slingshot.

"Did you hear me?" asked Joe McCoy.

"I'm thinking," I replied.

And I was. Joe McCoy's words struck a very strong chord with me. I remembered how I had felt when, during one sweet, soft Iowa sunset, a voice said to me, "If you build it, he will come," and I knew instinctively that I was meant to build a baseball diamond in my cornfield.

"Did someone tell you to do all the things you've done in the past few weeks?" I asked. "Have you been following instructions?"

"Not exactly. But no one's told me *not* to do what I've done. The thing is, no matter what the newspapers, especially the tabloids, say about me, nothing I've done has been in character."

I had never acted irresponsibly until I heard the voice. I had been unsuccessful, yes, but not deliberately irresponsible. If inexplicable events could happen to me they could happen to someone else whose roots were in Johnson County, Iowa.

"Are you telling me you're innocent? You didn't kidnap a baby? You're not on the run? You didn't hijack . . . ?"

"Not exactly. It's a long story."

"And you want to tell it to me?"

"I'd like to."

Karin, smelling like fresh ironing, kisses me on the cheek and bounds out the door, the screen slamming like a shot after her. Karin has her mother's red hair, green eyes, and ten million freckles.

"I don't think you should come out here," I said, not wanting the perfection of my life threatened.

"I don't intend to. I'm . . . I'm grasping at straws. I heard that unusual things happened with time out there . . . at your farm. Things concerning baseball . . . I played baseball, you know. Major-league baseball."

"I know."

"Will you meet me in town? In Iowa City?"

I watched Karin skip off toward the road and the school bus. Yogi Berra, her brindle cat, walked after her in stately procession, his tail raised straight in the air like a beacon, knowing that his advanced age wouldn't permit him to keep up with her, but if the bus were even a half-minute late, Yogi would arrive at the road in time to be petted before Karin left for the day.

"Where?"

"Pearson's Drug Store. The soda fountain."

"That's an awfully public place. You're a fugitive. You're known in this area. You come from Lone Tree, don't you?"

"Ray, one of the reasons I know something is out of sync, is that even though I'm at the top of the Most Wanted List, even though there are rewards for my capture that must total a half-million dollars, even though my picture has been on TV at least once a day for weeks and weeks, I don't think I could get arrested if I walked into a police station with a sign around my neck saying, 'Check the 10 Most Wanted List! I'm Joe McCoy!' If I did, someone at the police station would create a diversion, and eventually I'd get thrown out for loitering. I get the impression that either I'm invisible or every cop in the United States is dumber than a duffel bag."

"Pearson's in an hour," I said.

"I'm going to invite someone else, if that's all right?"

"Who?"

"I'd rather not say."

"Then how can I approve or disapprove?"

"You can't."

"Pearson's in an hour." I hung up.

"Who?" asked Annie, plunking herself and a cup of coffee down at the table. "Whew! It's gonna be a hot one," and she wiped her red curls back off her forehead.

"Joe McCoy," I said.

"You're gonna meet *him* at Pearson's?"

I nodded.

"But he's wanted for everything except . . . I can't think of anything he isn't wanted for. What if there's a shootout?"

"There won't be."

"But why meet him? Why don't you just call the police?"

"I don't think he's really dangerous. He just wants to talk."

"You don't have to call the police. I will."

"No."

"What did he say to convince you to see him?"

"He thinks there's something odd about all the things that have happened to him lately, that he isn't exactly in control of his life."

"But what can you do for him?"

"I don't know, but if you recall, I have a little experience in not being entirely in control, and in dealing with magic . . ."

"*You* didn't kidnap a baby. Maybe he's kidnapped the girl who's traveling with him, too. What's her name? Francie Bly?"

"Annie, I took a gun when I drove off to New Hampshire looking for J.D. Salinger. And I did kidnap Jerry, though I didn't use the gun. Maybe Joe McCoy is *not* entirely in control of what's happening."

"But hasn't Joe McCoy always been kind of a troublemaker?"

"According to some."

I was surprised to hear myself defending Joe McCoy, but then I remember the opinions of neighbors, God-fearing, generous, hard-working, but unable to grasp eccentricity, watching me plow under a portion of my corn in order to build a baseball field proposed by a disembodied voice.

"Don't forget the flack we took about me building the baseball field out there."

"I'll never forget *that*!" says Annie.

"Remember when I spent the last of our savings to buy the lawn tractor? You were the only person in the world who didn't think I was crazy."

"Who said I didn't think you were crazy?"

Annie reaches across the table and squeezes my hand, the smile in her green eyes letting me know she didn't think I was crazy then, or now, in spite of what people say or think. Annie is one in a million, she is, and I hope I appreciate her enough.

I fire up my road-weary Datsun for the twenty-minute drive to Iowa City. We have a new car since the ballpark has made the farm profitable, but I prefer the Datsun. It's like traveling with an old friend, as full of memories as it is food wrappers.

TWO

GIDEON CLARKE

MISSY LIKES TO KEEP THE WINDOWS OPEN IN SUMMER. She convinced me to take a hammer and small crowbar and pry open the windows at the rear of the house, several of them for the first time in their existence. In summer, in Iowa, the humidity itself is a presence, and the fragrance of honeysuckle is like a character in a drama. As the windows were opened, a breeze moved through my home like a cool hand, and as I pried open the side windows, cross breezes soothed and purified, carrying away odors and memories, letting in what I wished might be hope.

Eventually, all the windows on both floors were freed and oiled, and Missy could raise or lower them with the tips of her fingers. And my huge old house with the iron-spiked widow's walk was airy and cool, even in breathless high July.

Missy was eating the breakfast I had made, toast and marmalade, three fried sausages, two eggs and a glass of milk, when the phone rang. I raised my hand to indicate she needn't get up, then didn't make any move to answer it myself. It is a silly game we play: who can ignore the phone longest, but still get to it before the caller hangs up.

Before Missy came to live with me after her mother, Marylyle Baron, passed away, I seldom answered the telephone. The only person I hoped might call was my long-lost wife, Sunny. But Sunny did not like telephones, had never in the years we were married, in the dozen times she disappeared for days, or weeks, or months, or now, for years, ever called me.

Missy likes an ordered world. An unanswered telephone makes her agitated, for Missy, despite her Downs' syndrome, has, in many ways, more curiosity about life than I have.

The average caller, we have discovered, hangs up after the sixth ring. This time, after the fourth ring, Missy pushed her chair back, but I made as if to stand, a quality feint, deking Missy into sitting back down. The phone, the pure white of camelias, jangled a fifth time from the apple-green wall of the kitchen.

This phone is another concession to Missy's joy of living; we were walking past the phone store in Iowa City one afternoon when Missy was drawn in like metal filings to a magnet by the dazzle of multi-colored and miraculously shaped telephones. The camelia-white phone replaced the black-box table phone with a circular metal dial that had been in the house since I was a child.

I don't know who said, "Be careful, for you may get what you think you want," but it was certainly true in my case.

I labored most of my adult life to prove that information my father and I knew about a baseball league called the Iowa Baseball Confederacy was true and accurate. And, surprisingly, after a miraculous sojourn in the past, I accomplished what I had set out to do. My late father, Matthew Clarke, is now held to be one of the pioneers of American baseball research. His thesis, A Short History of the Iowa Baseball Confederacy, is considered one of the finest pieces of baseball research ever documented. But in the process of accomplishing what I thought I wanted most, I believe I lost whatever capacity I ever had for love, or at least true love, however that might be defined.

I thought when I first returned from the past (1908 to be specific) that I'd eventually be able to go back there, to take up where I left off, to somehow alter history.

I fantasized about returning to 1908 armed with nothing but a copy of The Baseball Encyclopedia, which I would use as a guide to betting on pennant races and World Series' winners. But as time passes, it appears that my excursion into the past was a once-in-a-lifetime experience. I've spent the dark of many a night walking the baseball spur on the outskirts of Iowa City, searching for the magical spot where my friend Stan Rogalski and I crossed the dimensions of time.

I've stood in the clover-smelling darkness at the end of that spur line, arms raised to the moon like some pagan warrior. I've pleaded with the night, with the voices and spirits that listened to me once. But there is only silence, only the touch of the velvet night on my arms, only the rub of the perfumed grasses on my ankles.

Sometimes I've broken the night open with the caterwauling of my horn, blasting out raucous Dixieland jazz or the ultimate sorrow of the blues. But nothing I could do would move the phantom listeners I knew were nearby in the long, black moonshadows of the abandoned rail line.

In the days when I thought of myself as a knight in shining armor, when I had a quest, it was I who reassured my life-long friend, Stan Rogalski, a career minor-league player, that he had a few more baseball games in him, that he still had a chance, albeit a slight one, of making it to the major leagues. But though I'm the one who got what he thought he wanted—the recognition that the Iowa Baseball Confederacy existed—it is Stan who has adjusted to life as I have never been able to.

When we returned from our adventure to our home town of Onamata, Stan had been cut by his team, forced into retirement, a situation that to my great surprise, he accepted. Stan didn't let his wife and brother-in-law talk him into a dead-end job with the railroad; instead he went to Onamata High School and applied for a job he was technically unqualified for, and he got it.

The baseball coach had just retired, but in order to coach baseball one had to have a teaching certificate and be able to teach health as well as physical education. But the powers that be wanted Stan to coach baseball. They forced the drivers' ed. teacher to teach health, and hired Stan as a custodian at a salary equivalent to that of a beginning teacher. It was agreed that as long as Stan coached all the boys' sports teams he didn't have to do any custodial work.

Stan has been at it for several years and is as happy as it's possible for him to be. His wife, Gloria, has supplied him with a square-built replica of himself, Stan Jr., now a toddler, and Gloria is pregnant again.

Just as children become guardians to aging parents, Stan and I, in the past year or so, have reversed roles. It is now Stan who assures me that I have something to live for, that my long-lost wife, Sunny, will return again someday. Or that I will be able to return to 1908, to Big Inning, Iowa, where Sarah will be waiting for me, and where I will be able to alter history by saving Sarah from the accidental death I know awaits her.

As the phone begins its sixth ring both Missy and I leap for it. I beat Missy by a stride and put the white receiver to my ear. Not many people phone us. We've calculated that for every call for me, there are two telephone solicitors. Missy and I have learned how to torture telephone solicitors with silence.

No matter what they are selling—magazines, travel opportunities, insurance, cookies, or cuckoo clocks—the seller's spiel can only be successful if the sellee co-operates by making acknowledging sounds at the proper moments. Missy and I listen to whatever pitch the salesperson is making, then, when they pause in their presentation for us to comment or grunt or answer a direct question, we simply stay silent.

After a long pause in which we can sometimes hear the heartbeat of the caller, the salesperson invariably says, "Are you there?"

We answer with the single word, "Yes."

The sales pitch then continues until the next pregnant pause. Followed by the next query. Followed by the next, "Yes."

Four or five pauses into the presentation the sweating, frustrated, suffering telephone solicitor succumbs to our silence, and forlornly hangs up the phone. Missy holds the record—she's kept a strangling solicitor going through seven pauses. Five is the best I've ever managed.

When the defeated sales representative hangs up, Missy and I give each other a high five, as if one of us has hit a home run. It is so much more fun than getting angry and hanging up.

I place the receiver to my ear. Missy is disappointed when I speak to the caller, and goes quickly back to her sausage and eggs.

"My name is Joe McCoy. Are you familiar with who I am?"

"I don't think so," I reply honestly, though the name vaguely rings a bell, a local politician or school board member, perhaps.

"I didn't think there was anyone who didn't know me," McCoy said, with what I detect as disappointment, "I've been in the news a lot lately."

"In what way?"

"I'm a criminal."

"Really?" Maybe this was a telephone solicitation after all. I could picture being victim of the first telephone armed robbery. The stranger saying, 'I'm covering you through your window with a high-powered rifle. Take all your money, your credit cards, and your cat, and drive to . . .'

"What kind of criminal?"

"Let me get to the point. I understand that you're a baseball historian. In fact I know you are. I was raised at Lone Tree. I used to play against Onamata High, though I'm quite a bit younger than you . . ."

"This is getting to the point?"

"I'm afraid I'm expressing myself very badly . . . I need to talk to you. Don't you watch television or read newspapers? If you did you'd know who I am."

"I don't, actually. I'm not much interested in the present."

I've let my subscriptions lapse. Missy watches *Wheel of Fortune*, and it's on at the same time as the national news. I've always avoided local news: trivial happenings presented in such detail and delivered with such sincerity, as if someone actually cared.

Missy loves *Wheel of Fortune*. There is something about its simplicity that appeals to her nature. She takes a folding chair and moves it closer to the television than it ought to be so she can stare right into the faces of the contestants. She laughs, and talks to them and the little man and girl who host the show. She loves the dinging sound whenever a contestant guesses a correct letter.

I don't know how much of the show Missy understands, and it doesn't really matter because it gives her pleasure. Since she came to live with me I've enrolled her in a life skills course up at Iowa City. Missy has learned to read at about a third-grade level, she can add figures, she has her own bank account. She helps me buy groceries.

"I understand if you're reluctant," McCoy continues. "I made this call in desperation. I've always thought of you as someone I could trust. I played major-league baseball for several years," he adds, hoping to hew out some common ground.

"I don't loan money to friends, let alone strangers," I say, putting distance in my voice.

"I'm not that kind of criminal. Well, actually I am. I held up a McDonald's in Los Angeles, but there was a good reason. Oh, I'm sorry. I sound crazy. I probably am."

I do recognize his name. I remember some controversy several years ago, ten or more, in which his name got yelled aloud at the local convenience store. Perhaps he threw a game or something.

"Just what is it you think I can do for you?"

"Will you meet with me?"

This *was* a telephone solicitation. It was my turn to answer a question, to acknowledge that I was still on the line. I remained silent.

"Are you still there?" asks Joe McCoy.

"Yes," I say, after another lengthy pause. Then he says the words that crack my telephone-solicitor-hating heart.

"I need to tell my story to someone who might believe me."

How many long years were there when that was exactly what I needed? Someone somewhere who would believe that the Iowa Baseball Confederacy existed, as I had always known it had. If it hadn't been for Stan's childlike belief in me . . . but suspicion toward Joe McCoy lingers like a thief.

"What do you know about me? Just tell me what you know about me." I say, a little too loudly.

"I know you weren't always considered an authority on baseball history. I remember when you were considered an oddball."

"You do?"

Now it was my turn to be surprised. In recent years I've been the only one who remembered that. Since I returned from the past, it's like the whole world has had part of its memory erased.

"Will you please meet with me? An hour is all I ask. Pearson's Drug Store in Iowa City, the soda fountain, in an hour?"

"I can be there," I say.

"I've invited someone else."

"Who?"

"Ray Kinsella."

"The fellow who built the baseball diamond that attracts tourists?"

"It's just that I feel you two have a lot in common. I'm surprised you're not close friends."

"Is *he* surprised I'm not his friend?" I say, but Joe McCoy doesn't catch the irony in my voice.

"I didn't tell him who you were."

"If you're a criminal, how can you meet me at a public place?"

"That's part of the story I want to tell you. Have you ever heard someone say their luck was so bad they couldn't get arrested?"

"Besides you?"

My tone eludes him. I've always known that politicians, clergymen, academics and accountants had no senses of humor. Perhaps I will have to add criminals and retired baseball players to the list.

"Will you meet me?" His voice rises in agitation.

"All right. Pearson's in an hour, then."

I turn to Missy.

"I have to go into Iowa City. Is there anything you want?"

Missy asks me to rent a video. She likes the movies about a little red-haired girl named Pippi Longstocking.

It will be interesting to meet Ray Kinsella. In the final days of my quest I considered contacting him. In my frustration at not being able to repeat my journey to the past I've considered visiting his farm. I've heard his baseball field has healing properties.

THREE
RAY KINSELLA

I'M GLAD JOE MCCOY HAS CHOSEN PEARSON'S as a meeting place. It is my favorite indoor spot in Iowa City. I discovered it soon after I arrived as a student, more years ago than I care to remember. Pearson's is a drug store; but at the back, dark and heavily air-conditioned, is a soda fountain, smelling deliciously of chocolate and lime, of cherry Cokes and malt.

From one of the dozen stools at the soda fountain one can watch a devilled-egg sandwich being prepared or see a chocolate malt—there are none better *anywhere*—being created by a waitress, one of whom, Doreen, has been working at the soda fountain for all the years I've been going there.

I have a habit of being early for every appointment: I arrive half an hour early to watch batting practice of a summer evening or to have a tooth filled on a depressing January afternoon. I order only coffee, but my resolve disappears quickly enough. Even though it is barely 9:30 in the morning, I order a half-sized chocolate malt, which at Pearson's is called a pony malt, a term I've encountered nowhere else.

I eat my malt slowly, dipping the straw in and licking the stiff, cement-like mixture off the end. That's the way I taught Karin, and later the twins Shannon and Crystal to love chocolate malts. When each was just old enough to accept that kind of food I would hold her in the crook of my arm and, dipping the straw in the malt, push the laden end of the straw into her mouth. Each baby would smack her lips and make wonderful gurgling noises that sounded vaguely Japanese.

The next person to arrive is Gideon Clarke. I have been watching everyone who came in, knowing I would recognize Joe McCoy, wondering who the mysterious third party could be. Gideon Clarke is a white-blond scarecrow of a fellow, tall and stoop-shouldered, who lives in Onamata, a dying town on the Iowa River a few miles south of Iowa City.

We've never spoken, but both of us patronize Pearson's regularly, and he was a denizen of the University of Iowa library all the while I was studying there. I know vaguely that he was involved in some dispute with the Department of History over a thesis his father had written in the 1940s. There was some talk he was going to sue the university because they wouldn't accept as fact what his father had written.

He must have been right all along, for a few years ago something happened, and since then he's been regarded as a baseball historian. He's given lectures at the university, though I've never attended, and I saw his picture, his long, bone-white hair combed tidily for the photograph, on the cover of *Sports Illustrated* a year or two ago.

There are three stools at the far left of the counter. I've occupied the middle one. Clarke swings a long leg over a stool near the center of the soda fountain. A group of coffee drinkers occupies the far end.

"Where's Missy today?" Doreen, the waitress, says to him. She is wearing a black uniform with a white collar.

Missy? Perhaps he has daughters, as I do, though I've never thought of him as being married. Or Missy could be a wife.

"She's at home this morning. Actually I'm here on business . . ."

"I thought it was a little early in the day. What can I get you?"

"A green river float," says Gideon Clarke.

"Sure," says Doreen. "This is usually coffee time," she says to anyone who cares to listen. "Takes a real drinker to down a green river this early."

A green river is something else unique to Pearson's, or at least to the Midwest, a sweet-tart lime drink that goes down best as a float with a baseball-sized scoop of French vanilla ice cream bobbing in the middle of it.

As she turns to work at the soda fountain I catch Gideon Clarke's eye and say, "Did you happen to get a mysterious phone call this morning?"

"Are you Ray?" he replies. "Joe . . ."

"I'm the third party, Ray Kinsella. Did he tell you there was going to be a third party?"

"He did. I've seen you here lots of times, and around town, I just never connected the name and the face," says Gideon.

"He didn't supply the third party with a name. I was just guessing. Though I know who you are, and I guessed that since all three of us have rather strong connections with baseball . . ."

Gideon moves over four or five stools until he is on the first stool around the corner. I move against the wall leaving an empty stool between us. The scene reminds me of the unwritten rule of washrooms: unless there is a crowd men leave one empty urinal between them. We shake hands. His hands are too large for his body, his skin as white as his hair.

Doreen appears with the green river float, long-handled silver spoon and straw. Doreen is about fifty with shoulder-length black hair, a long face and prominent teeth; it is a face made friendly by laugh lines acquired through years of bantering with her customers. Doreen and Lila, the other woman who works here regularly, are bossy and jovial in a motherly way; they each have several children. Doreen has a new grandson, and I, as a regular here, know of each new tooth and inoculation, while Doreen sees my Karin's report cards and monitors Shannon and Crystal's progress as three-year-old ballet dancers.

She plops the green river float and accoutrements on the counter in front of Gideon.

Norman Rockwell could have invented Pearson's, could have drawn its waitresses. "Pearson's is Iowa City," I tell Karin, almost every time I bring her here. The city expands, food and muffler franchises multiply, demolition crews chip away at history. Rows of elegant old houses are replaced by pink brick warrens that house stereo sets and university students; but Pearson's survives, a little piece of the past intact, cool, dark and chocolatey-smelling.

"Hey," says Doreen, bustling back from delivering a sandwich to the other end of the counter, "want to hear a riddle?"

"What choice do I have?" There is no choice. Doreen's riddle will be clean and simple, probably something to do with elephants.

"What's the one thing you can never do during your lifetime?"

I lick the end of my straw contemplatively. I have no idea, but I usually like to make a weak guess or two before giving up.

"Attend your own funeral?" I say finally.

Doreen snorts. "Tom Sawyer attended his own funeral. Lots of people have faked their deaths and attended their funerals."

"You're right," I say, pretending to be chagrined.

"See the back of your neck," says Gideon, stirring his green river.

"Can't you do better than that? Anyone can set up enough mirrors to see the back of their neck."

"We give up," I say.

Doreen waits a long minute before divulging the answer, savoring her triumph. "Don't care who you are, you never get to read your own autopsy report," Doreen chortles. "You can fake your funeral, but once you've been dissected like a biology-class frog, that's all she wrote. Ha!"

"I read mine," says a high-timbred voice behind us.

Gideon and I both swivel on our stools. Doreen raises her eyebrows, waiting for further explanation. There he is. He must have entered at the front, crossed the store and come down the far wall so he could sneak in behind us. He is a slight young man, with sandy hair. Too small to have been a major-league pitcher. His hands are slim and white. He doesn't look dangerous.

Doreen moves down the counter to where someone is signalling for a refill, while the three of us shake hands.

FOUR

GIDEON CLARKE

HAVING SPENT MOST OF MY LIFE BEING A RESEARCHER, instead of driving directly to Pearson's I stop first at the University of Iowa library and spend a fast fifteen minutes scanning recent issues of the L.A. *Times* and *Des Moines Register*.

Joe McCoy certainly wasn't lying about being a criminal. Reading of his exploits over the past several weeks makes me wonder how I could get so out of touch with what is happening in America. Not that anything McCoy's been doing is of great importance. He's an ex-major-league pitcher, working as a reporter in Los Angeles, who, for no apparent reason, was involved in a rather bizarre kidnapping. I vaguely remember his name—perhaps Stan has mentioned him—and I guess I knew, at least subliminally, that he grew up in Lone Tree, the next town down the line from Onamata.

McCoy looks very much as I had pictured him from the blurry mug shots in the newspapers. He is only about 5'8", wiry, with long reddish-blond hair and quick, almost furtive blue eyes. He is wearing faded jeans and sneakers, and a red-and-white satin baseball jacket, old and glazed with dirt, with LONE TREE in red, carpet-like letters on the back. He takes a long time to decide to sit on the stool between Ray Kinsella and me. He has that about-to-spring demeanor of a startled bird, the look of a second baseman caught napping on a bunt play, still at his position when he should have covered first, wishing that everyone would stop staring at him.

"The autopsy thing is true," he says. "But so routine as almost not to count. Remember that business in L.A. where they thought the body in the burned-out car was me?" He waits for a response, doesn't get one.

"You didn't read about it, did you?" he says with disappointment. "I've been away from the Midwest too long."

Ray and I remain silent. On the drive into Iowa City I had heard a song on a country station that was called, I think, "Here's a Quarter, Call Someone Who Cares." McCoy displays what seems to me a false bravado. I'm sure the autopsy thing is true. I don't like him very much.

"It's been ten years since I've been in here," he says, as Doreen takes his order for a chocolate malt made with chocolate ice cream. "I have, I had, a friend-enemy at LAPD. He let me read the autopsy report." He shrugs.

Doreen pays no attention to him as a person, it is obvious he means nothing to her, yet Doreen is one who keeps up on the news; she often asks me about local and national events I have no knowledge of. She would be aware if there was a nationally known fugitive at large who used to live at Lone Tree. She would recognize his face. But she goes to make his order without a backward glance.

While Joe and Ray talk quietly about where their paths may have crossed I remember who and what Joe McCoy reminds me of. A couple of months ago a salesman came to my door. I couldn't avoid him because I was sitting on the porch swing reading a book when he strode up the sidewalk and knocked on a porch pillar to attract my attention.

He was wearing a white shirt, black pants and tie. At first I thought he might be a Mormon missionary, but no, he was a salesman hawking encyclopedias, and since my body was warm, I was a prospect. He moved in for the kill.

He buried me in an avalanche of words. He was delivering a canned sales pitch, but even my all but ignoring him failed to deter him. He simply pretended that I had acknowledged the importance of what he was saying and crashed onward like a moose through a thicket.

I found him totally detestable. And when he finally finished his presentation, sweat running in his eyes, yards of brochures, and sample copies spread about the porch swing, the railing of the verandah, and the floor, I told him so.

"It doesn't matter what you're selling," I told him. "It could be carpet tacks, carpet itself, or a whole new interior to my house. If I like you, I'll buy any product from you that isn't totally fraudulent, and the average person will buy the fraudulent products too.

"What you've shown me this morning is a loud, self-centered, obnoxious, hot-shot salesman out to swindle a small-town rube. Now get off my property."

"But I'm not like that," the young man said. His shoulders slumped and he took a deep breath. For a second I thought he was going to cry.

"I'm not loud. I'm no more self-centered than anyone else. And I'm sure not a hot shot; I'm scared to death. I haven't made a sale in two weeks and I'm out of cash and every time I go to buy food or gas on my credit card I expect it to be seized, and I've got a wife and two babies back in Oklahoma, and the only money I've sent them this month is three cash advances I've taken on that same credit card."

That changed my opinion of the young man entirely.

"Are you selling a good product?" I asked.

"The best," he replied. "I researched it."

"Then why didn't you tell me that, instead of spewing all that foolishness designed to make me feel guilty if I don't buy? You never asked what I do. I'm a researcher of sorts. I need current geographical information, like what's the population of Houston at this minute? How far is it from Toledo to Cincinnati? Will your books have the answers to those questions?"

"Yes, sir, they will. And there's an atlas, a really good one, and a year book every year for five years with updates on current events and statistics."

We talked for another hour, not about selling but just about life in general. His name was Carsten Walgreen; his wife's name was Kitty and his daughters were Katherine Dowd and Patricia Darling.

I called to Missy and told her to change her dress, we were going to town, and the three of us drove into Iowa City. I sent Carsten to the university library to do some research for me while Missy and I came here to Pearson's for green river floats. Afterwards we met Carsten, and when he gave me the information I wanted I placed an order for fifty sets of encyclopedias. At over a thousand dollars a set, the bill, with taxes, came to over fifty-eight thousand dollars.

"You don't look rich," Carsten said, when he got over the shock. The research I'd asked him to do was to compile a list of small libraries in the eastern end of the state, fifty of them to be exact.

"I don't feel rich," I said. "My mother's second marriage was into a monied family. I inherited more than I ever dreamed. The money just sits and multiplies. I have trouble spending ten thousand dollars a year. My accountants will be happy to have such a healthy charitable deduction."

The odds, I suppose, were about even money that Carsten was a miserable little shyster, but he wasn't. He had been a university student at Norman, Oklahoma, working toward an MBA, when he got his girl-friend pregnant. They were married, but the money ran out; and his family weren't about to provide for three and eventually four. He dropped out and worked at the kind of miserable jobs a boy with three dependents and a year and a half toward an MBA can expect.

I'm jolted back to the present by Joe McCoy clapping his hands.

"I suppose you gentlemen are wondering why I've called this meeting?"

I'm tempted to say that I'm not wondering at all. I want Joe McCoy to be the boy from Tidewater, Oklahoma, with the pretty wife and daughters in white dresses, not the overzealous encyclopedia salesman intent on making an impression.

"Gideon," and he lowers his voice as he speaks, "let me begin by saying that I am on the FBI's 10 Most Wanted List."

Should I congratulate him? Offer sympathy? I glance over my shoulder toward the racks of greeting cards. Is there one that says, "Congratulations on Making the FBI's 10 Most Wanted List"?

"Well . . ." I say, not sure what to do. I don't like being entrusted with this type of information.

"If you gentlemen will bear with me I'd like to tell you my side of the story. Though you two don't seem to know each other, I believe you've each had experiences that while not totally alike, are similar enough that you might sympathize with me and be able to offer some advice on how to get out of my situation—alive and without doing a hundred years in prison."

"I've got an hour or so," says Ray.

"Why not?" I say. I owe him that much. My life was once terminally weird and I've been having some disturbing dreams lately, erotic dreams, but not about my long-lost wife or my long-lost girlfriend. I've been dreaming of kissing the pouty lips of a small blonde woman who speaks in a language I'm unfamiliar with, though it seems I can almost understand what she's saying.

Besides, Joe McCoy looks distraught enough that he might pull a gun and take us hostage if we don't let him deliver his monologue.

"Fair enough," says Joe McCoy. He dips his straw in the double chocolate malt Doreen has set in front of him. He looks uneasy, as if he doesn't know where or how to begin.

FIVE

JOE McCOY

"FAIR ENOUGH," I HEAR MYSELF SAYING. Gideon Clarke is not exactly what I'd hoped for, he and Ray Kinsella being my court of last resort, so to speak. Gideon looks at me from under his white silk eyebrows. I think he'd like to turn me in.

I play frantically with my straw, dipping the end in the thick mass, licking the chocolate off. I notice Ray eats his shake the same way.

Should I preface all this with an apology? "Look, I'm sorry, I've done what I've done," I could begin.

Here is another beginning: My name is Joe McCoy and I have lost my wife and family. I have a beautiful little girl named Charlotte, who hugs my neck and is all angel eyes and soft little kisses. I soak up her love like a sponge. I would give up my life for her, for my wife Maureen, for my baby son, Joe Jr.

At the moment all three are lost to me. I have been kidnapped and thrust into an alien dimension, where I am someone else. I am someone I don't even like very much. I am the someone else I would have been without Maureen Renn, without my roots in the quirky little town of Lone Tree, Iowa, without my passion for baseball, without my beautiful children.

The Joe McCoy I am in Los Angeles, the Joe McCoy in an open-necked white shirt, black slacks and a pair of hot-shot alligator cowboy boots, the Joe McCoy with a beeper attached to his waist, cannot be the Joe McCoy that Maureen loves. Maureen would laugh at this Joe McCoy.

"You buy those boots to compensate for a small dick?" Maureen would ask if I had the audacity to come home wearing them.

"I do not have a small dick."

"Of course you don't. And I'm the only one it matters to, and I've been happy with it for almost fifteen years and will be for another thirty, providing you lose those ridiculous boots."

"I'll drop them off at Goodwill tomorrow."

"Why not just park them under the bed for the moment, and tonight we'll pretend you're a six-foot-eight rodeo cowboy with a big dick . . ." Maureen puts her laughter aside and reaches for me, her mouth sweet and swarming. I grab a handful of her plum-colored hair, pull her even closer.

My wife Maureen is the love most men never know.

Then she's gone. The Joe McCoy even I don't like much is sitting in the newsroom late at night, trying to compose a story, wearing hot-shot alligator boots and a beeper.

What I actually say to Ray and Gideon is, "If I could live my life over, I'd pitch in the damned state tournament. I'd ruin my arm, forget about a career in baseball, attend the University of Iowa, study journalism, get a job with the *Iowa City Press Citizen*, marry my high-school sweetheart, Maureen Renn, and live happily ever after, okay? That's what I wish I'd done. But I didn't."

Well, baring my soul hasn't cleared the air any. These guys look at me as if I've spoken in Croatian.

"How long ago was this? This state tournament business?" asks Ray.

I name the year.

"Oh, well, I was working at an evil job then, selling life insurance to keep from starving. It was sort of like robbing convenience stores, only legal and less profitable. I was waiting for the girl I was going to marry to be old enough to propose to, hoping she wasn't going to run off with a brainless football player her own age. I didn't have much time to follow local sports."

"I was being thrown out of the offices of the Chicago Cubs," says Gideon. "I was writing letters, doing research, trying to find someone who would believe in the Iowa Baseball Confederacy. I didn't keep track of local sports. I was interested in bigger game."

I smile, but draw two bland, blank stares for my trouble.

When and how did my moderately orderly life, like a train gliding along, *bumpita, bumpita,* on a straight track, suddenly encounter an invisible switch and shunt without so much as a quiver onto a parallel track traversing a different and maddening country?

I have made some bad choices. Beginning in high school in Lone Tree, Iowa, through college and a mediocre baseball career, through my stint as a reporter for a major Southern California newspaper, there are so many things I wish I could change.

1. I shouldn't have refused to pitch on less than four days' rest in the Iowa State Baseball Championships.

2. I shouldn't have been so quick to abandon my high-school sweetheart, Maureen Renn.

3. I should never have shot my mouth off to *Sports Illustrated.*

4. I should never have believed my eyes that night in the desert outside Los Angeles.

After that, the list lengthens to infinity.

I was so certain the extraterrestrial story wasn't a hoax, but because of the extraterrestrial story I am unemployed and unemployable, as valuable as a stripped-down and rusting car.

I try another tack.

"Picture this, guys! Southern California. The not-too-distant past. I am thirty-one years old and living with a dental technician named Rosslyn Quinn, who is the sole source of income in our household. I have just been totally destroyed. Pounded into the ground by a herd of buffalo. Crapped on from a great height. Wile E. Coyote at the end of a cartoon. Can you guys relate to that?"

They nod. Maybe I'm getting somewhere.

"I was a reporter for a famous Southern California newspaper. Not a tabloid. We reported news. We didn't create news."

I had enough journalistic credits that the famous newspaper was not averse to hiring me. In the two years I was with the famous newspaper I was surprisingly successful, though, looking back, I think I may have overestimated both my abilities and influence. I made the age-old mistake of believing my own press clippings. As a journalist, I was a minor celebrity, something I had never been able to achieve in sports.

I have to admit I have a small flair for the dramatic and I enjoyed playing the part of a hot-shot reporter.

I started out doing person-on-the-street interviews. "What do you think we should do to achieve world peace?" "How do you feel about gun control?" In my spare time I began investigations into shady small businesses and discovered I had a unique ability to write up the results. The public loved it, and I got to feeling like Mike Wallace as I walked smiling into an office, backed up by a concealed tape recorder, ready to trap some grifter selling nonexistent graveyard plots in the desert to unsuspecting senior citizens.

What I suspect is that I've been living in two dimensions at the same time, or part time in each. Besides the frightening events that have happened to me, I believe I have received occasional glimpses of what might have been.

For instance, one night I saw myself and Maureen Renn walking down the steps of the great stone court house in Iowa City. It was late fall and the leaves were yellow, but the sun was blazing and the sky blue as tropical water. We were holding hands and had just come from getting our marriage license.

In Iowa when a couple marries, either one may take the other's name, or they may choose a neutral name. We could have become the McCoys or the Renns, or we could have decided to to be the Terwilligers or the Underwoods, or any of the billion possible names floating about. At Maureen's insistence we were going to become the McCoys.

"Don't you want to keep your own name?" I asked.

"Honey, I've been writing my name as Mrs. Joe McCoy ever since I was ten years old. Mrs. Joseph Michael Armbruster McCoy. Mrs. J.M.A. McCoy. I wasted half my school notepaper from fifth grade on practising variations of my married name, and nothing is going to take that away from me."

Maureen stopped in the middle of the long flight of stone stairs. She was wearing a yellow-and-white summer dress with white accessories; her plum-colored hair, which she usually wore straight, had been curled at the ends.

"It's not every day I get a marriage license," she had said that morning as she jumped into my car and bounced across the seat to kiss me. I was used to Maureen in jeans and a denim jacket. She was so womanly in her bright dress and white sandals with crisscross ties that rose several inches up her calves.

She stepped one stair above me so our faces were even. Then she hugged my neck and kissed me. And seeing her so happy made my heart swell with love, and I knew that marrying Maureen was right, no matter what our families or anyone else said.

Every morning, on my desk at the famous Southern California newspaper, I would find fifty phone messages alerting me to various shady business operations. Within six months I had every bait-and-switch advertiser within fifty miles of Los Angeles trembling in his suede shoes and shiny suit.

Readers loved what I was doing. One of my competitors described me a twenty-five-cent Ralph Nader, which I decided to take as a compliment. There was a rumor that A Current Affair was going to do a segment on me, that they were going to nickname me Fearless Joe McCoy.

I was just starting to snoop around the edge of organized crime, had established famous and unusual underworld contacts like Pico the Rat and Bulrush Moe, and, as any investigative reporter worth his weight in clichéd situations should, had developed an enemy on the police force: Detective Nathan Wiser, LAPD.

Then came the extraterrestrial thing. Before the extraterrestrial incident, I was an investigative reporter with a reputation for both honesty and competence. I was gathering a faithful readership. I was the senior editor's fair-haired boy. The extraterrestrial story ruined my life.

I received a telephone call from a teenage girl. Her voice was high pitched and breathless; in the background a radio blared rock music.

"You the guy does investigatey stuff?"

"Yes, I am," I said.

"McCoy?"

"Yes."

"I seen somethin' weird. I mean real weird, you know what I mean?"

"I'm familiar with weird," I said. "What exactly did you see, and where did you see it?"

"This here thing came down out of the sky. You know what I mean? We really seen it. Me and Buster."

"Buster?"

"My boyfriend. My old man, sort of, only we don't live together alla time. See, we just drove out to the desert to . . . you know, be alone. Buster parked his car, and we had this sleeping bag. We were down in this little arroyo, you know, outa sight sort of, when this thing fuckin' near lands on us. Pardon my French, but it scared us shitless . . ."

She rambled on for about five minutes. I listened intently and commented at appropriate moments. Her manner was straightforward, truthful, with a certain naivete. She put Buster on the phone. He was the strong, silent type. "Yeah," was the only word in his vocabulary. I recounted the story to him point by point, and he agreed with everything the girl had told me. Then the girl, whose name was Bertha, got on the line and told it all to me again.

I was intrigued because of the way she told the story. Here was a person who believed what she was telling me. There was probably a logical explanation, but this girl *believed*. I had taken enough hoax calls to know when someone was putting me on. I wrote down the address and drove out to see her and Buster.

Bertha lived in a dilapidated frame house in a lower-lower-class neighborhood on the edge of the desert. There were gaps between the houses like missing teeth, the bleached bodies of abandoned cars were strewn about, doorless refrigerators and freezers gleamed like patches of snow on the sand and brittle brown grasses.

Bertha was about sixteen, with a wide, pink face surrounded by lank, collar-length blonde hair. She was probably fifty pounds overweight; the top button of her jeans was undone and an inch of pink flesh showed between the jeans and the bottom of a black T-shirt that used to have glitter on the front in the shape of some rock star's face. She was barefoot, sitting at a filthy kitchen table covered with empty Pepsi bottles and full ashtrays.

We got into Buster's car, a sun-faded 1971 Ford that had been sky-blue, and drove about three miles into the desert. It was evening rush-hour on one of the hottest days of the year.

Bertha recounted her story again, yelling over the shriek of the car radio. The radio was cunningly hidden so I couldn't find a switch to lower the volume; and Buster, who turned out to be about twenty, long and thin, in tight jeans and cowboy boots, didn't look like the type you asked on first acquaintance to turn down his radio.

I couldn't catch Bertha in any lies. Buster confirmed everything she said. In person he nodded and grinned, instead of saying "Yeah." He had a raw, high-cheekboned face, and hair that he must have oiled at a Texaco station. "Born to lose" was tattooed on his left forearm. A dragon's head on his right bicep peeked from the sleeve of a gray T-shirt mottled with grease and sweat stains.

I felt uneasy. Hadn't there been a guy and girl like this in Phoenix who drove people out into the desert and murdered them? But Bertha didn't appear to have the ability to con anyone. Both she and Buster were a little in awe of me, thrilled that a well-known investigative reporter would take them seriously, after their friends, families and, I'm sure, other newspaper people had dismissed them as lunatics.

"I was gonna call the *National Enquirer*," said Bertha, "but I couldn't figure out how. I've never made a long-distance call."

Buster grunted, grinned and nodded.

What had been somewhat of a road dwindled to a trail, then to tire tracks on sand. We drove another half-mile through sage, brittlebush and creosote trees, and parked in a gully.

We tramped over barren sand hills, past small hummocks sheathed in bleached grass. A lizard scuttled out of our way; some kind of large insect thumped against the knee of my pants.

"See, here it is," said Bertha, as we arrived at the base of a dome-like hill. Two oblong, grid-like patterns were burned into the earth.

"That's where it landed."

I knelt down and examined the tracks. Each one was the size of a very large snowshoe. The patterns had burned through the sparse grass and into the sandy soil, a heavy brand perhaps three-quarters of an inch deep.

"We were laying right over here," Bertha said, shaking out a cigarette from a beat-up pack she extracted from the front pocket of her jeans. She pointed to a small, natural shelf in the side of the hill. "Fuckin' near scared us to death, right Buster?"

Buster grinned and nodded.

I tried to imagine what could have made the imprints, tried to guess what Bertha and Buster had actually seen.

"Well, do they look like flying saucer tracks?" asked Bertha.

"I've never had any first-hand experience," I said.

Bertha looked disappointed. Then she grabbed Buster's arm, rubbing her nose against his bicep.

"Tell him the surprise," she said.

Buster just smiled, a shifty-eyed, shit-eating smile.

"They came back," said Bertha. "We first seen 'em two nights ago. They came last night and I bet they're comin' back tonight. I think it was because we didn't run and didn't have a gun or nothin'. Last night, they came and looked us over again. They kind of measured us, if you know what I mean."

"They?" I said.

"Well, you know, I could feel them. That machine made comforting sounds, like a baby when it's talkin' itself to sleep. But the light that came out of it touched us, like all over. Right, Buster?"

Buster smiled and nodded.

We drove back to the rickety, basementless house. The home belonged to Bertha's mother, who arrived in a rusting Pontiac, accompanied by a couple of unkempt, tow-headed boys she must have retrieved from a babysitter.

The mother wore a grayish waitress uniform; her mud-colored hair was limp. She wasn't much over thirty, but everything about her, including her clothes and hair, looked wilted and tired. She had probably been beautiful as a teenager, but now every part of her was slouching. I decided she had probably had a long succession of boyfriends, husbands and lovers just like Buster.

"Geez, I thought reporters had better things to do than listen to dumb kids," she said, after Bertha introduced us. "Don't tell me you believe this flying saucer crap. These kids are just looking for some attention."

"I photographed the tracks out there on the hill," I said a little defensively. "They're unlike anything I've ever seen before. Besides, I make a point of checking out every lead," I added, trying to sound professional and gracious at the same time.

"Suit yourself. Hey, I loved the way you nailed that little rat who was selling phony water softeners. He worked this area, you know, sold to the old lady in the yellow house across the way . . ."

Bertha's mother served canned tomato soup thinned with water, and sandwiches containing one slice of a pinkish substance that may or may not have had a protein base, followed by instant coffee served in cracked mugs, accompanied by Carnation milk with two yellow lines dribbled down the label.

I phoned Rosslyn to tell her I'd be late. Looking back, I realize she didn't even ask where I was or what I was working on. But then, I didn't ask her how many people's mouths she'd immortalized in plaster of Paris that afternoon. Our relationship was not in wonderful shape even before I became terminally unemployed.

I have no idea why I got together with Rosslyn. I suspect she had no idea why she chose me. After I retired from organized baseball I took a long holiday. I went to Honolulu. I wasn't worried about finding work; I had a journalism degree to fall back on and a few dollars in the bank, though I'd never made big money in baseball. I was to some extent at loose ends, suffering, in a mild form, from the terrible letdown professional athletes undergo when they are suddenly thrust into the civilian world.

I met Rosslyn in a singles bar. She had her own business, was two years older than me, sensible, dedicated. She was, as they say, upwardly mobile, the direction I intended to be traveling. Rosslyn was everything the women I'd known throughout my baseball career were not. We also had Southern California in common; I had made my home there every off-season. A week after we returned from our Hawaiian holiday we moved in together. We both thought it was time to settle down; the fact that we weren't the right people for each other was incidental.

At Bertha's we watched TV on a dusty, finger-marked black-and-white set until the sun went down. Then the three of us got in Buster's car and again headed for the desert.

We sat on the ledge above where Bertha and Buster had been when the spaceship first landed.

"I wonder what they thought of us," Bertha said. "We had the sleeping bag and we were, like, going at it, if you know what I mean."

"A much better introduction to Earth than being met by a dozen armored tanks and a trigger-happy SWAT team," I said.

"You do believe us, don't you, Joe?" Bertha asked.

I paused for a long time. "I believe you've seen *something*. I believe you believe what you're telling me."

Bertha smiled, and, as she did, her wide, placid face was suddenly lighted the color of pink neon by the spaceship flitting over the nearest hill like a gigantic firefly. It landed in the tracks it had previously established.

"Son of a bitch!" said Bertha.

The only other time I experienced anything similar was when I was sent into a game in Yankee Stadium in the ninth inning, before fifty thousand screaming fans, the bases loaded, two out, and our team up by two. I remember feeling like I might faint, then imagining how ridiculous I'd look, a couple of runs scoring as the third baseman tried to pry the ball out of my glove. I got out of the inning and game with one pitch: I hung a curve ball that Graig Nettles hit in the gap in left-center to empty the bases.

What did the spaceship look like? Visualize one of those egg-shaped, plastic containers in which pantyhose are packaged. Picture one fifteen feet long and five or six feet high; then imagine it full of pink cotton candy.

It glided in like a cartoon insect. Bertha had been remarkably accurate in her description of the vehicle. Once it landed it sat silently, glowing baby pink, for what must have approached ten minutes, emitting comforting sounds.

The three of us just stood, awe-struck. For the first five minutes Buster and I each held one of Bertha's pudgy hands. I wanted to touch the craft, but I don't know if I lacked the nerve or if I was prevented from walking forward by some force within the machine.

Finally, I remembered my camera, and I began photographing the craft. I scurried around snapping photos like a Japanese tourist.

All the time the spaceship was there I had the feeling I was being touched, investigated, "measured," as Bertha had said, by gentle, loving hands.

Gradually I relaxed. I finished photographing, or, more accurately, ran out of film, and ended as we had begun, the three of us holding hands. I have never felt so at peace.

Then, the craft lifted one snowshoe-like foot up into its body, lifted the other, hovered an instant and was gone in the direction it had come from, leaving us bathed in a sweet, pink glow.

"So now you've seen it," said Bertha, letting go of my hand, fumbling in the pocket of her jeans for cigarettes. "You believe us now, don't you?"

"I believe," I said, moving forward to feel the tracks, which were deeper than they had been, and many degrees warmer than the surrounding sand.

As I finish, I look expectantly at Ray and Gideon to see if they are any more sympathetic to my plight.

"What you experienced," says Gideon, "was a close encounter, which, if you've described it accurately, seems legitimate. It also appears that you documented it with photographs, and had witnesses. So what went wrong?"

"Can you spare me a few more minutes?"

They both nod.

"What we have here are two people who between them do not display sufficient imagination to perpetrate a hoax." Those were the exact words I used in presenting my case to my managing editor. I had read in some self-improvement book that it was best to speak formally when conversing with superiors, and that I should never be afraid to show I possessed a vocabulary.

Later, the entire editorial board studied my photographs.

"Those tracks look like a blow-up of a waffle iron," one said.

The photographs of the craft itself were, in spite of their number, of disappointing quality. They looked like a side view of cotton candy or the usual fraudulent shots of supposed ectoplasm, taken by your basic raving lunatic.

"I have no control over the conveyance they travel in," I replied.

Three days had passed since my evening with Buster and Bertha. The next evening several senior staff members were out in the desert hoping for a glimpse of my extraterrestrials. Nothing. They all took their own photographs of the tracks.

"Are your sources clean?" management wanted to know. They meant Buster and Bertha.

"Nathan Wiser himself ran them through both adult and juvie," I said. "Clean as the day they were born." Wiser had growled. "Buster has five traffic charges as an adult, but nothing criminal."

I had put the same question to Bertha and Buster right after our close encounter.

"You two clean? Any arrests? Any convictions?"

"Well . . ." said Bertha, as my heart sank, "I been rousted for hanging around a shopping mall. Fuckin' security guards think they own the world."

"That's all?"

"Yeah. What'd you expect? And Buster ain't been in no more trouble than anybody else."

Largely because I was personally involved in the case and was such a credible witness, management decided to run the story and photographs.

If there's one kind of story that every rival journalist and reporter wants to discredit it's one about UFOs or extraterrestrials. But I wasn't worried. I knew what I'd seen. If I'd been smart I'd have remembered that I'd seen Reggie Jackson strike out a few hundred times, but he had three homers in four at-bats against me.

If there's one kind of story the general public wants desperately to be true it is one about aliens or UFOs.

I appeared on TV a couple of times, but I was just another newspaper guy. It was Bertha and Buster the public were interested in. They could relate to Bertha and Buster. Three days after the story broke all three of us were on "Good Morning, America."

Bertha, in a dress, with her hair permed, looked like everybody's babysitter. Even dressed up and washed Buster looked like your average neighborhood hoodlum. In the aftermath, one of the more facetious tabloids would nickname them Big Bertha and Hoodly McHotrod. Never mind what they called me.

The first inkling I had of trouble was right after we got off the air from doing "Good Morning, America." There was an urgent message for me to call my managing editor.

"Get your ass in here, McCoy," he growled. He was a gentlemanly managing editor who didn't use alcohol, tea, coffee or profanity. It had never occurred to me that ass was in his vocabulary.

Nathan Wiser was in the managing editor's office.

"Your sources are contaminated, McCoy," the managing editor said. "Tell him," he said to Wiser.

"Buster has more arrests than Willie Nelson's had hits," said Wiser, smiling like a hairy bagel.

"But you checked," I wailed.

"I don't know what you're trying to pull, McCoy, but I never heard of these people until your boss called my boss."

Why was he lying?

When a veteran police officer calls a reporter who has written the UFO story of the decade a liar, the charge is likely to stick.

"It's worse with the girl," said the managing editor, looking so pale he could have been in shock.

My insides felt as if they were melting.

"A phony rape charge," said Wiser, smiling amiably. "She should have been charged. Instead, we just put the fear of the Lord in her and dropped the whole mess."

I telephoned Bertha, turned on the speaker phone.

"Listen, Joe, I'm a bitch sometimes, okay? I've been in a little trouble. I didn't want to tell you 'cause then you wouldn't run the story, and we both know one don't have nothin' to do with the other. It's just that when I'm in a jam I lie though my fuckin' teeth. Know what I mean? Honest to God, we weren't jerking you around. Me and Buster seen what we seen. And so did you."

"What about the phony rape charge?"

She exhaled audibly.

"It did happen, you know what I mean? But not the way everybody thinks. I was home alone one afternoon when this guy from down the street showed up, Orlando something—I never did know his last name—he's twenty-six and he lifts weights and he had a bottle of wine. One thing, like, led to another, you know, and we had a nice time in my bedroom, and that would have been that except the son of a bitch laughed at me. After we was all finished, this guy tells me I'm fuckin' lousy in bed.

"I mean I done the best I could, and no son of a bitch should be able to talk to me like that, right? So after he left I called the cops and I said he raped me. Served him right, you know what I mean? They hauled his ass away in handcuffs and everything. I stuck to my story all night, scared him good. I bet he won't laugh at the next poor chick who done her best for him.

"The cops were so fuckin' mad at me. They threatened me with all kinds of charges. You'd have thought I was the criminal. But I was just so tired, I said, 'I don't care anymore. Do whatever you want to me.' They sent me home. Didn't drive me home like they drove me to the station.

"'Get out of here and don't ever waste our time again,' they said. The big-push detective was a fat, hairy bastard with a broken nose."

I looked at Wiser, who I'm certain bared his teeth at me. My managing editor had slid down in his chair until his face was even with the top of his desk.

"Would you have done the story if I'd told you the truth?" asked Bertha.

"I'd have still seen the spaceship. If I'd known the truth I could have been prepared to defend you. Things are going to get rough," I said.

I had no idea how rough.

"UFO PHOTOS PHONY," trumpeted our competitors. They blew up my photo of the spaceship tracks and ran them beside the blow-up of a General Electric waffle iron. The photos were identical. Even I could see the G.E. emblem in one corner of my track photo.

The photos of the spacecraft were diagnosed as a pantyhose container stuffed with cotton batting, shot from an advantageous angle.

"You're fired!" the managing editor said.

"You were out in the desert. You saw the tracks. Why didn't the waffle iron show up when we blew up the photographs?" I asked.

No one had any answers, and highly embarrassed managing editors don't want to hear unpleasant questions. The newspaper had kept the exact landing site a secret until the photographs were exposed as a hoax. Then a hundred reporters drove into the desert in a long, dusty caravan to find the hill where we had seen the craft land, as dry and bald and barren as it had always been. The only life they found were a few grasshoppers snicking about in the crackly grass.

I'll spare you any more details of my disgrace. The hoax appeared so blatantly dumb that I realized I was going to be without income possibly forever. I had a brief fantasy that one of the more scurrilous tabloids might hire me. They wouldn't.

Fortunately, I am not suicidal. Rosslyn has remained stonily silent throughout my ordeal. I'm sure she would be happier if I moved out, but she has the grace not to dump on me while I'm down.

"I'm glad we didn't decide to marry," she did mention, somewhat more than casually. We had actually discussed marriage. Rosslyn would have kept her own name. There was no stigma attached to R. QUINN DENTAL LABORATORY. Only her closest friends knew she was living with 'that guy who wrote the phony story about the UFO.'

"There's an aura of danger about you," Rosslyn had said once, after my investigative reporting brought down a crooked district attorney.

I wonder what my aura is like now?

SIX

RAY KINSELLA

MY INCLINATION IS TO TRY TO SPEED UP Joe's story. It's like he has many coins hidden on his person, if I just picked him up by the ankles and shook him the coins would fall in a silver shower at our feet. But then, I'm beginning to feel a little sympathy for him. He is somehow being manipulated by forces beyond his control. At least he hasn't been visited by disembodied voices.

I don't think he realized how much story he had until he started. He looks from me to Gideon, shrugs helplessly.

"This is going to take a lot longer than I anticipated."

"I want to hear it," I say. "Gideon, how about you?"

"All right. I can see why you've asked us to listen. I don't know what we can do for you . . ."

"Just understand," says Joe. "I've barely scratched the surface. I want someone to say to me, 'You're not crazy. No matter what the rest of the world thinks.'"

"It took me about twenty years to accomplish that," says Gideon.

"Over three years for me," I say. "Look, I've got to get home. Joe, can you come to the farm this afternoon? Gideon, how about you?"

"I'm not doing anything much except being a fugitive," says Joe, with a wry grin.

"I can't leave Missy alone for long," says Gideon.

"Missy is your wife? Daughter?"

"Neither. She's the adult daughter of a close friend who passed away. Missy has Downs' syndrome. I'm her legal guardian."

"Bring her along. She'll enjoy my daughters. They have a whole menagerie of pets."

Gideon nods.

"Say three o'clock at my place," I say.

"There's one other thing I'd like to mention right now," says Joe. "On top of everything, there's this feeling that I've been living two lives, maybe ever since I left Iowa all those years ago. I don't know how to put this clearly, but do either of you suppose there might come a time in a person's life when they have a choice, only they don't know it's a choice, at least not consciously; when they either follow the life they're in or veer off in a completely different direction? Do you think it's possible, that those who veer keep on living their original life in another dimension or a deep inner life?"

"You're experiencing that, too?" I ask.

"I shouldn't have brought it up just yet. But I keep getting flashes, like an amnesia victim must when they're starting to recover, scenes of the life I'd have lived if I'd stayed in Iowa. What I wonder is, if those who live their straight-arrow lives get little glimpses of the unknown, little fragments of eternity dropped on their heads, so they get an inkling of what would have happened if they had veered?

"Anything can happen," says Gideon.

Joe laughs, causing the waitresses and the few remaining customers to stare at us. We have been speaking so quietly for so long most of them have forgotten we were there.

"'Anything Can Happen,' that was the Seattle Mariners' slogan the year I played for them," says Joe. "It didn't work."

"What you're saying," I ask, "is that you think you're living or recalling bits of your life as it would have been if you'd stayed here in Johnson County? I know there was some kerfuffle about you not playing in the State Tournament. The story made it all the way to *Sports Illustrated*, didn't it?"

"I'll get to that. I'll get to everything if you give me time. Three o'clock, then. At Ray's farm."

Karin is home from school by the time Gideon arrives with Missy. Gideon drives a very old pick-up truck. I fix coffee, and thaw some of Annie's strawberry muffins.

"You're not," Annie had said to me before anyone arrived, "going to get us into something crazy? I mean this Joe McCoy is wanted. *Wanted.* Dangerous."

"We're going to listen to the rest of his story. That's all. No involvement. Nothing."

"You're not a good liar, Champ. You've already decided this guy's legitimate or you wouldn't have invited him here. Watch yourself, okay? Don't do anything *really* foolish."

But at the same time she is admonishing me, Annie is hugging me, letting me know she trusts me. Annie is sunshine, she is. And when I see how few people have someone who truly loves them, I realize for the thousandth time how lucky I am to have her.

Late in the evening, after Joe has related several more adventures, after Gideon and Missy have left in Gideon's truck, I suggest to Joe that we have a look at my baseball field.

"I feel privileged," he says.

The floodlights bathe the field in gold. A few wisps of ground fog cattail about the outfield. The players are warming up, playing catch; a grizzled coach hits fungoes. The sounds and smells of baseball envelop us, frying onions, fresh-cut grass, newly watered infield dirt. There is the low buzz of fans, as the bleachers begin to fill. Joe doesn't seem to notice, but there is a line-up of perhaps thirty cars waiting to cross the cattle guard onto my property, park their cars and visit the field. Gypsy, my brother's lady, dark and mysterious as her name, collects fees from the visitors, money they willingly hand over, for what they lack is peace and harmony, not ready cash.

We find a spot a few rows behind first base.

I can't decide about Joe McCoy. Listening to his tales has been like scouting a rookie, trying to decide if he deserves a positive scouting report.

"I don't know when I've felt so relaxed," he says. "Being on the run takes a lot out of a fellow. You know some of those players look familiar. What are they, local guys in old-time uniforms? Where do the fans come from? Are they locals, too?"

What wonderful, reassuring questions. Joe McCoy sees. I feel much better about him.

"Those are the 1919 White Sox on the third-base side."

"Go on!"

"That's Shoeless Joe Jackson down in the corner tossing balls with Happy Felsch."

"For whatever reason, I believe you," says Joe.

I offer to buy him a beer and hot dog and he accepts.

"The opponents are often different. A couple of weeks ago it was the 1927 Yankees. Murderers' Row. Gehrig had four hits. Ruth hit a home run down each foul line."

"Who's playing tonight?"

"I think my desires have some effect on who plays here. And you don't have to be dead to play on the dream field. One of my favorite World Series was 1946. I always wished I could have seen Harry "The Cat" Brecheen and Howie Pollet pitch, Enos "Country" Slaughter and Whitey Kurowski hit, Marty Marion play short stop. Every once in a while I get my wish, like tonight."

"Is that Joe Garagiola catching?"

"You got it."

"The 1946 Cardinals against the 1919 White Sox?"

"That's it."

"I heard there was magic here, but Stan Musial, Terry Moore, Dick Sisler. Wow! Thanks for trusting me enough to show me this. I know you must have had misgivings."

"Thanks for seeing."

He looks at me, smiles slightly and nods. We settle back to watch the game.

SEVEN
JOE McCOY

I TRIED TO BE HONEST WITH GIDEON AND RAY, and I've done a pretty good job. Sort of. The things I haven't told them frighten me. For instance, more than once, when I've been talking with someone, I suddenly feel what they're thinking about, events in their lives that I couldn't possibly know. It started with Rosslyn. We had just finished a dinner that I had cooked—stuffed green peppers, coconut-cream pie, Starbuck's chocolate-almond coffee—I was pouring cream into my coffee, when I suddenly knew Rosslyn was brooding about an impression she had made that afternoon of the teeth of a man with a bad overbite. "I'm going to have to redo Mr. Waller's impression, and I'm going to have to have a talk with his dentist about what I should do when I get the perfect impression," was what she was daydreaming.

"You're thinking about Mr. Waller's overbite," I said.

Rosslyn jerked to attention, like she'd just been wakened from a nap. "How could you possibly know that?"

"I don't know," I replied. "I was hoping you could help me out."

Rosslyn stared at me fearfully. I wonder what secrets she's been keeping from me. There are thousands of my thoughts I wouldn't want Rosslyn to know about. Thousands, millions.

"I'm sorry," I said. "I didn't do it on purpose. It's the first time. I'll try never to let it happen again." Rosslyn kept staring suspiciously at me, as if she'd just caught me rifling her purse.

"There's no way you could have known. Mr. Waller was just referred to me this morning." She left the table, taking her coffee with her. Rosslyn slept in the spare bedroom that night.

"Adam and Francie are coming from Boston for a visit," Rosslyn announced one morning a few weeks after the extraterrestrial fiasco. "Adam says the story barely made the front pages in the east."

That was all I needed. Adam is Rosslyn's brother, a tall, square-jawed, pipe-smoking accountant with a pernicious ardor for detail who, like a raccoon, washes his food before he eats it. I've seen Adam holding a block of cheese between two forks under the kitchen tap. Adam won't eat an ice cream cone because it has been touched by human hands. I wonder where *his* hands have been?

Adam's fiancée, Francie Bly, is a pert little thing with pale, taffy-colored hair whirlwinding about her face. She is slim and fair-skinned, with a saucy nose that has about fifteen freckles scattered across it. Her eyebrows are sun-blonde, and she has a small crease in the middle of her bottom lip that enlarges when she pretends to pout, or when she looks quizzically at someone as if she is staring over the rim of eyeglasses.

I like Francie, but feel she is hiding some serious character flaw, otherwise why would she have agreed to marry Adam the raccoon? Perhaps there are women truly attracted to men like Adam Quinn. I dismiss the thought. Adam gets up at six o'clock every morning to jog. I have read that jogging plays havoc with one's sex life. If Francie was my lady, I'd do my jogging in bed.

Cute was the word I would use to describe Francie—in spite of her eastern-girls'-school-looking-down-on-the-rest-of-the-nation-especially-California, mentality.

She didn't appear unhappy; she openly teased Adam about his stuffiness, made fun of him in person and behind his back, a steady stream of good-natured pinpricks to try and keep Adam from taking himself so seriously. She did not succeed.

"Since you don't have anything to do, you can meet Adam and Francie at the airport," Rosslyn said. She was just stating an obvious fact. I don't think she had any idea how cruel her words sounded.

Ever since the night of the extraterrestrials, I have been having the most detailed, clear-as-life, you-are-there, this-is-happening dreams. I have always been a daydreamer, but, though experts claim everyone dreams extensively every night, I seldom remembered my night dreams, until now.

In my dreams I am driving my red, 1956 Lincoln Continental convertible with the classic car plates: MCCOY 1. My Lincoln is the only extravagance from my baseball days. I paid $15,500 for it, and treated it with more concern than my teammates showed for their showgirl-model-trophy wives, their Ferraris, Corvettes, Mercedes, or Porsches. I was never in their league in salaries. If I had had just a little more ability, or a lot more desire, or Maureen Renn waiting after the game . . .

Eight weeks after the fiasco, when it appeared that my term of unemployment was going to stretch to infinity, I sold my Lincoln to a leering Armenian with gravy stains on his vest. That left me driving Rosslyn's second car, a 1972 Ford that a transient cousin had abandoned in her carport. It left a black trail of pollution behind it; neither its air-conditioning nor its emission control would ever work again.

Last night I was back in Iowa, but in that way dreams have, I was driving my Lincoln. I was married to a woman who was very much in love with me. We had a child.

At times the woman was Francie Bly. I have no reason to believe Francie has any interest in me, she seems relatively happy with Adam, who is only slightly less interesting than lint. I rationalize that I dreamed of her because I knew she was due to visit. On other occasions the woman beside me in the convertible seemed to be Maureen Renn. Dreams, memories, wishes, interweave like the colors in variegated thread.

In one dream I was seventeen and Maureen's arms were tight about my neck, her thighs locked about mine, her mouth hot and thrilling as we made love on a blanket spread over a stack of grain sacks behind the manger in her father's barn. The scent of dried hay was mixed with the thick, wet odor of cattle. A cow lurched forward in her stanchion, her pink nose protruded beyond the manger wall, her dull eyes stared at us, green straws bristled on each side of her mouth.

Maureen climaxed violently, taking me with her. She slowly unlocked her arms from around my neck, our mouths parted.

I still can't imagine how, at sixteen, Maureen could instinctively have known so much about sex, and I could have been so unknowledgeable.

Maureen was a tall, strapping farm girl with a mop of dark-red hair. She pitched hay, did farm chores and drove tractors and combines alongside her hulking brothers. My father made his precarious living from his second-hand store in Lone Tree. The most physical duties I performed were helping my father move an oak table or bookcase from the shop to a waiting truck. Though I was athletic, I was neither large nor particularly strong. My older brother worked for an insurance company in Des Moines until my father retired and sold him the business. My sister, Agnes, a year younger than me, was as my father said, "Homely as a mud fence and proud of it."

"So how did it feel to have my virgin body, McCoy?" Maureen asked, staring into my eyes in the dim light of the barn, half smiling in the way she always did, so I couldn't tell if she was making fun of me.

"Well . . ." I said. I was watching a tine of sunlight that pierced the roof like a golden laser and angled to the far wall. She had just had my virgin body. It had never occurred to me that it might also have been Maureen's first time.

She seemed to know so much more than I did. She had been so calm, apparently privy to knowledge I had no access to. I won't detail the embarrassing struggle I had with one of the contraceptives I carried in my wallet until Maureen pointed out how it should be used. When I was between her thighs, after Maureen had used her hand to guide me into the heat of her, I came almost immediately, but she imprisoned me with her strong limbs.

"Lie still, Sugar," she whispered. "It's gonna be so good," and she twitched involuntarily as the sheer heat of her revived my desire.

"Am I better than the second baseman?" Maureen asked, a lilt in her voice.

I was too surprised to answer. "Well . . ." I said eventually.

"Kiss me, Sugar. Make us so close." I did.

"'Well . . .' What kind of an answer is that? Am I better than fucking your second baseman?"

"Much better than my second baseman," I said, watching the arrow of sunlight. "You were wonderful. He shaves and chews snuff."

"All right," said Maureen, "that's better."

I swallowed hard. Everything about me was so incredibly awkward. I have no idea what Maureen saw in me. It was easy to be rowdy and raucous with my friends, my teammates, but put me alone with a girl and I might as well have had a garrote around my neck.

"I wish you'd look at me, Joe. You never look at me, never make eye contact."

She shifted out from under me, pulled herself to a sitting position. "When we kiss you close your eyes, otherwise you look at some spot in the distance over my left shoulder."

"I like to look at you," I said lamely.

Maureen had thrown her plaid shirt over her shoulders so she could lean against the outer wall of the barn without scratching her back. She was peeking through thick strands of plum-colored hair, almost as if peering between her fingers.

"You don't believe this was my first time," she said, fishing in her shirt pocket for a pack of cigarettes and a book of matches. The shirt hung just to the outside of each nipple. Her large, freckled breasts rose and fell rhythmically with her breathing.

"I never thought about it," I said. But I had. She talked so freely and openly of sex, I'd just assumed she'd had other lovers, though I couldn't think of who they might have been.

"I want you to know you're the first outside the family, McCoy." She glanced at me, that same wry, enigmatic smile on her face.

I couldn't keep a surprised expression off my face.

"Shit, that's what you expect me to say, isn't it? A brother has his sister in bed and says to her, 'You're better'n Ma.' And the girl answers back, 'That's what Pa says.'"

Maureen drew deeply on her cigarette, let the smoke out slowly between her teeth.

She had read my mind. The Renns were, as my father often said, a wild and woolly bunch. 'Disreputable,' would be the consensus of the community. Her father was a prodigious drinker. One of her brothers was in jail; the other two were terrors, roaming the countryside in souped-up cars. They drank, fought, fucked, stole anything that wasn't nailed to the earth. Only the wildest white girls or Indian women from the reservation near Tama were ever seen with Harley or Magnus Renn.

"I thought only men got grouchy after sex," I said, hoping to distract her. The statement was something I had read in a pretentious book about teenage sex. I had to get a note from my father before the school librarian would let me take it out.

Maureen laughed. I tried to look her in the eye, but only managed the briefest of contact.

"Do you want to go one more round? My folks won't be home for at least an hour, longer if the old man hits the bars in Iowa City."

I reached for her, and her mouth was sweet and smoky. This time I knew how to handle the contraceptive. I was just arching above Maureen's spread thighs, her cool hand about to guide me into her again, when I awoke.

I wondered if what was happening to me was in some way a defence mechanism. My present life was a shambles. Had I unconsciously retreated to days when life was less complicated?

I could recall with perfect clarity those scenes, emotions, conversations, all of which had happened some thirteen years earlier. They became clearer and more detailed each time I dreamed or relived them. Yet, there I lay, in a darkened bedroom, beside a woman swathed in a flannel nightgown who I barely knew. Try as I might, I couldn't recall for sure the color of Rosslyn's eyes.

"What do you fantasize about?" Maureen once asked me.

"How do you mean?" I replied, a little suspicious.

"Oh, I don't mean sexual fantasies. Anybody with blood fantasizes about getting laid. When you're walking out to my place, or when you're alone for hours at a time, what do you daydream about, besides sex?"

I had to think for quite a while, trying to see if any pattern developed. One did.

"I fantasize about being on the run, being a fugitive, police and FBI chasing after me, and me always eluding them."

The fantasy had been with me from early childhood, grew stronger as

I grew older. I used to sit in bullpens all across America, on hot, boring afternoons, and cold, windy evenings, dreaming of being on the run, dreaming that I was actually hiding out in the bullpen, police and security guards closing in on me, imagining how I would leap into the stands and elude them.

I never asked Maureen what she fantasized about. But once, not long after we got together, I asked Rosslyn. She didn't have to stop and think before coming up with an answer.

"I design wallpaper," she said, smiling dreamily. "I fantasize about rearranging the furniture in our house and creating the perfect set of dentures."

"Of course," I said. "I should have known."

On more than one occasion I have dreamed of Rosslyn accepting the Nobel Prize in the newly created category of Perfect Dentures.

Okay, now how am I going to explain this? There is a difference between recalling a scene, like Maureen and I having sex in her father's barn, in which you're a participant, and seeing yourself in a scene from the past, as a spectator. I am embarrassed at being a spectator. I see Maureen and I making love, but instead of recalling the event with pleasure, remembering Maureen's sexual warmth and fiery energy, I observe myself and my inexperience. I see my smooth teenage face, my inept hands. What in the world did Maureen ever see in me? And how could I have been so arrogant as to think there were dozens, no, hundreds, of other women out there waiting for me? Callow. That is the perfect word to describe me in those days. Besides "inexperienced," *callow* means "without feathers."

I'm going to have to talk about baseball sooner or later. I get depressed just thinking about it.

I loved the game, don't ever think I didn't. It was just that I had the ability to see beyond it. I was cursed with a very good estimation of my ability. I pitched well enough in high school to get five scholarship offers, including one for the University of Iowa, fifteen minutes from my front door. Pitchers generally have egos as big as the Grand Canyon. They have to. A pitcher is, as Reggie Jackson said of himself, the straw that stirs the drink. A pitcher has one of the loneliest jobs this side of the cross. An arm against the world. Pitchers need their egos, like hockey enforcers need anger. A tired pitcher will swear on his mother's grave that he still has good stuff, he has to be dragged kicking from the field, furious that he has been removed, even though he has given up five consecutive hits. The arm may be dead but the ego lives on. A quality catcher can make life easier, a really knowledgeable one will have a sixth sense when it comes to calling pitches, a sense that can make a mediocre hurler look good, and make a Hall of Famer of a really good pitcher.

In the end though you're the one out there alone with your ego.

I didn't have that giant ego. I knew after I'd seen three balls hammered off the outfield fences that my curve wasn't working, that I wasn't spotting the ball where I wanted, that I was high in the strike zone. I had no qualms about looking the pitching coach in the eye and saying, "I don't have my good stuff. I'll stay or go. It's up to you." Coaches and managers however, are partial to pitchers who lie on their mother's eyes. In baseball, being honest is seen as a weakness.

Those beautiful, humid Iowa evenings when all my joints felt full to bursting with warm oil, those evenings when my father, after a day of driving around Johnson County back roads looking for antiques, or sitting around the store, maybe idly sanding a piece of furniture he was restoring, talking crops and baseball with friends who dropped in, talking Iowa with tourists who usually looked at big items and bought small, there being no way to cram a chiffonier into the trunk of their Buick, would rise from the table, often after having cooked supper, for my delicate mother was indisposed more often than not, sighing, saying, "Who's for tossing the ball for a while?" and all three of us kids would be raring to go. This was when I was perhaps seven or eight, small for my age, all skinned knees and missing teeth, but able to burn the ball in twice as hard as Billy, my older brother.

Agnes, tough as a weed, loved to run the bases. Billy would cover second, I'd pitch to Dad, and Agnes would lead off an unguarded first base and try to steal. She'd slide into second in a cloud of dust, trying to kick the ball out of Billy's glove, her blonde pigtails half a step behind her like exotic reins.

A few months ago Dad wrote to say Agnes and her friend, Grace, who looks like Martina Navratilova, have applied to adopt a child. I hope my recent infamous activities won't hurt their chances.

I was concerned about performing well, but not with winning for the school, or the coach, or my teammates. In fact, the reason I chose base-ball was because it is essentially *not* a team sport; I have never had a fanatical dedication to team. Though I played hard, I had a high regard for my body and my personal safety. Had I played the outfield I would never have run into a wall trying to make a catch. There is no single play worth jeopardizing a career. During my career, I never criticized a teammate for not risking life and limb.

"Running into walls or blocking the plate is for fools and football players," I had the nerve to tell my coach.

As early as my freshman year in high school, I discovered I needed four full days rest between pitching assignments. I absolutely refused to work any oftener.

My senior year in high school I faced the wrath not only of my coaches, but of my teammates and the citizens of Lone Tree and vicinity. We had a chance to win the state championship but I would have had to pitch three times in a week.

"I wouldn't pitch on less than four days' rest if we were playing for the championship of the world," I told my coaches.

Maureen was the only one who stood behind my decision.

Inexplicably, by my senior year I was tiring of Maureen. I was eigh-teen, had a long life in front of me, and didn't want to share it. Also, I didn't know how good I had it. It never occurred to me that I could have struck gold on my first try, that the world wasn't full of prettier, sexier, more sophisticated Maureens just waiting for Joe McCoy to come along. That single misconception has done more to shape my life than any-thing except the extraterrestrial business.

Even my mother, that delicate, thin-as-paper woman, whose failing health was always a mystery, pressured me, gently of course, to break my pitching regimen.

"Lois Glenville says her Dougie wants to win the state championship very badly, and she says you're the only one who can take them there."

I explained my position again. My mother was wearing a filmy bed jacket with large, lavender angels on it; she always smelled of Evening in Paris cologne. I longed to say, "If Dougie Glenville wants to win so badly, let *him* pitch," but there was no use upsetting Mother, who had never attended one of my games—the outdoor air brought on her asthma. Besides, Dougie Glenville was a weasel-faced third baseman who smoked dope and had a particularly foul mouth.

The state championships were held in Cedar Rapids that year. I was roundly booed by fans from Lone Tree when I was introduced during pre-game ceremonies. I pitched a three-hit win in the first round. After that, I didn't pitch again, and we were eliminated in two straight games. Each time the fans booed me I vowed to leave Lone Tree and the small-minded people who thought I should risk my future to bolster their pride.

I turned down my scholarship to Iowa. Even then, I knew baseball was not going to be my whole life. Maybe I just lacked confidence in my ability. Maybe, deep inside, I knew I didn't have what it took to be a star. I accepted a baseball scholarship from the university with the best school of journalism, which turned out to be in the deep South.

I remember my first meeting with the baseball coach, a short, box-like man with a crewcut, who had never played in organized baseball.

His second sentence was, "Y'all believe in the Lord Jesus Christ, Boy?"

"I beg your pardon?"

"I asked if you've given your life to Christ, Boy?"

"My religious beliefs are personal and private," I said. Actually I had none; but that, too, wasn't any of his business.

He spat tobacco juice on a paper spread on the floor beside his desk.

"Those who are dedicated to the Lord have nothin' to hide, Boy. A true believer professes his belief at every opportunity, witnesses often, and works unstintingly to convert the heathen."

I stared at him with as much contempt as I could muster. There were other schools, I decided.

"Let's get down on our knees and pray to the Almighty for guidance."

He sent his chair rolling back toward the wall and dropped to his knees right next to the juice-filthy newspaper.

I walked out of his office and slammed the door.

That afternoon the university's board of governors and a gaggle of good ol' boy alumni were out to watch me.

My curveball sent hitters leaping out of the batter's box as if they'd been pushed. The ball then zapped across the corner of the plate, leaving the hitters both embarrassed and angry.

The powers-that-be decided anyone with that much stuff on the ball didn't need an active affiliation with the supernatural.

A portly alumnus with a droopy suit jacket and a cigar that looked like eight inches of hoe-handle offered me ten thousand dollars a year expense money, under the table, of course. The coach, in addition to full tuition, offered to arrange it so I never had to attend a class.

"But I want to attend classes," I said. "I'm here because you have an excellent school of journalism."

"What the hell you want to go studyin' for?" Coach asked. "It'll interfere with your baseball, and you'll have to *read*," he said contemptuously. "A boy with as much talent as you could easily ruin your eyesight readin'."

"Hell, boy," the cigar-chomping alumnus said, "you're here to pitch baseballs and nothin' else. Just let Coach here take care of your education. If you agree to do as Coach says, you run on down to Faith Pontiac–Buick and pick out any vehicle that strikes your fancy. Sales manager will let you take it out for a drive. You don't have to bring it back 'til June. If anyone asks, you're just givin' it a thorough test."

I refused the car and the money, on the grounds that the less I owed them the more likely they'd be to understand or at least tolerate my refusal to work on less than four days' rest. I also took a full load of journalism courses. No one ever mentioned religion to me again, though the rest of the team prayed together before games, and for most of the players there was a direct relationship between innings played and the alleged strength of their Christian faith.

I put in an interesting four years. I watched with some fascination as the players around me continued to grow physically and improve their baseball skills. I, on the other hand, stayed the same. I was 5' 8½" and 155 lbs. I lifted weights, tried every strength program known at the time, but I couldn't gain an ounce. The curve that baffled hitters my freshman year had not improved an iota by graduation. Where I had been able to pitch complete games in high school and my early university years, by graduation I was lucky to get through six innings.

I was the center of a brouhaha my senior year when I backed out of a start in a regional tournament because I had to study for an exam. My coaches, teammates, and school authorities were livid. There wasn't a term evil enough to describe me. A redneck queer was a boy who liked girls better than sports, but for an athlete to be interested in learning . . .

My preference for academia over athletics made several regional newspapers and *Sports Illustrated*, which dredged up my refusal to pitch in the Iowa state championships.

The *L.A. Times* assigned me to write my side of the story in a thousand words. I was paid $200, and introduced to the art of dictating a story, long distance, into a machine manned by recorded voices doling out precise, mechanical instructions.

I received hate mail from thirty-one states, several unsigned and badly spelled pieces coming from my old home town, Lone Tree.

I graduated with a degree in journalism. I was drafted in the eighth round, signed a contract and was shunted to a AA team in Knoxville, where it became clear I didn't have the stamina to be a starter in professional baseball. At Knoxville, my ERA for innings one through three was .091. My fourth-inning ERA was 5.77. I became a reliever. If the manager and pitching coach agreed, I could be called on to pitch six nights in a row. I considered quitting. I looked at the salaries star players were earning. I accepted my lot. But my heart was never again in it.

I only went back to Lone Tree once, for my mother's funeral. She passed away suddenly in the February of my junior year.

"She just fluttered away," my father said, scratching his head in puzzlement.

To this day I don't know what killed my mother. The doctor used and reused the word *attrition*, but the word is not in any medical dictionary.

Maureen was at the funeral and the grave-side service. She looked solemn in a wine-red coat, her hair tied down with a black scarf. I stole a number of glances at her; but our eyes never met, and I was glad she didn't stop to offer condolences. It would have embarrassed us both.

Shortly after my mother's death, my father sold his business to my brother, William Armbruster McCoy, for a small down payment, and moved south to Miami where he took a job as a night clerk at a small, exclusive hotel with an ocean view from every room. He was given a room, as well as breakfast and supper in the hotel's dining room.

In my senior year he wrote to say he had married a widow vacationing at the hotel. I pictured a nice, fiftyish grandmother with blue-gray hair and a midwestern twang.

Elena, it turned out, was barely forty, a tall, healthy-looking woman with naturally yellow hair and a lot of teeth. She was of Greek-Italian ancestry, had once been Miss Rhode Island, and had learned to smile with her mouth open, her highly glossed lips glowing red as polished apples. She also had five teenaged children.

"Thank goodness my family is grown up," Father said over the phone. By this time my sister, Agnes Armbruster McCoy, was sharing an apartment in Iowa City with her girlfriend, working as an ambulance attendant while attending university part time, working toward a nursing degree.

Elena did not have to move her family into my father's room at the hotel. Her deceased husband had borne the name of one of the better-known crime families in America, and his demise, at age forty-two, had been caused by someone pointing a machine gun at him and pulling the trigger perhaps fifty times.

"Men in bulletproof limousines drop bags of money off at the back door," my father told me in a letter. He enclosed a picture of the house Elena had purchased for them. I mistook it for the hotel where my father had worked. He also sent a photograph of his five stepchildren, all boys, sitting in a row, wearing undertaker-like suits and conservative ties.

"The five little assassins," I said, showing the photo to Rosslyn.

"I think they're very handsome boys," Rosslyn replied.

I can't remember their names, but choose from the following: Tony, Rocco, Guido, Demos, Georgio, Christos, Aristotle, Nunzio.

"They learned how to make cement overshoes at their father's knee," I said to Rosslyn.

"What would your father say?" Rosslyn has no sense of humor.

I felt that if my father could handle the situation it was none of my business. Still, it was memories of my stepmother's late husband, the ventilated Greek tycoon, that got me started investigating the Syndicate in Southern California. A fatal mistake if there ever was one.

The head of the Family is one Carmine Anthony "Tony the Pianist" Bablioto. He controls everything illegal west of Kansas City. I was just uncovering some precise and interesting details when the extraterrestrial fiasco body-slammed my career.

Could my downfall have been engineered by the Syndicate? Doesn't seem likely. They would have needed the special effects department of a motion picture studio in their pocket. Still, I know what I saw, and who else would go to so much trouble to discredit me?

I bumped around the Bigs for seven seasons.

Instead of vegetating in the bullpen, shooting beaver with infrared binoculars, engaging in spitting contests, and having semi-obscene conversations with women looking for trouble, I wrote a number of articles for newspapers and magazines about what it was like inside baseball. I wrote a non-fiction baseball book that was rejected by fifty publishers. I wrote a second non-fiction baseball book that was rejected by even more.

"Earn yourself thirty saves in a season and we'll publish both books," an editor told me. "You're not bankable. What you say lacks authority because you're a marginal player. When you're critical of management or your fellow players it sounds like sour grapes. Only if you're a star is it okay to be critical of baseball."

Though I had one magnificent post season, my career was unspectacular. I was lifetime 8-23 with thirty-seven saves, and an ERA of 4.47. I'm listed in *The Baseball Encyclopedia* as Joe McCoy, followed by my full handle, Joseph Michael Armbruster "Kid" McCoy.

No one ever called me Kid except Jim Murray, the *L.A. Times* columnist, my hero, the best baseball writer in the world, in one column the day after I bounced a ball off Jim Rice at Angel Stadium and he charged the mound. I landed a pretty good left on his face before I retreated, both benches cleared and the players duked it out for about five minutes. There was an old-time boxer named Kid McCoy, who was pretty hot stuff in his time. Jim Murray quoted from a song about Kid McCoy.

My final year in the Bigs I was the number-ten pitcher on the ten-man staff of a last-place team. I was the guy who came in in the seventh inning when we were behind 9-1. I'd get the first three men, then give up two or three runs. The hometown fans, what few there were, loved to boo me. Our opponents' fans used to cheer when I came into a game. A New York sportswriter tried to nickname me White Flag McCoy, but I didn't remain in baseball long enough for the name to catch on.

No matter where I played, I was supposed to clear every article I wrote with the front office. I seldom did. Usually I tried to be careful not to offend my teammates even though most of them were innately suspicious of me because I was literate. I stayed on their good side by writing little paragraphs of praise, with colored felt pens, and sending them in from the bullpen. BARNWELL WALLOPS TENTH HOMER! I'd headline in green ink. I'd write five lines of superlatives and hope that someone in the dugout would be able to pronounce all the words correctly when they read the piece to Barnwell. Flattery is a great peacemaker.

My downfall came about not because of what I wrote, although the trouble started with a thousand-word column I wrote for *The New York Times* on the essence of pitching. It was unspectacular, inoffensive journeyman prose. But I didn't clear it.

I was summoned to the front office where a petty little Harvard Business School type, being strangled by his school tie, pointed out in his best Newport-$500,000-summer-cottage accent that I should have ballyhooed our star hitter in the column. Our star hitter, Player X, was a fat drunk with an IQ lower than his uniform number and more brushes with gonorrhoea than home runs. Those of us who valued our health brought bottled water to the clubhouse. Player X was earning $2 million a year.

"The article was on pitching," I pointed out logically.

"I'm afraid I'm going to have to suspend your writing privileges," the bean counter said.

While "Get fucked!" was not the most original response I could have come up with, it served the purpose. I stormed into the clubhouse just as a famous writer from *Sports Illustrated* was coming out.

He could see the wrath in my eyes. He put an arm around my shoulder and said soothingly, "Tell me, Joe, how does it feel to be an intelligent player in a game where intelligence isn't valued?"

I ran off at the mouth for forty minutes.

Management got a copy of *Sports Illustrated* before it hit the news stands. I was summoned.

"Betrayed!" screamed the owner, a dumpy, cigar-chewing man.

"I didn't say anything that wasn't true," I replied. "At least eight players on our team are functionally illiterate."

He turned a deep purple.

"We can't have the likes of you on our team," he roared.

I found myself on a plane heading toward our Triple A franchise in Hawaii. I decided that was not the worst thing that could happen. I had been there before, I deserved to live permanently in a warm climate.

After nine hours in the air and a five-hour time change, I arrived in Honolulu. A grinning idiot from the front office was waiting with a one-way ticket to Salt Lake City.

That was the worst thing that could happen to me. I had been traded as I flew. They didn't even have the decency to put me up in a hotel for the night. I sat in the airport for three hours, then endured another endless flight.

Salt Lake City, as some sportswriter once wrote, is the most uptight city between Cleveland and Asia.

In Salt Lake City it was made plain that even if I pitched three no-hitters in a row I'd never get promoted back to the Bigs. The word was out: Joe McCoy was poison. The threat proved empty, for our parent team was the Seattle Mariners, a club that probably wouldn't have been leading the Pacific Coast League if they'd played there full time. They were so desperate for a live body to hurl the ball toward the plate that they'd have promoted Charles Manson if he had an ERA below 4.00.

I finished the season and my career in Seattle. My contract and enthusiasm expired at about the same time. I retired as gracefully as an unwanted player can retire. I was perceived to have bitten the hand that fed me. I've never quite understood why one shouldn't, especially if the hand is sanctimonious, arrogant and opinionated, the food cold, greasy, full of empty calories.

"Organized baseball is not *that* organized," my number-one snitch, Pico the Rat, pointed out to me one day when I was whining about my bad luck.

"If you'd been an owner who stepped out of line, somebody like Bill Veeck who pissed on what the stuffed-shirt owners thought was decorum, that would be another matter. Then I could believe you. All you did was embarrass a few players and managers. You overrate your importance."

"Thank you, Pico," I said. "It's always nice to have one's place in society clarified."

"Think nothing of it," said Pico.

Behind the secondhand store in Lone Tree was a half acre of white poplars. Sometimes Maureen would ride into town on her horse, a big bay with a white blaze on its forehead. The horse's name was Matty-Lou, named for Maureen's grandmother, Matilda Louise.

I remember the way Maureen would swing down out of the saddle and into my arms. We'd tether the horse and stroll among the fluttering, silver-leafed poplars, seldom talking, stopping frequently to kiss, Maureen's denimed belly pressed tightly against mine, the heat of her radiating through.

I could never take Maureen to my room. I wouldn't have even if the opportunity had presented itself. My mother had an animal's sense of smell. I could picture Mother, in her pale, frilly bed jacket, sniffing delicately as a rabbit, saying: "Joey, there's been someone in your room who smokes. I hope you haven't been smoking. And I smell horses, and . . ." How she would have described the odors of sex? I didn't want to know.

Between the store and the poplar grove was an unpainted garage stacked high with dusty collectibles, boxes of depression glass, churns and three-wheeled wicker baby buggies. In the middle was a 1941 Pontiac, long and sleek, painted gray and silver. It had come with the property when my father purchased it and the business immediately after the Second World War. The car was supported by railway ties under the axles, the wheels stacked crookedly in the back corner of the building.

"It'll be worth somethin' some day," my father said vaguely.

If it's still there it probably is worth something.

I pilfered the key to the garage, had it duplicated, and Maureen and I made love in the dusty-smelling, velvety back seat of the Pontiac.

"Why do you like me?" Maureen asked, one warm September evening. There was no electricity in the garage, so after the sun died down it became pitch black. A few seconds before, Maureen had lit a cigarette, the flare of the match revealing her hair wild about her face and her speckled breasts beaded with sweat, for we had just made love slowly and sweetly for what seemed like an hour, our bodies pressed together so closely our own juices lubricated us until it was as if we had been soaped. "Other than the fact that I'm the best fuck you'll ever have in your mealy-mouthed life," Maureen went on, when I didn't answer quickly enough. What she said was true, though I certainly didn't know it then.

My silence continued for a long time. I knew what I should say but the words choked in my throat.

A few weeks ago, after the extraterrestrial business, but before the shit, as they say, really hit the fan, I told Maureen, in a dream, the words I should have spoken to her all those years ago.

In the dream, I relived that gentle fall evening, the odor of burning leaves in the air. I told Maureen the truth, instead of just pulling her face into the crook of my neck, kissing her sex-damp hair. Whether it was the truth then, I don't know. But it was the truth a few weeks ago, and the truth now.

"I don't just like you, I love you. I love you because you complement me—you're everything I'm not. You're tough, and a little bit wild, and mysterious. And you have a touch of evil. I love you because you delight in sex, and you aren't afraid to let yourself go when we make love. And you're not afraid to talk about sex.

"And I love you because your family is rough and ready and dangerous, while mine is bland as pudding. My mother douses her natural odors, if she has any, in Evening in Paris. My father always smells of Aqua Velva.

"I love you because you wear denim, and smoke, and whisper 'Fuck me, Joe. Fuck me, hard,' while we're making love. And I love you because the chemicals are right. You smell right to me, you taste right to me. I love you so much that I don't care what anybody else thinks. I am fatally and forever turned on by tough, sexy, big-thighed women."

* * *

"Don't you want to know why I like you?" Maureen asked, that September night.

It didn't matter to me. I knew that what attracts one person to another can't be explained. And even if it *is* explained it is still a mystery.

"I like you because you're gonna be somebody," Maureen said. "You're smart and you're a great ballplayer. My family's all beer and hard times, and yours is nothing special, but you are. And it's a turn-on, McCoy. I fucking tingle all over thinking about you being real successful. And then I get awful scared that I won't be able to hold on to you."

She waited for me to reassure her. But I've never been a convincing liar. I already knew I was going to accept a scholarship to a university far from Iowa. I knew Maureen probably wasn't going to be able to hold on to me.

I didn't have the guts to make a clean break with Maureen. I just sneaked away. It must have hurt her to know I was leaving because our relationship was too perfect, too easy, too natural.

She eventually married a local boy named Tucker Wegman. They live on a farm about seven miles south of Lone Tree.

I want to tell you a little about Pico the Rat, my most useful source of information on the streets of Los Angeles.

Pico the Rat is small and chinless, about ninety pounds of scruff and beady eyes. Pico is the perfect informant. He is seemingly capable of being in more than one place at a time. Both cops and criminals hold him in mild contempt. A street hustler like Pico is a hyena; he scavenges. Cops and crooks throw him their leftovers.

Pico is about 5'3", sink-chested, with scraggly hair, dirty fingernails, a perennial two-day growth of beard. He has large, sorrowful, protruding eyes. My archenemy on the police force, Nathan Wiser, describes Pico as a terminally unwashed Woody Allen. The Mob uses Pico to find out what the police are up to, the police use Pico to keep tabs on the Mob. I used Pico to keep track of both.

He served in virtually every police line-up in the greater Los Angeles area. Pico looks like the guy who snatched your wife's purse, the scum who sold drugs to your daughter, stole your car, or broke into your apartment. He is the man who always stands next to the guilty party. If John Q. Citizen can pass over Pico and pick out a perpetrator, the police feel the charge is likely to stick.

If Pico the Rat had lived in biblical times, he would have stolen the burning bush, figured out how it operated, and sold it faggot by faggot as Pico's Perpetual Firestarter.

Perhaps the weird dreams I was experiencing had something to do with a conversation I had had with Pico just a few days before my life started its uninterrupted downward spiral. I was, as usual, making inquiries abut organized crime.

"My advice, McCoy, is to stick to exposing bait-and-switch advertisers. You'll live longer."

"I'll take my chances," I said, handing Pico two ten-dollar bills, surreptitiously, the way I felt an ace investigative reporter was supposed to pay off his number-one snitch.

"You know there are better lives than this," Pico said suddenly, hopping on one foot until he leaned against a wall in the deep doorway where we were meeting. We were on a street of bars and rooming houses, pawn shops and frequently-robbed liquor stores. A couple of bare-legged black whores strolled by, their hard eyes touching us, dismissing us in a glance.

"I imagine there are," I said, anxious to leave.

"No, you don't have any idea," said Pico. "We all live other lives. Parallel dimensions, know what I mean? Other worlds, whatever you want to call them. Two, three, maybe more. I got psychic powers," and he grinned through his widely spaced, yellow teeth. "How do you think I get so much information for you and my other sources?

"I'm not a scummy little street hustler in my other lives. Listen! There's one in particular I'm getting closer to all the time: it's like there's a thick, gauzy curtain keeping me away from it, but sometimes I can see into that life, catch glimpses of what it will be like. Only when I try to attract my attention the other me isn't aware because he can't see or hear me.

"But let me tell you one thing, McCoy, I'm successful in my other life. I'm in the movie business, the real thing, none of this getting some amateur hooker to pose for a porno postcard, or go two rounds in front of the camera with some dumb stud and Rusty the Wonder Dog. I wear thousand-dollar suits, have a desk big as a fucking pool table with a posh leather chair. And there's none of this Pico the Rat shit. It's 'Yes, Mr. Piccolino,' and 'No, Mr. Piccolino, sir.' And I tell you, McCoy, instead of a casting couch I got a round, fucking waterbed, twelve feet across. And all them little starlets parade into my office, and I say, 'Show me your titties, Honey,' and they do. We get up on that bed and perform like we were on the U.S. Olympic Gymnastic Fucking Team."

"It's called having an active fantasy life, Pico."

"And I got a beach house in the Malibu Colony. More glass than you ever seen in your whole life, and a view of the ocean that'd make you cry, it's so beautiful. I'm gettin' close, McCoy. One of these days I'm gonna slip through those curtains. Then I'm gonna be somebody. You wait and see if I don't."

By the time he finished he was wild-eyed and there was a bead of sweat on the end of his ugly nose. He believed what he was telling me.

"Invite me out to the beach house some time, please, Mr. Piccolino, sir," I said, as I slipped him another ten.

"I'm this close, McCoy," shouted Pico the Rat, his small, stained hands held an inch apart. He hopped away in an ungainly dwarf's walk, disappearing down the paper-strewn street.

EIGHT

JOE McCOY

"YOU CAN PICK UP ADAM AND FRANCIE at LAX at 2:40 this afternoon." Rosslyn said as she was getting ready to leave for the dental lab.

Even though I'd known for weeks that Adam and Francie were planning to visit, the imminence of their arrival surprised me. Time also flies when you're not having fun.

Adam and Francie have a four-bedroom house in an affluent suburb of Boston. Their home has thick carpets, Japanese wall hangings and a glass coffee table that must be eight feet across. They live in a semi-rural area, crisscrossed by winding, tree-shaded roads. The houses don't have numbers and the roads, if they have names, do not have street signs. Visitors have to be met at "The Village," which as I remember was a camouflaged Conoco Station, and guided as if to a guerrilla leader's hideout.

While visiting L.A., Adam and Francie behave as if they are slumming. "Quaint," is the way Adam describes the endless rows of garish and greasy-smelling fast-food restaurants that line the boulevards of Los Angeles. Adam is chief assistant bean counter at some firm of actuaries and accountants who have been in business in Boston since 1776. Accountants do not have a sense of humor. Adam is my age and a thousand times more successful; Francie is four years younger.

I never knew what to make of Francie. I felt she shared Adam's opinion that Rosslyn had chosen a co-vivant several classes beneath herself.

Francie is one of those girls who appear to have been born without sweat glands. She graduated from Vassar with a degree that serves no practical purpose. Since she became engaged to Adam Quinn she decorates their house and cooks gourmet meals. Adam doesn't believe a wife should work. Francie, it seemed to me, was the perfect choice to be Adam's wife—white wine, designer jeans, dinner parties, charity masquerades. She kept her recipes in a kitchen computer. I teased her once that her Vassar degree was in shopping. She was not amused.

Not long after we met for the first time, Francie said, "I've never quite understood why you and Rosslyn got together. You don't seem to have anything in common."

"Honolulu," I replied.

"Honolulu?"

"Rosslyn was responsible in an irresponsible situation. I found that charming. Most people who vacation in Hawaii go there to drink too much, get laid, get too little sleep and terminal sunburn, and come away depressed because they try too hard to have a good time. I met Rosslyn in a dark little bar called The Crow's Nest, where they have barrels of free peanuts. Ex-baseball players like free food. When I asked her what she did back on the mainland she explained the whole process of casting and manufacturing dentures. There was something terribly sweet and sad about someone really interested in false teeth.

"And when we went to dinner she ordered a balanced meal; she actually said that—'a balanced meal'. I asked if she had a copy of America's Food Guide, or whatever they call it, in her purse. She answered as if I'd asked a serious question. After dinner she excused herself and went to the ladies' room to floss her teeth."

"Still, why did you get together?"

"Hawaiian moonlight, people far from home. Besides, no one is ever quite who they seem to be, including me and maybe even you."

"I wouldn't know," said Francie.

"For instance," I said, "I've always had the feeling that Adam quotes the statistical probability of your getting pregnant in relation to the type of birth control you're practising. My guess is he does it while the two of you are making love."

"How did you know?" cried Francie, laughing musically. Was she appreciating my joke, making fun of Adam or making fun of me?

That conversation happened when I was still marginally respectable. Now, when I cross a street I expect to see a car, driven by me, shrieking toward me, attempting to run me down.

I arrived at LAX several hours early and moved from coffee shop to coffee shop, reading newspapers, studying passengers, watching Airport Security watch me. By the time Adam and Francie's plane arrived, a whole contingent of security men were following me.

The plane from Boston arrived on time. Adam wouldn't have had it any other way. Unfortunately, one of their bags was lost. Adam filled out forms, complaining in a nasal but intimidating voice.

"We are expediting our search," a harried-looking man in a red jacket told Adam. We went to a coffee shop to wait. I was still under surveillance. The coffee shop had deep purple upholstery, the coffee cups were white china, low and wide as grapefruit halves.

Francie was beautiful in a white sundress, her shoulders tanned to the color of oak. I was both surprised and confused at the way Francie greeted me. I was waiting by the baggage carousel when they appeared from the bowels of the airport. Francie, looking cool and refined as ever, strolled toward me smiling in a friendly but noncommittal manner.

But when she got to within about fifteen feet of me her face burst into a joyous smile and she ran the last few steps before throwing herself into my arms, something she had never done before. She kissed me on the lips, something else she had never done before, for what I interpreted to be much longer than a brother's fiancée should kiss his sister's boyfriend. And as she kissed me, her little pink tongue grazed my upper lip, several times. She tasted a little—lemony, like those scented napkins airlines pass out toward the end of long flights. Adam waited patiently, dressed in actuary pinstripes and tasteful tie, to shake my hand firmly, but not too firmly.

If anyone had told me that that sweet, unexpected kiss would lead to Francie and me being on the FBI's 10 Most Wanted List, and that I, an undistinguished ex-jock, ex-investigative reporter would, in a matter of weeks, become an American folk hero of sorts, known as Kid McCoy, and that Adam Quinn would compile a cookbook of Francie's recipes called *The Francie Bly Cookbook: Recipes for People on the Run*, well, as far as I'm concerned, wishes, in that case, might really be horses, and I don't believe that either.

I have a terminal fascination with airports. Ha!

Airports are so private. There is something sensuous about the chrome, the marble, the various-colored imitation leather chairs, the perpetual air conditioning. For an instant I fantasized Francie and I together, in hiding in an airport. We could check into an Airport Hilton, a Ramada, or a Holiday Inn, perhaps a Hyatt-Regency—check in each evening, check out each morning.

An airport is a city unto itself containing everything necessary to sustain life and spirit: there are food, clothing, newspapers, magazines, toys, insurance, a post office, a gift shop. There are no neighbors to complain that the grass is uncut, the windows dirty, a car abandoned in the back yard, the gate unpainted and hanging by one hinge. Broken hinges, dirty windows and abandoned cars are not allowed in airports.

As long as I had my credit cards, those little biscuits of God, we could eat three meals a day, walk our dog if we had one, push our children in strollers along the miles of labyrinthian corridors or let them play in departure areas, and we would owe explanations to no one. Perpetual travelers, we would move in utter anonymity.

In the airport coffee shop, Adam Quinn washed both his food and his cutlery. Francie smiled at me over her creamed coffee. Under the table, her small, white-shod foot brushed my instep. The harried man in the red jacket delivered Adam's suitcase. Had it been mine it would have arrived twenty-four-hours after I had left on my return journey. Adam grumbled thanks, tipped the man a quarter.

*　*　*

My dreams. Realer than real. Sight, sound, taste, touch, smell. My dreams whirling, advancing and retreating, changed subtly from reliving incidents that happened to me, if in slightly different form or time frame, to dreaming a past that never occurred.

My dreams more and more concern Maureen Renn. For instance, though I know Maureen wouldn't have wanted a church wedding, there we were kneeling at the altar in a large, cold church, the air heavy with incense. I sneaked a glance at Maureen; she was wearing an expensive and beautiful creamy lace bridal gown. She had on lipstick and make-up. The church was full but we were alone at the altar. Where was the wedding party?

I couldn't imagine who my best man might be, a high-school baseball teammate? One of Maureen's orangutan brothers? Whoever it was, I knew he had printed HELP ME! on the soles of my shoes, and that those words were now exposed to the churchful of people who sat silent as pillows, waiting.

"What church is this?" I whispered to Maureen.

"Easy, Sugar," she said, squeezing my hand.

A priest or minister appeared, dressed in a long, white cassock with bands of bright embroidery encircling it.

He raised his hands as if calling time out. The wedding guests maintained their deathly silence. I couldn't even hear them breathing.

"I'm sorry," the churchman intoned, "but the tests show that the bride is not only not a virgin, but is nine weeks pregnant. The ceremony is canceled."

There were harsh whispers and a ritual shuffling of feet among the guests. Anger rose in me like mercury in a thermometer.

"Who the hell needs this?" I said to Maureen in as normal a voice as I could muster. I scrambled to my feet. But when I glanced to my right, Maureen was gone, and in her place was Francie Bly, sweet as frosting, a lacy veil covering her face.

"What are you grumbling about?" she whispered. "The service is about to begin."

I woke with a gasp, feeling as if I had fallen a great distance. I fully expected to have disturbed Rosslyn, but she slept peacefully at my side, dreaming of overbites.

I'm relatively certain that that really was a dream. Some other events I'm not entirely sure about. My marriage to Maureen, for instance; I feel so sure it happened. We are leaving on our honeymoon, Maureen and I, but I'm driving my Lincoln, which I didn't acquire until after Maureen had married Tucker Wegman. Yet, being married to Maureen feels so right.

There are other dreams about flight, being on the run—cliffhangers, I'm often left in life-threatening situations. When I wake, bedclothes tangled about me like restraints, I wonder if, in another life or dimension, I haven't been out there engaged in some dangerous activities, on the run, pursued by law and outlaw.

See what you think of these dreams:

In Dallas, we—we being myself, Francie Bly and our baby—are just about to start the first leg of a journey that will end in Honolulu.

At Love Field, the gum-chewing girl on the X-ray machine runs the baby's diaper-bag through the machine three times, lazily studying the outline of articles that show up on the screen. She opens the bag, feels around, rearranging his bottles as if they were hand grenades. Though the metal detector didn't beep, I am pulled to one side and the electronic wand passed over my body several times.

Immediately behind us at security, three swarthy young men, looking like the best man and ushers from a Middle Eastern wedding party, are scarcely glanced at, even though they carry overly large flight bags that bulge ominously.

The plane is not large and is less than a third full when the largest and flashiest of the Middle Eastern wedding party leaps—the best man? — into the aisle, brandishing a weapon and shouting in what I assume to be a foreign language.

"What now?" says Francie, looking up from the baby.

"I suspect we're being hijacked."

"Oh, no."

"Everything else has happened to us, why not?"

The other hijackers—they must be the ushers—force their way into the cabin. They make the crew close the door, leaving probably fifty passengers outside. The ushers station themselves one forward, one aft.

The best man is conducting a dramatic monologue in heavily accented

English about the thousand years of oppression his people, who may or may not be Palestinian, have suffered. He is certainly not fond of Jews.

But there is something askew. He is ranting at us as if we were Jews, his gun to the neck of a very small flight attendant who looks like somebody's kid sister dressed for Hallowe'en. The passengers are gabbling like they were at a Tupperware party.

The best man moves the flight attendant down the aisle until they are opposite us.

"You will convey our demands to your Zionist Captain," the best man says to the flight attendant.

"This is my first day on the job," the girl whispers. She is so pale I suspect she may faint.

"Excuse me," I say, loudly enough for the best man to hear. His eyes are large and brown and protrude slightly. He has a neatly trimmed mustache above very thick lips. "I'd like to offer my services," I say. "I'm used to working in difficult situations."

"You have perhaps commandeered an aircraft?" he says, placing the muzzle of his gun directly above my heart.

"Not exactly," I squeak. "But I'm a reliable messenger."

"I am thinking you are an employee of this El Al Airline?"

"El Al?"

"You are thinking I am stupid? I have studied one year at Tulane University. Of course, El Al! We plan to deliver this planeful of Jews to Libya."

"Oh, dear," the flight attendant whispers. She stares up at the terrorist. "I'm afraid you've made a terrible mistake. This is a domestic flight, out of Gate 16. The El Al flight to Israel departs from Gate 60."

The hijacker tries to pretend he is not devastated.

"You lie!" he shouts, pushing the gun hard against my chest. He looks questioningly at me.

"This isn't El Al," I say. I don't add, "You'd probably be dead if it were, as they have ten times better security than other airlines."

We are interrupted by a pop, like a wine bottle being uncorked, followed by about three seconds of dead silence then screams from the front of the plane.

"Ali!" shouts the best man, delivering a couple of dozen ugly-sounding words in his own language.

Word drifts back, in musical snatches, like childrens' voices from a playground, that Ali has accidentally discharged his gun.

"Go tell the captain we are going to Libya," he says to me.

"The El Al flight doesn't depart for forty minutes," says the flight attendant. "If you hurry you can still make it."

The hijacker actually considers the possibility. He leans across me and glances out the window. There is a SWAT van on the tarmac, and a dozen men who look like astronauts in asbestos suits are piling out.

"I'll deliver your message," I say. "My name's Joe. And this is my wife, Francie, and our baby. What's your name? It will make for easier communication, give negotiations a personal touch."

"I am thinking you are odd, Joe," says the best man. "I am Fazi. Ali and Assad," he goes on, pointing first to the front, then to the rear of the plane.

From across the aisle, a sixtyish man with a hearing aid grabs me by the arm. He is wearing a spiffy western shirt and string tie.

"Ain't you Joe McCoy? I seen you play for the Rangers a couple of seasons back."

"Never heard of him," I reply, trying to pull loose.

"The hell," says the man. "I seen you. You couldn't pitch a strike if you was throwin' at a boxcar."

"Sorry," I say.

"Ain't you been in the news of recently?"

"Not until now. We're being hijacked."

"Well I know that," the man says. "Ain't nothin' to worry about, they'll just send in the real Texas Rangers, blow the asses off these A-rabs. You're not in cahoots with them, are you?"

"No, sir, I'm not."

"No offence. I was just hopin' y'all hadn't turned to a life of crime. You sure never could pitch a baseball."

"Horses! Horses! Hijackers!" I scream. Francie is shaking my shoulder. I stare wildly around. I'm on a plane droning tranquilly over an ocean.

"You've had a bad dream," says Francie. I am sweaty. My mouth tastes like Courteguayan insurgents have been marching through it for eight hours.

I look across the aisle. There is the old man in the western garb. He is squinting at me in an ominous way.

"We're not being hijacked?" I say to Francie.

"Of course not. Don't say 'hijacked' so loud," she replies, placing her fingers over my lips. "You could get in all kinds of trouble."

The old man touches Francie on the arm. "You taking this fellow home from a loonie bin?"

"Yes," hisses Francie.

"Don't bode well for that poor baby, insanity in the family and all. Is he the father?"

"I have no idea," says Francie. "I am promiscuous beyond your wildest dreams. You might even be the father. We have met before, haven't we?"

The old man goes back to his airline magazine. His wife, who has upswept white hair lacquered in place and is dressed for square dancing, glowers at him suspiciously.

I am staring wildly about the plane.

"Why don't you read for a while," says Francie. She hands me a copy of the airline magazine. On the cover is a flat-deck truck piled high with merry-go-round horses in various states of disrepair.

Or this:

The motel room in Tulsa is stuffed with moonlight. I see the door-knob turn, watch in horror as the thin silver jaws of a cutting device snake in and snip the chain. Two shiny-suited figures cross toward the bed. What would be better for Francie and the baby—if I let them kill me or if I create a distraction?

I decide on the distraction. I brace my ankles on the mattress, and, with arms spread wide, rise like the phoenix.

"What the fuck?" mumbles one of the suits.

"HY-YAAAAAAH," I scream and pitch myself on the intruders.

"Run, Francie," I cry.

Someone lands a body blow but I'm protected by bedclothes. I knee something that groans.

The baby cries out as Francie snatches him from his crib. The door slams. I hear my Lincoln grind to a start. I relax and let the intruders overpower me.

They are too well dressed and barbered to be police or Mafia. Either could be a shill who gives testimonials on Sunday morning religious broadcasts, except that the seated man holds a gun on me.

"The baby is gone," I say. "Unless you had back-up out there."

"We're not interested in the baby. We're interested in you," says the shorter of the two who is blond and apple-cheeked.

"Are you bounty hunters?"

"In a way," says the seated man, who is dark and trim. "We have a document for you to sign."

"No need for you to read it," says the pacing man. "It's a formal apology to organized baseball. We've included every imaginable cliché. You admit your guilt, beg forgiveness, ask for the prayers of all baseball fans. You hint that you intend to end your life because of the disgrace you've brought to the national pastime."

"You're going to aid me in doing the honorable thing?"

"Your statement will wring tears from even your most furious detractors," says the gun toter.

"Because of your unconscionable acts, diplomatic relations between the USA and Courteguay may be broken off," adds the other.

"I thought you were with organized baseball? What do you care about diplomatic relations?"

"Baseball players. We lost the Cubans. We still spirit the odd player out of Cuba, introduce him into organized baseball as a Venezuelan or Courteguayan. We can't afford to lose Courteguay. Eighteen of the twenty-eight teams have middle infielders from Courteguay."

"Would you consider letting me do the job myself? You wouldn't have a poison capsule on you?"

Both men shake their heads, but there is a vague light of understanding in their eyes.

"Here's what I propose. You guys carry a second gun, right?"

They nod.

"Well, leave me a gun with one bullet. Check the bathroom, there's no window. Allow me five minutes to get my thoughts together. When you hear the shot, rush in and discover my body. As a gesture of good faith I'll sign the confession, only you've got to leave it with me."

We reach an uneasy agreement. They leave a gun with one bullet on the TV, back out the door slowly.

The motel is one long row of units with arches for doorways. While there is no window in the bathroom, there is a trap door in the ceiling, which I have just climbed through, after tearing the confessional document to shreds and flushing it down the john. I crouch on the roof for a few seconds.

There is about twenty feet of potholed parking lot and a slack chain-link fence separating the motel from a private residence. The private yard is heavily treed, large limbs drooping onto the parking lot. When I jump from the roof my shoes sound like hands clapping as they hit the asphalt. I cross the lot and vault the fence. I can hear the feet of my would-be executioners pounding on asphalt. Fortunately, my unit was in the middle of the motel; my enemies had to run half a block to get behind the motel. There are a number of popping sounds like single kernels of popcorn exploding, something strikes the leaves of a tree right next to my left ear.

I skulk through several yards, barely avoiding a yellow-fanged dog tethered to a tree, who sets up a wow-wowing that will provide a good clue as to my location.

NINE

JOE McCOY

AS ADAM AND FRANCIE'S VISIT TOOK SHAPE, my improbable life became more improbable. It looked as if Francie Bly was falling in love with me. It wasn't my imagination. I'd catch her staring at me out of the corner of her eye, the way girls used to look at boys in high school, furtive, exciting little glances. We became a couple at dinner, at cards, when we went for a late-evening stroll. Adam and Rosslyn don't seem to notice, but then Adam and Rosslyn were not very observant. They were having a marvelous visit, they talked about family and friends, their childhoods. They talked business. Adam manages Rosslyn's investments.

What I couldn't comprehend was that when I was modestly successful and reasonably well known, Francie acted as if I was Rosslyn's gardener, but now that I was disgraced and broke she suddenly found me irresistible. I wasn't sure I liked Francie very much, but I *needed* someone to care.

I wondered if I had day-dreamed Francie into my arms at the airport? Between the time their plane arrived and the time they appeared at the baggage carousel I had the strangest fantasy. I envisioned Francie as my wife; I was meeting her alone. She would be dressed in Easter mauve, my favorite color; she would give a little squeal of joy when she saw me, rush across the room and throw herself into my arms, our mouths colliding.

"Let's get a hotel," I whispered to her.

"I'm with you, Lover," Francie said. "Who did you bring down while I was away?" she asked as an afterthought.

"Only the Mayor," I said nonchalantly. "But next week, if all goes well, Tommy Lasorda and the Dodger infield."

"After we make love, let's go to Disneyland," said Francie.

With Francie loving me it was impossible to be unsuccessful.

And, when they arrived it was as if Francie had read my mind, for she threw her arms around my neck, and there was that kiss, sweet and intimate and personal. She was even wearing mauve, a scarf, and she was dressed more attractively than usual—like a beautiful young woman on a holiday rather than as if she had just escaped from a business seminar on computer hardware.

"Rosslyn says you've been having a run of tough luck," Adam said, as if my troubles would disappear if the Dow-Jones gained seven points.

"Joe will bounce back, won't you?" said Francie.

"All that's bouncing right now are my checks," I said, smiling for the first time in weeks, the lemony taste of Francie's lips still on mine. I looked at Adam, hoping he wouldn't misconstrue my joke as a request for a loan.

My dreams continued during Adam and Francie's visit: past and present, fantasy and reality pounding around in my head. Since Rosslyn was at work, and Adam spent his time on the phone to Boston, I spent my days with Francie. She *was* coming on to me. Inexplicably, she was fascinated by the junky car I was driving.

"Mother would never let me ride in a car that was more than two years old," she said. "I always wanted to date a guy in a leather jacket, who had a car like this, with foam-rubber dice hanging from the rearview."

"I'll buy a leather jacket," I said. And I did. I wheeled off the freeway into a shopping mall, and put down my about-to-expire, highly over-extended MasterCard to purchase a $199.95 leather jacket with six silver studs on each shoulder.

"This is fun," said Francie, hugging my arm.

Back in the car she slid over beside me as if we were out on a date, her expression making clear what *her* intentions were. I wheeled the car into a Jack-in-the-Box and ordered chocolate milkshakes.

That evening the four of us went out to dinner, Adam and Francie's treat in return for the use of the guest room. Francie slid into the restaurant booth, grabbed my hand and pulled me down beside her. Rosslyn and Adam sat across from us. Francie was rubbing around me like a hungry cat. We watched a couple in another booth toast each other. Francie then insisted we entwine arms and wine glasses in the embarrassing ritual of sipping from each other's glass. Adam and Rosslyn were not offended.

For the ride home, Francie pulled me into the back seat of Rosslyn's Volvo, sat with her head resting on my shoulder, her small hand tightly clasped in mine.

When Rosslyn came to bed I fully expected a lecture on proper decorum in public places and the evils of flirting.

"I thought it was awfully nice of Francie to try to cheer you up," Rosslyn said, pulling her flannel nightgown down over her head.

"Is that what she was doing?"

"You might have at least tried to enjoy yourself," she went on. "You spent the whole evening shifting in your seat and looking guilty."

The next night our jolly foursome went dancing.

"It's a motif cabaret called Jungle Jim's," Francie said. She had picked it from an ad in an entertainment guide.

Francie insisted we take separate cars.

"I want to ride in Joe's rickety old car," she said. "It makes me feel like a teenager. It's liable to break down on the freeway or run out of gas, or take off for Las Vegas."

"Rosslyn's rickety old car," I reminded her. "I sold my Lincoln to buy luxuries like food and paper to print my résumés."

Maybe I should have a close encounter and get fired from my job more often, I thought.

The interior of the cabaret was like a rain forest. There were roots painted on the floor, so realistic I at first tried to step over them, and a tree growing out of the middle of each table. Mechanical cockatoos and furry monkeys chittered in the branches above us. The waitresses wore clothing that intimated that their plane had crashed in the cabaret in 1942. The band was dressed in khaki Bermuda shorts and pith helmets. The doorman looked exactly like Mandrake the Magician's faithful sidekick, Lothar.

"I can't go in," I said at the door. "I haven't had my malaria booster." No one laughed.

Francie and I found a table for two behind a plastic banyan tree. I ordered a Cheetah's Revenge, which was coconut milk with something floating in it. We checked in with Rosslyn and Adam once, but their heads were close together, oblivious to the music. He was offering her advice on buying securities.

After two drinks, I danced Francie into the darkest corner of the room and, first checking carefully to make certain we were out of view, bent to kiss her. The shock of her tongue touching mine straightened my back as if I'd been kidney-punched. Francie moved her arms up around my neck and we pressed our bodies close together. We kissed again, long and slow.

"We shouldn't . . ." I began, when our mouths finally parted.

"Shhhh," said Francie. "We're all alone on a strange continent. There's no one in the world but us."

We shut our eyes and danced and kissed for the rest of the set.

When we returned to our table, Francie plopped down on a log chair, lit a cigarette, and smiled at me in a love-struck yet impudent way that increased my heart rate fifteen beats a minute.

"I can't help myself," she said, shaking her taffy-colored curls. "And if something can't be helped then I'm going to enjoy it."

The music started again, and we danced, kissed, and stared into each other's eyes, the way lovers are supposed to do. Francie was wearing an ivory-colored dress, her right shoulder bare. There was a mauve-colored orchid imprinted on the material just above her left breast.

Later, as we were leaving, Francie waved gaily at Rosslyn and Adam. "We'll see you at home," she called.

As we were going out the door I was accosted by a staggering alcoholic, about thirty-five, developing jowls and a belly.

"Didn't you used to be somebody?" he slurred, his ninety-proof breath making us both turn away.

Just what I needed, a drunken sports fan. Or did he recognize me from my more recent escapades?

"I certainly did," I said, ducking by him, as he leaned a large paw on the wall to block my exit, "but a couple of months ago I died and went to hell."

Francie and I sat for several minutes in the dark parking lot. We were all over each other like teenagers at a drive-in movie. Francie draped her legs over mine as we kissed wildly. I slipped a hand inside her dress and cupped one of her small, naked breasts. Francie locked one hand in the long hair at the base of my neck, applying sweet pressure to keep our mouths together. We engaged in a considerable amount of heavy breathing and the snapping of various elastics. Francie had her hand in my pants and we both knew we were not about to stop when a car backed out of a nearby parking place, its headlights flooding our car interior with light, and stopped so the driver could talk with someone. A half minute later, we straightened our clothes and prepared to leave.

Instead of the freeway I choose to drive home by regular streets. We kissed away red lights, two or three if there was no traffic behind us. We sat at stop signs, sometimes for delightfully long periods of time, until a car finally zippered up behind us and honked.

"What if a car never comes along?" Francie whispered into my mouth. "What if the street behind us is closed forever?"

"In thirty-four years I'll get out of the car and apply for Social Security," I replied. "I declare this road closed."

A yellow Corvette grumbled up behind us, sat for a few seconds, then honked a scratchy-sounding horn.

"Liar," said Francie, untangling her legs from mine. "I wish what you were saying was true. I've wished it so hard . . ."

"If wishes were horses . . ." I said.

For just an instant, in the pattern made by the Corvette's headlights in my rearview mirror appeared the shape of a rearing horse. How strange.

"I beg your pardon?" said Francie. "Horses?"

"An old poem or nursery rhyme," I said. "Don't tell me you've never heard it?"

"All right, I won't," said Francie.

Rosslyn's Volvo was in the driveway, the house ablaze with lights.

"I hope you two didn't stop to eat," Rosslyn called as we entered. The air was heavy with the smell of coffee and grilled cheese sandwiches.

Adam, who has short, blue-black hair, baby fat and a perpetually self-satisfied expression, had changed into striped pyjamas and was gargling obscenely with Listerine as we passed the open bathroom door.

At the kitchen table Francie and I were properly subdued, feeling guilty for what we had almost done. But Rosslyn and Adam continued talking business. Adam had figured out how to shelter some of her income, something about tax-free bonds, and was holding forth on how Rosslyn could claim me as a tax write-off.

Like a typewriter that's been replaced by a computer, or a machine that's died on the job? I wanted to ask. But they were both so jubilant at Adam's genius that I said nothing.

That night I dreamed a past not with Francie, who occupied my thoughts as I drifted into sleep, but Maureen. We lived in a big, old house on Johnson Street a few blocks from downtown in Iowa City, a house with a swing on the verandah, a fireplace, a glassed-in sunporch that we used as our bedroom. I worked for the *Iowa City Press Citizen*, a slim daily newspaper that, competing as it did with the *Des Moines Register*, *Chicago Tribune*, *Cedar Rapids Gazette* and *USA Today*, stayed in business only because it had super-aggressive advertising salesmen. I was a sportswriter.

I was on my way to cover a high-school baseball game between West High and a team from Onamata. I was driving my red Lincoln Continental convertible; Maureen was sitting close by my side. We were very much in love. Our son, Joe Jr., was asleep in a basket on the back seat.

Onamata is not far from my home town. I was surprised that I had no animosity toward Lone Tree or its people, and I became vaguely aware that this was because I had lived a totally different life for the previous thirteen years.

It was a perfect June evening, the cornfields, lilacs and honeysuckle in bloom.

Maureen glanced into the back seat, where a small, maple-colored nose was all that was visible of Joe Jr. We passed several white horses grazing in a verdant pasture. They galloped beside us for a while, teeth flashing, swift as moonlight.

My little family sat in the bleachers behind first base, Maureen hugged my arm, Joe Jr. asleep in his basket. I made occasional notes on the baseball game. Once or twice Maureen got excited enough to cheer for the Onamata team. She liked them because they had only nine players and their uniforms didn't match.

Beyond the outfield the cornfields glowed emerald in the evening sun. The air was moist with the odors of growth. Beyond the third-base foul-line the Iowa River twisted silently toward Missouri; it never does get to Missouri, the Iowa is absorbed by the Mississippi near a town called Toolesboro, Iowa. The river was so close that a schoolboy with a glove was stationed on its bank to keep foul balls from rolling in and bobbing away like white corks in the silk-green river.

Surprisingly, Onamata was winning. They had pitiful pitching, mediocre fielding, and no particular skill as base runners. But they could hit. I suspected one, maybe even two, would end up in the Bigs. I had alerted my friend Bill Clark, a scout for the Atlanta Braves, and he had promised to come by for a look before school adjourned for the summer.

Onamata's coach resembled a bear walking upright. His name was Stan Rogalski and he had played fifteen years of undistinguished outfield in the minor leagues. His first words to me when he took over the team four years ago were, "Hi, I'm Stan Rogalski, and I hate Polish jokes. If you tell any Polish jokes when I'm around I'm liable to break your face."

"I'm Joe McCoy," I said, "and I'm Irish, and I don't mind Irish jokes. They're all about my relatives. And they're funny, both the relatives and the jokes. Did you know my brother married into white trash to improve his social standing?"

Rogalski grinned. "Different strokes," he said. And we've been friends ever since.

"How come you're not a hitting instructor in the Bigs?" I asked.

"I've only been coaching for four years," he replied. "Sports people are slow to recognize talent. I've got one kid in Triple A this year, Kansas City will call him up before the season's over. Word is getting around. The Phillies offered me a job as traveling minor-league hitting instructor, but I turned it down. I spent fifteen years on the road as a player. It'll take a better offer'n that to get me to leave Onamata."

Maureen nuzzled my arm. Joe Jr. opened one eye then closed it.

"There is the finest of lines between fantasy and reality," Maureen said without warning.

My stomach dropped sickeningly. I felt as if I've just been picked off first. Like I'd realized a split second too late that the throw was coming, had dived back in a cloud of dust only to have the first baseman's glove slap my forearm while my fingers still stretched toward the angel-white base.

"I wish you hadn't said that, Maureen."

"Life with you is so good it's like I wished it. That's all I mean. We could be somewhere else. I could be somewhere else, married to an accountant in some horrible place like Boston, where there are ten diesel trucks and a bus without a muffler ahead of you at every light."

"I know what you mean. In another dimension I might have to work in a machine shop," I said. "That would be my idea of hell. But you don't live in Boston, and I'm not a machinist, so let's not worry about it."

But I was worrying about it. Everything seemed impermanent, as if it might be a dream. I felt as if I had sneaked into my life from somewhere else.

The sunporch of our house on Johnson Street faced east. In the early morning, whoever had changed Joe Jr. and given him his bottle crawled back under the covers and cuddled the other one awake. We then made love with the sunshine playing through the screen, covering our bodies with sinister masks and scars. The morning sunshine warmed my back and a soft breeze cooled it. Maureen crooned her love, her arms locked about my neck. We joked that we provided the entertainment for that block of old frame houses, disguised by trees, yards choked with lilacs and honeysuckle. Maureen's voice carried in the early morning air. Joe Jr. was the only child on the block. Walking home from work in the humid late afternoon I could hear him fussing or crying from at least four houses down the street.

Now, on the bleacher, Maureen, her face and arms deeply tanned, dressed in blue jeans, the arms of a denim jacket loosely tied about her waist, ran her hand inside my shirt, her long fingers counting my ribs, but when I looked over it was not Maureen but Francie. Francie in her cool sundress, wearing the mauve scarf.

"It's time to change the baby," she said, kissing my cheek. She stood and turned away from me to pick up the basket in which the unseen Little Joe lay gurgling.

*   *   *

Somewhere out in the night my other life revolves around a different planet. I want to phone Maureen. Occasionally I call information for Iowa City, for Onamata, for Lone Tree, for Cedar Rapids, just to be positive that I'm not listed, that nothing has changed, that I'm not back in Iowa City working for the *Press Citizen*, sitting at my terminal just before deadline, anxious to get home to Maureen and the kids.

Three more days and nights of dreams passed, and I was driving Francie toward LAX. Two days before, Adam had been called to Boston, where some conglomerate whose investments he mothers surprised everyone by filing Chapter Eleven Bankruptcy. The night Adam left, Francie and I stayed up late and, over coffee at the kitchen table, talked vaguely of our dissatisfaction.

"He does up the collar of his sports shirts," Francie said, making further cataloguing unnecessary. What it amounted to was that we were dreamers and our companions were not. Francie wanted babies, Adam wanted AT&T.

"I have never been able to find romance in the construction of false teeth, though I admit there is no poetry in being an unemployed reporter."

My temptation in the desert seems never to have happened. I am still employed, my beautiful '56 Lincoln Continental has not been driven into the sunset by a warty father-figure from a Saroyan novel.

I am entering a Kentucky Fried Chicken. There are only two people ahead of me, but I notice as I enter that people are heading for the door from all corners of the parking lot—teenagers, working people, business men—converging like columns of ants. The man in front of me is paying for a large order, nineteen dollars and some cents worth. He is a working man, probably picking up lunch for several co-workers. As he accepts his change he says something in a low voice to the pretty Hispanic cashier. She says something back in an equally low voice.

"What?" the man shouts, outraged.

The line behind me now runs all the way to the door. There is a black couple in their twenties, both beautiful and attired as if they had just stepped out of *Ebony*, there are three teenaged girls and a sad-looking man in baggy trousers.

"You want twenty-five cents for salsa?" the man shouted. "I just spent twenty dollars on chicken. You should give me a salsa." He is about thirty.

The buzz of conversation stops. We all look toward the commotion, toward the glass case just inside the door, which holds milk cartons, packs of coleslaw, and a stack of small containers, each holding about an ounce of salsa that looks only dark, not red, through the translucent plastic.

The girl says something we can't hear, even though all ears are straining toward the commotion.

"I want the manager," the man states loudly.

The clerk scurries away.

"Way to go," I say.

A few seconds later the clerk returns trailing a surprised-looking woman, another teenager.

"It's company policy," the young manager says, shrugging disinterestedly. "I don't have any control over it."

"Nobody's ever in charge," I hear myself saying. There are murmurs of approval.

"Give him the salsa," says the handsome young black man. Applause.

"Give me a salsa or give me my money back," says the man.

"Give him the salsa," says the black woman.

"May I take your order?" a second clerk says to me.

"Not yet," I say. "I want to see how this turns out."

Suddenly, Maureen is directly behind me in line.

"Still tilting at windmills," says Maureen, her ironic smile taking me in.

"It's a living," I say.

"You've turned into a real asshole, Joe. I'm glad you dumped me. I'm glad you fucked off to college without me." I don't know what to say. Memory is like a dappled mirror. How old is she, anyway? Is she the girl I left behind? The woman she would be today?

I touch Maureen's wrist and the thrill of contact is so strong it is like I am iron filings and she is a magnet.

"I've never loved anybody but you," I hear myself saying.

Maureen's face crumples, her bottom lip trembling.

"Help me get away from here," I say into her plum-colored hair, the scent so familiar it is like walking into your childhood home after a long absence.

We have one long, wild, teary, tongue-touching kiss.

The people around us are stamping their feet and chanting rhythmically "Give him the salsa! Give him the salsa!"

The young manager goes to the cooler, takes out one of the tiny containers of salsa and hands it to the man. Everyone applauds.

"One small step for man," the black man says.

More applause.

"May I take your order, please?" the clerk says to me.

I turn back to face her. Maureen is gone, but her taste is still on my lips, her scent in my nostrils.

"I have fantasies about you," Francie said, sliding across the car seat until our bodies touched. "I've undressed you so many times this past week that I'm tired from unbuttoning all those buttons."

She gently undid one of the buttons on my shirt. Only the points of her nails were painted, a pearly vermilion. There was something incredibly erotic about the touch of her paint-tipped nails.

In the parking lot at LAX, I slumped down behind the wheel. Three of Francie's fingers rested where the button used to be. My heart beats into her fingertips. My impulse was to pull back on the freeway, find a motel.

"We're never going to do anything about the way we feel, are we?" asked Francie, reading my heartbeats.

"Probably not," I said, adding quickly, "but never is a long time."

There was a lengthy silence.

Two thugs in a purple van with teardrop windows parked beside us. Drug dealers, I decided. Maybe I would interview them after Francie's plane left. The driver was stocky and scarred, with muscles and tattoos.

"I would," said Francie. "If it weren't for . . . everything. I want to make love with you more than anything I can think of. Adam and I will be back in a few months. You and I will sneak a few kisses in the downstairs hall, make ourselves feel just guilty enough not to do anything foolish. Adam and I may even be married by then."

She wrapped her arms around me, kissed me wildly, but only for about five seconds, then slipped to her side of the car, smoothed her clothes and hair and opened the door. I had the feeling the thugs had been watching us from behind purple-tinted windows.

At the check-in counter, Francie asked for a window seat.

"Leave the aisle seat vacant," I said to the clerk. "My wife gets air sick and she's a projectile vomiter."

The asexual clerk needed a facelift. It stared at us for several seconds to see if we were joking, then turned the number of the aisle seat upside down on the seat-assignment chart.

Outside the security gate, like a shy suitor, I took Francie's hand. She glanced at me, smiled a tough little smile that could have melted metal. Here we are, I thought, duty will win out over lust. A fine pair of dreamers we are.

Francie was about fifteen minutes away from passing through security and flying out of my life when, seemingly from nowhere, a flight attendant, whose sky-blue uniform was covered in jewel-like buttons, pink epaulets and medals, appeared and presented Francie with a pink blanket, which, by its shape, and the fact that a large, blue diaper bag accompanied it, gave the impression that there was a baby inside.

Francie let go of my hand and accepted the baby. She looked puzzled, made a mild protest, but even as she did so she was arranging the baby in a comfortable position in the crook of her arm. I appraised the flight attendant's gaudy uniform, trying to spot an airline insignia. Her accent was vaguely Spanish.

"I'm not . . ." Francie said.

"We're not . . ." I protested.

But, like a plump blackbird, she whirled away into the awesome depths of the Los Angeles International Airport.

Francie and I looked at each other.

"My goodness!" said Francie. "What do we do now?"

"We could send out announcements."

Francie's smile was sudden as fireworks, her face full of love as she raised the point of the blanket and kissed the baby's small, cinnamon-colored nose, which was all I could see.

Francie's flight was announced.

We both stared around the waiting room. There was no one who looked as though they were expecting a baby to be pressed into their arms.

"Here we go," said Francie. As she stood, her eyes locked onto mine.

"You can't," I said.

"Only if you'll come with me," she said. "Come for the ride, Joe. Do something totally lunatic," she whispered.

She had one arm around me, standing against me so we were both holding the baby.

"We'll pretend. For the next four or five hours there'll be no one in the world but our little family." Francie's lips were slightly parted. Lust superseded common sense. "Pretend with me, Joe, please?"

"I'll get a ticket."

I bolted away, trotting the long, translucent corridors of LAX.

As I walked, each step a commitment to something bizarre, foolish, dangerous, illegal, I remembered my long-standing fantasies of being on the run. I have always felt I am smart enough to outwit anyone searching for me. A kind of up-beat, real life, TV-series game of hide and seek appealed to me.

In my fantasies, there was never a specific reason why I was a fugitive. I imagined long, intricate scenarios in which, always innocent, I was forced to flee for my life, from police, FBI, CIA, or the Mob. More recently I have envisioned those emissaries of organized baseball, well-scrubbed young men in pinstriped uniforms, hunting me down, wreaking revenge on me for slandering the national pastime.

By the time I returned to the departure lounge, I figured that someone would have shown up to claim the baby. Still, the idea of being a fugitive excited me. It must be a terrific aphrodisiac to be on the run. What was it Willie Nelson sang? Something about ladies love outlaws? I wondered if they were the same kind of ladies who loved ballplayers. I hoped not.

TEN

JOE McCOY

THE WOMEN OF THE ROAD. Maureen spoiled me. I was never well enough known as a baseball player to have famous groupies, movie starlets, fashion models. I'm the kind of guy who got stopped outside the player's gate after the stars had left.

"Are you anybody?" I was often asked.

"Once, when the hand grabbing at my sleeve belonged to a very pretty girl, I replied, "Yes, I am somebody," and I named a star player. There was a long pause as the information made its way slowly to the girl's brain.

"But he's black," she said finally.

"Only on the field," I said.

I never lacked for female companionship. I had a girl or two in every city. But I discouraged relationships. The words *settle down* held an unpleasant picture of a building settling, disappearing into the earth, covered with moss, ravaged by termites.

In my early days at university, I missed Maureen a lot. I often thought of calling her, of asking her to forgive me, to come to me, but the months slipped into years.

Once, outside the Astrodome, a pretty young woman in a leather skirt asked for my autograph (a subtle way to find out if I was anybody) flirted a lot, and ended up in my bed. We were having what I considered a good time when she whispered, "Would you mind hurrying up a little, like I got a late date with Billy," and she named our star outfielder.

I charged my ticket on my MasterCard, holding my breath, trying to project an image of honesty and reliability. I smiled like a beauty contest finalist, stared the agent straight in the eye. Because there were eighteen people in line behind me she did not check my card.

Rosslyn, understandably, refused to pay my bills. She said being in debt would teach me responsibility. Actually, she was cross because I had recently turned down my only job offer: a chance to write ad copy for a rock radio station. Rosslyn would have considered me responsible if I wrote advertising jingles for crooked used-car dealers, to air on W–HIT.

After I bought my ticket, I had to jog about a mile through the hallways of LAX, wait at security while they went over the three guys in front of me, all of whom looked as though they could be carrying hand grenades. I recognized one from the van in the parking lot.

One lonely attendant was left at the departure gate. I raced down the ramp and reached the plane just as they were closing the door.

"Is it a boy or a girl?" I asked Francie, as I slipped into my seat.

"You must have known you were coming all along," said Francie. "Otherwise why did you save the seat?"

"I used the vomiting story when I played baseball, saved me from sharing a seat with some bozo who chewed snuff. Now, boy or girl?"

Francie flashed me a smile so sweet it could have fed a starving army, converted a heathen, started a stalled car.

"Let's make it a game," she said, staring down at the baby. "Guess the right sex or we don't get to keep him."

"I notice you've decided already."

"Women can tell about things like that."

"The blanket is pink."

"The diaper bag is blue," she said, producing a blue bottle. She peeled back the blanket to expose the head of the sleeping child, its face bland as a pancake.

"A boy. Then it's decided?"

"Should we peek?" Her blouse was the color of strawberry wine. Francie pulled up the knitted sweater, delicately raised the top of the diaper so she alone could see. The baby, in its sleep, waved its left hand; the nails were translucent, like the claws of a tiny bird.

"What will we call him?" asked Francie.

"I'm sure he already has a name."

"He's ours until we arrive in Boston."

As the plane began to back up, making my journey to Boston irrevocable, I was struck by the thought that Adam would be waiting for Francie at Logan Field. What was *he* going to think of Francie turning up with a baby? How would he react to my being there?

"He won't be at the airport," said Francie, after I voiced my fears. "Time is money," she added in Adam's clipped, Bobby Kennedy accent. "Adam once spent most of an evening demonstrating with a pie graph on his computer why it is more economical for me to take a taxi from the airport than for him to take time off work to drive there."

Our plane was taxiing down the runway.

"I keep expecting a flight attendant to take this baby away," said Francie. "The back of my neck tingles. I feel like when I used to smoke in the washroom at school."

I tried to imagine Francie, wearing a green-and-white uniform and flat, brown shoes, smoking in a school washroom.

"It's exciting, though. I've never done anything illegal."

"You could call a flight attendant, say that a woman asked you to carry the baby on board, but now you don't see her anywhere."

Francie acted as if she didn't hear me. "If he were ours, yours and mine, what would you name him?"

"I've always been partial to Shawn."

Francie pouted. "He's our first. I want to name him after you."

"Joseph is so heavy for a baby."

"He can be Little Joe, then Joey. We'll increase the weight of the name as he grows."

When we were airborne, Francie walked the length of the plane in both directions. She uncovered the baby's head, making sure anyone who might be looking for him could see him clearly.

"So much for that," said Francie. She slipped past me and into the window seat.

"Someone will be waiting for him in Boston," I said.

"And if not?"

"We have a ready-made family." I leaned over and kissed Francie's cheek. The baby was asleep, one eye half-open, as if he was engaged in a prolonged wink.

We were silent for several minutes.

"What happens when we get to Boston? About us, I mean."

"We have nearly five hours to plan our strategy," Francie replied. "We can turn the baby over to the proper authorities . . ."

"No," I heard myself saying. "But I hope you have lots of money and credit cards. You're going to find life with a terminally unemployed investigative reporter will require a lot of improvision."

"I can improvise like nobody you've ever met," whispered Francie. "Everyone should pretend they're someone else."

She moved Little Joe to a more comfortable position, then slid closer to me, until her head touched my shoulder. The baby stirred.

I can't believe I'm doing this, I thought.

"Mommy loves you," Francie whispered to the bundle.

About two weeks before Francie and Adam arrived, I visited the Los Angeles Police Station. Ever since the extraterrestrial incident I had been feeling empty as a deadheading truck, as if I didn't exist, as if people were staring straight through me.

At the police station, I stood in the middle of a hallway and made people walk around me. It was comforting to see them making a conscious effort to avoid bumping into me, to hear the change in cadence of their heels on the marble floor.

One set of steps, approaching from behind, didn't slow down. I was afraid the person was going to walk directly through me, but at the last second he pulled up and nuzzled his vulture-shaped nose against my back. I turned around. Nathan Wiser smelled of cigar smoke and Brut.

"What the hell are you doing here, McCoy?"

I sighed with delight. I existed.

"You're not welcome here."

"The last time I checked, this was public property."

"If I said the word, McCoy, you would disappear." Wiser has a bald spot, like the opening of a volcano. He has scrub-brushes for eyebrows.

"I've heard rumors that you can turn water into wine," I said, smiling wryly. I was ecstatic about existing.

"It's easier the other way around," said Wiser, his chuckle like the cocking of a dozen revolvers.

"Something big is going down, Nathan, and I'm close to finding out what it is," I said. I, of course, had no idea what was going down, but perhaps if I was melodramatic enough . . .

"You watch too much TV, McCoy. Unemployment is addling your brain." Wiser lifted one eyebrow until it merged with his hairline.

"Are you off the Mob kick? You couldn't spot a Mafia foot soldier at an Italian Anti-Defamation League benefit."

"What's Tony the Pianist up to these days?" I referred, of course, to Carmine Anthony "Tony the Pianist" Bablioto, his nickname derived not because he is musical, but because of a length of piano wire which he uses as a garrote, or, sometimes, to slice off the ears of people who have offended him.

"The Mafia doesn't exist," Nathan Wiser assured me. "Santa Claus, the Easter Bunny, the Great Pumpkin and Tony the Pianist are all figments of overactive imaginations. Do I make myself clear, McCoy?" Then, over his shoulder as he walked away, "My best to Maureen and the baby."

I scratched my head, watching as he disappeared through swinging doors at the end of the hall.

The plane snores on. I am overwhelmed by possibilities, unwilling or unable to formulate a plan of action, something I always envisioned I would be able to do instantly.

Francie and the baby sleep.

I sink into a daydream about Maureen.

Maureen and I never made love in a real bed. We loved each other in the antique car in my father's garage, in her father's barn, in the backseat of a friend's car at a drive-in movie in Cedar Rapids, several times we took a blanket and walked deep in among the five-foot-tall corn of summer, and lay pressed together, completely isolated in the deep, sweet shadows as wind rustled the corn fronds.

Maureen, her hair wild across her face, our bodies slick with sweat: "I need a shower. This cornfield smells like somebody's been fucking in it."

Or, her voice sad: "You never look at me, Joe."

And towards the end: ". . . I'm tryin' to pick a fight with you, McCoy. Come on, fight with me. I'll be unreasonable on any subject. It'll give you an excuse. I'll go away mad. Then you won't feel guilty."

Maureen sent me an invitation to her wedding. She married Tucker Wegman, a big, muscular, man's man a couple of years older than us. He fished, hunted, chewed Redman tobacco, wore gray-striped railroad coveralls while he hummed over the fields of his father's farm in the air-conditioned cab of his combine.

"It would make me feel special if you could attend," she wrote.

I'm sure I wasn't on the official guest list. The Wegmans were stable, successful farmers, and it must have been an embarrassment for them to have their son marry into Maureen's family.

I considered attending the wedding, but I had a summer job with the *Baltimore Sun*; I had had to compete fiercely to get it and I didn't want to take time off. Besides, it was a long way from Baltimore to Iowa City.

I thought about Maureen on her wedding day. I wondered if she and Tucker had wedding pictures taken at Fairfield Cemetery, in front of the mysterious Black Angel statue. That was another place we made love, on a June evening with the perfume of apple blossoms in the air, beneath the dark, feathered wing of the eerie Black Angel.

Maureen had written to me about six months before the wedding invitation arrived: "I guess you're never coming back to Lone Tree, or to me. I guess I'd better make a life for myself. You remember Tucker Wegman? He's asked me to marry him. I've put him off. If there's any chance . . ."

I intended to reply, but days became weeks.

*　*　*

A few days before Francie and Adam's visit, the phone rang.

"This is Bertha." She paused. "I just want to say how sorry I am."

"It's okay."

"It was my idea to call you and all. We didn't mean no harm. Ma read in the paper the other day about how you haven't been able to get a job or nothin'. Buster's sorry, too."

"It's okay. I know what I saw. I don't blame you for anything."

"Still, we're sorry you lost your job. Those call-in shows on the radio said such awful things about all of us."

"It wasn't your fault, Bertha. We all have to get on with our lives," I added, but without much conviction.

Bertha took a deep breath. "Me and Buster talked it over, and we figure I could, you know, go to bed with you. Like it's all I got to offer. And it's okay with Buster, you know what I mean?"

"That's very sweet of you. But you don't owe me anything. Not that I wouldn't like to. And you thank Buster, too. It's a lovely gesture."

"If there's anything either of us can do."

"I'll let you know."

They've talked me into bringing Francie to the farm. We three baseball outcasts have developed a rapport, like brothers, I suppose, fictional brothers. For Gideon has no brother, my relationship with mine, at least in my West Coast years, has been noncommittal, and Ray and his twin, Richard, are light and shadow. But, here we are, sharing the camaraderie of soldiers? Convicts? Teammates?

As Francie climbs out of the car, Annie and Karin help her unbuckle Little Joe. Gideon hulks nearby like an albino Igor, rubbing his hands together, staying on the periphery of Francie's vision. I saw him yesterday waiting for us in his truck outside Pearson's. He was reading *The Francie Bly Cookbook*, or rather he was staring open-mouthed at the smiling photo of Francie on the dust jacket.

Francie glances at him, glances at me. I shrug. I introduce them. Gideon smiles like an idiot. He's fallen for her. He seems to belong to another era.

Within an hour Francie and Annie are like sisters. I thought Francie a little too Eastern to fit in well on this down to earth (pun intended) Midwestern farm. But Francie, Annie, Missy, and Richard Kinsella's wife Gypsy are all in the kitchen, the conversation punctuated by shrieks of laughter. Richard is away, something about a new floodlight for Ray's ballpark. The twins, Shannon and Crystal, have placed Little Joe in a Fisher-Price swing set and are taking turns pushing him.

Gideon is missing some of my stories this afternoon because he keeps venturing into the kitchen for water, notepaper, muffins, anything to be close to Francie for a few seconds.

I still have stories to tell. Telling them to these two men who seem to have some cosmic connection to me is uplifting, a word I never thought I'd use. Purifying. Are Joe and Gideon capable of absolving my sins of both omission and commission?

SECTION TWO
AT LARGE

ELEVEN

JOE McCOY

NO ONE WAS WAITING FOR THE BABY at Logan Field. As we walked the long airport corridors, I waited, tense as a guitar string, for the law to descend.

At the baggage carousel, Francie chattered like a sparrow to hide her nervousness. My stomach felt like a washing machine half-full of ball bearings, the sounds of my heart stampeded across my chest. I glanced around. I could spot a security man from a hundred yards. There were two sleepy detective-types, like surreal coat racks, leaning against pastel walls, waiting for their shift to end.

"Where to?" I said. "I don't know Boston very well."

"I'm not sure," said Francie. "I don't suppose I can go home, can I?"

"Adam would probably not be thrilled."

"I should call him. Otherwise he'll report me missing."

Francie deposited the baby and diaper bag in my arms. The baby stared at me skeptically. He smelled like talcum powder and milk. Francie deposited a quarter in a pay phone.

"Adam, this is Francie," she said. "I've decided not to come home . . . ever." She waited a couple of seconds for the impact of her words to sink in, then added, in a cheerful voice, "Take care of yourself," and hung up.

"That was the answering machine," she said. "Adam likes straight statements. Accountants don't understand teary goodbyes." She rubbed her hands together, a gesture of finality. "Now, I suppose, a hotel . . ."

"Where do police check first for criminals?"

"Are we criminals? That woman gave us the baby."

"I think it's like when the computer deposits a million dollars in your bank account. You're supposed to give it back."

"Where do you suggest we go?"

"We could sit around a laundromat pretending to wash clothes."

"There are all-night porno movies."

"The baby's too young to get in," I said. Francie laughed, a sound that reminded me of dew sparkling. A few of the ball bearings churning within me begin to melt.

"A motel, then. Only we'll use our real names. Kidnapping is not my idea of the way to start a life together."

"She gave him to us," Francie insisted.

"How are we going to feed him, once these bottles run out?" I had asked Francie, soon after we were airborne.

"He's not a newborn," Francie replied. "He's got to be four months old, maybe more. Don't worry about it. Women know about these things."

"Really? Don't expect any mechanical knowledge from me just because I'm a man. I'm not even sure where to find the engine of a car."

"You hunt, I'll take care of the cave," said Francie.

"Right, I'll go off in the morning searching for a herd of McDonald's, a covey of Pizza Huts, a pride of Kentucky Fried Chicken outlets."

We talked of my fantasy of being on the run. Francie's idea was to hide out, to rent a small apartment in a quiet area of a large city and try to fit in.

"I don't think that would work," I said. "People who are anchored to one place are curious about newcomers. If you've got anything to hide, somebody usually finds out about it. Keeping on the move is best. Suppose you're walking in a park and a thug pulls a gun on you. Do you stand a better chance if you stay in one place and let him take a shot at you, or if you break into a zig-zag run?"

"It would be better to run," said Francie.

"Case closed," I said. "Moving targets are always harder to hit. There aren't many unsolved murders because most people are killed by someone they know, but breaking and entering, fraud, auto theft—a very low arrest rate."

"Joe, have we gone crazy?"

"Yes." I replied without hesitation.

My MasterCard paid for a taxi and a room at a first-rate hotel.

Francie was bathing Little Joe when I got back with the groceries and baby supplies. While I was out I bought mirrored sunglasses. I considered gloves, except that it is summer, and they would tend to make me more, instead of less conspicuous. Francie had one hand under Little Joe's back; he laughed and kicked water. Little Joe was the color of warm sand.

The hotel provided us with a crib. We registered as Mr. and Mrs. Joseph M. A. McCoy.

"I'm having a little cash flow problem," I told the person who brought the crib to the room. "I'll tip you as soon as I cash a traveler's check." He glowered and closed the door.

Not since Maureen had I felt that lighter-than-air, nothing-in-the-world-matters-but-this-moment feeling. Not since Maureen had I truly felt I was going to be loved back. I wanted to do much more than make Francie's body vibrate with passion. I understood what drives explorers and adventurers, I wanted to pile the spoils of war in front of her, to bask in her admiration.

The spoils of war. I had $28, three credit cards, and not one change of clothes.

"I'm not ready," she said as we came up from a long kiss.

"Not ready?" I said. Was she telling me she was not sufficiently stimulated, or was she telling me she was NOT READY.

"Trust me on this," she said. "I don't think we should make love until everything is perfect."

She meant NOT READY.

"Define perfect. To be truthful, I would not have whisked myself off to Boston with my live-in's brother's fiancée and a more-or-less kidnapped baby if I hadn't thought there was going to be a great deal of sex involved."

"You're in love with somebody else," Francie said.

"I don't think I've ever been in love with Rosslyn," I said truthfully.

"Our relationship has been like marking time for both of us."

"I didn't say it was Rosslyn you were in love with."

"Who then?"

"I don't know. I think I could really love you, Joe. But . . ."

What could I say? I have never stopped loving Maureen. But except in my dreams Maureen is back in Iowa, married for going on ten years, I assume happily.

"But you seemed so ready . . ."

"That was different, an opportunity for a little fling . . . but now we've taken a serious step forward. I don't think it would be right until you get your feelings straightened out."

There is no solution to my problem.

"You don't have to stop kissing me," Francie said, "unless you want to. I just think we should be sweethearts for a while longer."

Later, side-by-side on the bed, we watched a late movie with the volume turned down. Francie was smoking a cigarette.

"I can't believe this is happening," I said, for probably the tenth time.

"It is," said Francie.

I leaned over and kissed her. Across the room, Little Joe turned and fussed in his sleep, his tiny hand touching a bar of his crib. I could feel Francie's scarlet-tipped nails pressing against my shoulders as she kissed me, her tongue exploring like a curious cat.

"Did you ever see me play?" I asked suddenly, realizing we had never talked about my first career.

"Not until now," said Francie. "I never saw you play baseball, at least I don't think I did. You were with a lot of teams, weren't you? But I know all about baseball. There are the Boston Red Sox . . . and some other teams, maybe even another league."

"We're incompatible," I said. "You don't know baseball."

"Sure I do. There's something I want to ask you. You don't really need four days' rest between starts, do you?"

"Try me."

"When the time is right."

* * *

Eventually, Francie slept. She turned slightly, her tongue lazily licked her upper lip. I hoped she was dreaming of me. I paced the room. The blinds were closed, the door locked. We were on the eleventh floor. Yet I started at each sound from the hall or the street. Little Joe woke, fretful. I changed him and he went back to sleep. In my mind, the world outside the room was a dark, sinister street with hands grasping from doorways. What the hell would we do in the morning?

Ten days have passed since the flight from Los Angeles to Boston. I feel like a figure in a political cartoon, the politician dodging bombs: INFLATION! UNEMPLOYMENT! WASTE! CORRUPTION! Mine would read POLICE! FBI! THE MOB! The newspapers are full of speculation concerning my sanity.

I don't feel crazy. However, wherever Francie and I are holed up, when I contemplate the fact that two supposedly normal people accepted a baby thrust at them in an airport, abandoned family and friends, present and future prospects, and became outlaws for no apparent reason, I have a lot of second thoughts.

Everyone in the world seems to be looking for us. Our faces dominate the TV screen each evening, yet if I attempted to give myself up, I know I would be turned away like a professional confessor.

When I was first called up to the Bigs, I was vaguely afraid of the giants who were my teammates, those hulking, seed-spitting, tobacco-chewing monsters who sat on the bench and crowded the bullpen. It never occurred to me that I belonged.

I fulfilled my first fantasy of being a major-league baseball player, and that did not turn out very well. I was now fulfilling my second fantasy. The difference was I could retire from baseball.

I remember Francie and I standing on the sidewalk near a park.

"I wish I hadn't gotten you into this mess," I said to Francie, when suddenly, at the curb, where before there had been only grumbling traffic, there appeared a horse, sad-faced as an old scholar, a top hat tied on by green ribbon. I know the horse was not there the previous instant.

There is something I didn't mention before because I thought it would sound too bizarre. I recall assuring Bertha that I was familiar with weird.

How wrong I was. That night on the desert with Bertha and Buster, the extraterrestrial touched me. Not as I said earlier, *measured*, but really touched. As Buster, Bertha and I stood holding hands, something pink as a cactus flower, ephemeral as ground mist, the shape of a small tumbleweed, moved toward us. It rubbed around my ankles, soft as pink angora. Gradually, it worked its way up the inside of my pantleg. I was not the least frightened, for the comforting sounds the spacecraft emitted lulled me as if I were in a down-filled bed. When the angora got to my waist it was like an electric shock: it touched me and brought me erect.

I glanced at Bertha and Buster, wondering if they were experiencing the same sensation. Were they glancing at me, knowing what I was experiencing, laughing behind their hands? I felt the most enormous sexual desire, but the object of it was unclear. I thought of Maureen, for not since making love with her had I *wanted* so violently, while desiring the contact to be delicate and loving. I was held in thrall for several seconds, my heart drumming, my chest full of heat, my whole body burned by an intense rush of love.

The first thing I said to Francie when we awoke in the old hotel in Boston was, "I think we should get out of Boston immediately."

"As far as we know, no one is looking for us," Francie said.

"I'm afraid the first person I'll run into is Adam. I'm not up to saying, 'Your fiancée and I have borrowed a baby, and we've decided to run off together. Hope you don't mind.'"

"Adam is a geek," Francie said, and smiled disarmingly, the freckles on her nose rearranging themselves.

"I didn't think the word *geek* would be in your vocabulary."

"It isn't," said Francie, smiling even more broadly. "It's what you think he is, though."

"I don't remember telling you that," I said. But Francie had hopped out of bed and was turning on the television.

"Let's see if we're on 'Good Morning, America.'"

*   *   *

Ironically, it would be Adam who was on "Good Morning, America" a few weeks later. He would be doing a book promotion for *The Francie Bly Cookbook*, which he had created by going through Francie's recipes in her kitchen computer and using an acquaintance, an editor at a large Boston publishing house, to facilitate the matter.

Francie and I went to a restaurant called Aegean Fare, a place I used to go after games in Boston. It is not really a breakfast place, but they make the best Greek pastries in America; we both had *bougatsa* and sandy-tasting coffee for breakfast. I bought a newspaper and scanned every page, hoping not to find anything, but at the same time longing for an explanation of our situation.

Buried on an inside page was the following:

> LOS ANGELES (A.P.): Local police and FBI agents are investigating the disappearance of the infant son of the Courteguayan ambassador to the United States. The child was last seen yesterday afternoon at the Los Angeles International Airport.
>
> Circumstances surrounding the disappearance of the child, Jose Joaquin Alvarez Mendoza Blanco, are unclear. FBI report they have no suspects in the case.

I showed the item to Francie.

"I knew his name was Joe," she said brightly.

The son of the Courteguayan ambassador. Curious.

Toward the end of my career I played one season of winter baseball in Courteguay, a country about as big as Delaware, shaped like the moon of a fingernail, squeezed in between Haiti and the Dominican Republic on the island of Hispanola.

Courteguay is a bizarre, baseball-mad country, ruled by a president-dictator, also named Blanco, who had, at least when I was there, twenty-three first names. President Blanco claims to be a wizard, dresses in a dashiki-like coat of many colors, festooned with stars, asterisks, and other symbols that American cartoonists use to designate four-letter words.

I was assigned to a team that, as near as I could translate, was called the San Cristobel Anthurium Rapists.

The country is engaged in a perpetual civil war. The guerrilla leader, Dr. Lucius Noir, the offspring of a Haitian prostitute, has a degree in chiropractic medicine from a college in Davenport, Iowa.

It is said that President Blanco hired Bill Veeck to supervise the construction of the scoreboard at the San Cristobel stadium. Under the guise of security, the entire army got to watch games for free. The public address announcer had to repeat between batters, "Please do not point loaded weapons toward the baseball field."

The soldiers, supposedly on alert for insurgent snipers, had to watch the games with their necks swivelled. Baseball neck was the most common injury in the Courteguayan army. I suggested to our manager that they employ Dr. Noir to treat the necks of the soldiers, thus ending the civil war, but he did not take me seriously.

In New York we used Francie's American Express card to register at a charming old hotel in the theater district. We hired a babysitter, went to a Broadway play, ate dinner at a Greek restaurant, cuddled deep into the night while Little Joe slept in a crib at the foot of our bed.

"Here we are!" I called to Francie the next morning, almost jubilantly folding open a page of *The New York Times* so she could read the small article.

LOS ANGELES: FBI today named the suspects in the disappearance of the infant son of the Courteguayan ambassador to the United States. Wanted for questioning concerning the alleged abduction are ex-major-league baseball player, Joseph Armbruster "Kid" McCoy, of Los Angeles, and Mary Frances Bly of suburban Boston.

The article went on to reiterate what little information was available to the authorities, mentioned my lifetime 8–23 record, and included a quote or two from President Blanco of Courteguay, something about him not accepting any more American foreign aid until his nephew, the ambassador's son, was restored.

"I'm beginning to get scared," said Francie. "Maybe you're right about taking this situation seriously?"

"You should have thought of that a couple of days ago, back at LAX," I said. "We have committed ourselves to be fugitives."

After breakfast we rented a car, bought a car seat for Little Joe.

"We're wanted by the police," I told the clerk, a sour-faced woman in a green smock. "A week from now you'll be able to get your picture in the newspaper just by recalling that you waited on us."

"What does it pay?" she rasped in a voice that had smoked a hundred thousand cigarettes.

"What?"

"Getting your picture in the paper."

"Nothing. It's news. Newspapers don't pay for news."

"Then they can forget it."

During the next two days we drove in the general direction of Chicago. I insisted that we travel the main roads, eat at busy truck stops, stay at heavy-traffic motels. Warrants were issued for our arrest on charges of kidnapping. Our photos, but not the baby's, were on the "CBS Evening News." Mine was from my baseball days; in my uniform I appeared wide-eyed, startled, even a little foolish. Francie, it turned out, was not one for being photographed. The picture of her was supplied by Adam, his large hand, severed from his body, clasped grotesquely on her shoulder.

I told Francie about my ace snitch, Pico the Rat, and his theory that he is only one curtain of time away from being a Hollywood mogul.

"I wonder if there might *not* be parallel dimensions," I said to Francie as we hummed along an Interstate. "What if, a few months ago in the dimension where I used to live, a plump young girl named Bertha, who had been taught at her mother's knee how to use long distance, phoned her story of extraterrestrials to the *National Enquirer* thus depriving an L.A. investigative reporter named Joe McCoy of the story that would ruin his life and career?

"I suspect I am still living in that dimension, still writing meaningless stories, still going home at night to my fiancée the dental technician, still dissatisfied with my life, lusting after a girl named Francie Bly, but too inept to do anything about it."

"Would you like to be back there?"

"Sometimes."

Francie pouted. She lifted Little Joe out of his car seat, held him toward me; he reached out his tiny brown fingers, exploring my cheek. The baby looks a bit like me, my forehead. He doesn't look like Francie, but he does resemble Maureen Renn. His nose, large hands and dusky complexion remind me of Maureen.

"I think you'd be crazy to want to go back," said Francie.

"I have to admit there is something very exciting about being in the spotlight again. I told myself I was happy to be out of sports . . . but the attention is rather like applause . . ."

Ah, yes, life on the mound. The sun is setting. The entire western sky is a swathe of scarlet silk. We are in a close game. There will be no pinch-hitter for me. I stand in the on-deck circle waiting to wave my bat in total futility. I rest the bat across the back of my neck, a hand on each end. I feel disoriented. My shadow, like a Japanese character, is brushed black on the reddened earth. Waving the bat like a noodle, I strike out on three pitches.

The opposing hitters are ravenous for base hits. I take turns throwing a fastball out of the strike zone, a change-up painting the black on either the inside or outside of the plate. Sometimes they hack at the fastball and foul it off, the hitters are consistently out in front of the change-up. I strike out all three batters. Apparently it is the final inning. We win again.

Adam's reaction to Francie's disappearance. From a story in the *Chicago Tribune*:

> "The cryptic message she left on our answering service clearly indicates that my fiancée, Mary Frances Bly, is being held against her will by this Kid McCoy," an aggrieved Adam Quinn said today at a press conference.

"Kid McCoy?" I said.

"Wait until you see this." Francie was reading *The New York Times*.

"'Kid is not the most stable person I know,' his girlfriend Rosslyn Quinn told this reporter."

"*She* called me Kid?" I fairly shrieked. "She used to call me Joseph in moments of passion."

I keep dreaming a remembered past, a past that, during waking hours, I am sure I never lived. The more time I spend with Francie, the more I dream of Maureen. I remember being married to Maureen. We were in Iowa City. It was a warm Indian-summer day, the leaves the yellow of firemen's raincoats, and we were standing on the porch of a very old frame house. The real estate agent had just showed it to us. We walked through the chill, hollow rooms, heard the floor groaning beneath our steps, smelled the odors of mice, mold and abandonment.

I was in my junior year, studying journalism at the University of Iowa. As I watched from a distance, I tried to fathom how I could have enough money to think of buying a house. Neither of our families, particularly the Renns, had any financial aid to offer. Then, as we talked with the real estate agent, the situation became clearer, though it was as if I were hearing the information for the first time.

Maureen and I have been living in married-student housing, a one-bedroom apartment in a slum-like project near the golf course on Mormon Trek Road. I have just won a hefty scholarship. If we use the entire scholarship as a down payment on the house, and if I continue to work part time (I am assistant editor of the the student newspaper, *The Daily Iowan*, a position that pays), and if Maureen helps out when she can, we would just about be able to keep our heads above water.

It was then that I noticed Maureen was pregnant. How could I have not noticed? She walked splay-legged across the porch and adjusted her multi-flowered maternity dress.

"I'm thinking of getting a job as a flower bed on the lawn of the Old Capitol," she told the real estate agent, who was slightly embarrassed by her condition. "When I lie down I look like a Volkswagen Beetle."

"My favorite car," I told him.

The house had been vacant for several years, something to do with a contested will, and was badly in need of paint. The gingerbread trim was weathered and a piece or two hung dangerously loose. Several shutters had fallen off, others hung askew. The verandah, which ran around three sides of the house, sagged, listed, drooped and slumped.

"We have one piece of furniture for each room," said Maureen.

"Maybe I can park the car in the living room. It will take up space and be a conversation piece."

"We'll have to have lots of babies," said Maureen.

I am about to answer her, suggest we get in some final practice, when I awake with a start. The odor of the motel room where Francie and I sleep on a sagging mattress is similar to that of the house on that long-ago day.

On another occasion, though I can't remember what precipitated it, Maureen is flaming mad. She is stomping about our small apartment, presumably the one in student housing. She raises her long, maroon hair from the back of her neck, a gesture as familiar as one of my own, her long, thick hair making her neck hot. She is barefoot, wearing one of my white shirts, faded jeans.

"You think you're the center of the fucking universe, McCoy."

It is about 2:00 A.M. I have put the *Daily Iowan* to bed, then walked home. Maureen is pissed off at the smallness of our apartment, my weird hours, the cockroaches that defy every chemical.

Now I remember. Maureen, in a frenzy of cockroach hate has sprinkled chili powder along the baseboards. I stepped in some, wiped it off my sock, a moment later wiped my eyes. Somehow my crying out, rushing to the bathroom where I wash a scalded eye in cold water for several minutes, does not arouse sympathy. Maureen details her every dissatisfaction, all of which are my fault. I am, to put it kindly, a stupid, sanctimonious son of a bitch. The apartment is unfit for human habitation. Maureen paces. She lights a Winston, inhales deeply, continues her tirade. I sit on the sofa. I come from a mild-mannered family.

"If you hate it here so much why don't you move back with your family. I bet you'd be thrilled. Lots of room in a drafty old house, where the windows have been cracked and cardboarded for twenty years, where the whole downstairs smells of sour milk and full ashtrays."

"Fucking right," Maureen screams, and she stomps out of the room. I hear her slamming about in the walk-in closet off the bedroom, bags and boxes bouncing off the hardwood floor.

I can't leave well enough alone. I toss out a few remarks about how much she'll enjoy dodging her felonious brothers in the hallways of her parents' home. Bad choice.

Maureen brings up every grievance she has ever had against me, from my seldom looking her in the eye, to the way I clip my fingernails, to the way I drive (too cautious for her), to the size of my private parts. Bad choice on her part.

"Why wait!" I yell. "Go now. I'll put your stuff out on the patio."

Maureen packs loudly. She emerges at regular intervals to announce some new grievance or elaborate on an old one. She wants to be sure I won't get a moment's sleep.

I am shirtless, lying on the sofa, face in, one arm around a cushion. I am freezing but will never admit it. Maureen moves her suitcases and boxes to the patio one by one, leaving the french doors open the whole time.

"I'm going now," she says.

"Mmmfff," I reply. I should have feigned sleep. I've probably already contracted pneumonia.

Maureen thumps into the bedroom, thumps back, stands over me.

"Here," she says. She pulls the sofa cushion from my grasp, replaces it with a pillow from our bed. I can smell the scent of her skin on the pillow. I reluctantly turn over. She is holding a badly worn green blanket, one I brought to the marriage. She spreads the blanket over me in one motion. Before she can turn to the door, I grab her hand. I ease her toward me. She falls to her knees beside the sofa, buries her face in my chest, sobs so loudly and uncontrollably I'm afraid it will wake the neighbors, if our shouting already hasn't. We cling to each other fiercely as I kiss her wet cheeks, my own eyes overflowing. Eventually, her sobbing subsides, she eases up under the blanket, we crush our bodies together, lie that way for a long time.

"I don't want to lose you," I whisper.

"Take me to our bed," says Maureen, her voice still full of tears.

We love away the remainder of the night; we do nearly everything sexual a man and woman can do to and with each other.

* * *

I know that happened. But when? Maureen and I have never lived together. At least I don't think so.

I remember the first time I saw my daughter, the first time I held her, the unconditional love I felt for her. Unconditional love was a new emotion for me. I stared down at her in the hospital basket, her eyes scrunched shut against the light. She wasn't beautiful, like some newborns: her face was radish-red, her legs too long, her feet thin, the tiny nails translucent. I looked at her and fell in love, totally and completely. I visualized her walking away from me on her first day of school, I saw her with ragged pink hair and a safety pin through her nose, on the arm of a Cro-Magnon lout, and still I loved her. I pictured her a member of some radical terrorist cell, in the prisoner's dock, fist raised in defiance. And yet I loved her. I knew at that instant that my feelings for everyone else in my life could be altered by time, by the way they treated me; but that my feelings for my daughter could never be altered. I was hopelessly, passionately, unalterably in love, forever.

At a time when men were expected to clutter delivery rooms, like rubberneckers at a car accident, Maureen had understood why I couldn't be present at my daughter's birth.

"You're a coward, pure and simple."

"You've found me out."

"You're responsible for my condition. Now, you chicken out on your responsibility."

"You took something seriously that was poked at you in fun."

"And look where it got me."

It is 4:00 A.M., and Maureen, big as a house, waits, flat on her back on a cot in the hallway of the hospital. I have to turn away while a blood sample is drawn from her arm. I grow queasy at seeing someone else's blood. As a cub reporter on the traffic beat I approached the window of a damaged car to find a lacerated face staring blankly at me, the iron-like odor of blood causing me to turn away and retch. Yet, now I know that if it had been my daughter injured in that car, bleeding profusely, I would do whatever had to be done. I would tie a tourniquet, staunch her wounds with the sheer power of love.

"I think I'll go wake up some of my buddies," I whispered to Maureen, "brag about my sexual prowess. Maybe we can suck back a couple of beers for breakfast and get in an early eighteen holes of golf. I'll check back in a few hours."

Maureen managed a laugh.

"You're a true chauvinist swine."

"Thank you."

I don't have a daughter, or a wife. All I have are dreams and memories of a life I can't prove I've lived.

TWELVE

RAY KINSELLA

"WHAT DO YOU THINK?" I ask Gideon while Joe is on a washroom break.

"I gather we three do have something in common. Missy's mother, Marylyle Baron, used to say, 'Things are out of kilter in Johnson County.'"

"Joe McCoy has carried 'out of kilter' to new lengths, little to do with Johnson County."

"I know from both happy and sad experience that things are indeed out of kilter in Johnson County. And so do you. Do you believe Joe? A lot of what he's telling us is more or less documented by the newspapers, but the double life? The parallel dimensions?"

"He's experiencing more than his share of weird," I say.

Joe reappears.

"Well, how do you like me so far?" he asks.

This is the Joe McCoy I imagined from the newspaper accounts, brash, smart-ass, acting that way because he thinks it is expected of him. The hot-shot ex-athlete tells us of his baseball career, of his life with Rosslyn Quinn; but there is another Joe McCoy who recalls his life and times with Maureen Renn. When he speaks of Maureen, of their passionate love, I have no trouble relating to him. I think my Annie and Maureen have a lot in common. My love for Annie knows no bounds. But what if

I had run off to 'seek my fortune,' left Annie behind while I tried to carve out a career with some multinational insurance firm? It seems implausible, but no more so than Joe abandoning Maureen by choosing his good right arm over what his heart and community desired him to do.

I grit my teeth at his obnoxious question, until he smiles disarmingly, and I see he is kidding. I feel for his helplessness.

"I think it's pretty obvious what's happening," Gideon says. "Surely you recognize it," he says to Joe. "You're living out your life-long fantasy of being on the run. You've become a fugitive."

"Not of my own volition," says the befuddled version of Joe McCoy. "I'm not in control of my own life."

"That, I think, is a matter of opinion," says Gideon. "You've chosen to become a criminal."

"Didn't you guys ever do anything criminal?"

"I know a certain amount about kidnapping," I admit. "But it seemed like the proper thing to do at the time."

"I kidnapped a few records from the offices of the Chicago Cubs," says Gideon, staring at us both with a shy, sly smile.

"Let's say you've piqued our interest," I say.

THIRTEEN

GIDEON CLARKE

THEY'RE NOT SLEEPING TOGETHER. Well, they're not making love. And not making love is Francie's idea. I have to admit I missed a little of his story after he told us that, my attention wandered. Francie and Joe have not made love. Francie doesn't want to. I feel like doing a jig, from the sunporch to the living room to the kitchen. I feel like sweeping Francie Bly into my arms and dancing around the kitchen counter. I can't ever remember doing a jig. I hulk. My hips are high, my shoulders ungainly. I move like a movie monster.

Without realizing it I have moved from the porch through the living room, where Missy and Ray's twins are engaged in some game that involves hitting what looks like milk bottle caps with a hammer, to the kitchen, which smells of cinnamon and roasting meat. Francie Bly, in black jeans and a black blouse with a couple of yellow sunflowers on it, is sitting on a stool at the counter drinking coffee and laughing with the girl named Gypsy.

"Missy is such a sweet person," Francie says without warning, interrupting something Gypsy was saying, smiling up at me.

"She is," I reply. "She attends a life skills course in Iowa City. She has her own bank account. She studies the grocery flyers and picks out the specials she thinks we should shop for."

"That's wonderful," says Francie. "When I was in high school I volunteered in a home where a lot of people had Downs' syndrome."

Gypsy, when we were first introduced, glanced at me like someone she was never going to see again. She sits next to Francie, smoking, staring at me but not seeing me at all, simply waiting for me to go away so she can continue her conversation with Francie.

"Would you like to see my house, our house?" I hear myself saying to Francie. My mouth is dry.

"I'd love to," says Francie. Gypsy scowls, I assume trying to imagine what possible interest Francie could have in me and Missy.

"I have to take Missy home soon, she gets overexcited playing for too long with other children."

"I'll ride along," says Francie, "if it's not too much trouble."

I assure her it isn't, then head back to listen to more of Joe's fantastical story. Too much trouble! I'd pave the road from here to Onamata by hand if she'd ride with me, I'd sprinkle camelia petals on the fresh black asphalt, I'd push the truck, I'd . . . well, you get the idea.

FOURTEEN

JOE McCOY

I PHONED MY FRIEND AND CONFIDANT PICO THE RAT. His office is a pay phone outside a Wendy's on Sunset Strip.

"You're hot, man. Poison. You shouldn't have grabbed that baby. Lindbergh Law and all that shit. Listen, I've never seen the streets blanketed like this before, dozens of guys in pinstripe suits, dark glasses, shoulder holsters. And those are the tourists. Seriously, there's a fed on every corner, a local cop in every alley. The Mob keeps a low profile. There are other guys looking for you, UPH, you know—unidentified plainclothes hitmen—and Latin-type guys in army fatigues and long sideburns."

I stay silent.

"I'll be honest with you, Kid. I've always thought you were a stumble-fuck. A pleasant stumblefuck nonetheless."

"Thanks Pico, I appreciate your honesty, though you don't have to call me Kid. What I want from you is advice and I.D."

"Stay on the move. Don't eat yellow snow. What kind of I.D. and what can you offer in return?"

"What have you got that you can courier to me quickly?"

"Old couple went into a nursing home. Their family don't even know these credit cards exist: American Express, Carte Blanche, MasterCard, Visa, a car rental, seven oil companies, three department stores, even a library card. These cards won't even whimper for weeks. The Mob will give me ten thousand cash. What about you?"

"An even trade for our cards. No, don't hang up. Our cards are collector's items. Think about it. There are crime freaks out there, Pico. Guys will pay four or five thou for Kid McCoy's driver's license. You could auction them. 'What am I bid for Mary Frances Bly's Bonwit Teller charge card?'"

I rattled on until my voice penetrated to his monetary glands.

"I'm gonna take a chance on you, Kid."

"I owe you."

"You're fucking right you do."

"How's the movie business?"

"That's how you can repay my kindness, McCoy. I want the rights to you and your lady's story. Fifty percent of everything."

"Fifteen. All you're giving up is a potential ten thousand."

"Twenty. There may never be a movie deal."

"Ten. If you can come down, I can come down."

"An agent gets fifteen percent."

"Exactly what experience do you have as an agent?"

We settle on twelve-and-a-half.

"I'm already talking to moguls about the concept. It will be the greatest fugitive movie of all time. I'm inching closer to Hollywood. I've priced a Mercedes, used to belong to a drug dealer, and I'm investigating cosmetic surgery . . ."

I can see the new Pico, sleek and sinister after his daily facial and manicure, hair styled, his beak smoothed down like a mountain under a road grader. I wonder what he'll see when he looks in the mirror? No matter how cosmetically suave he becomes, will the old, scraggy, street hustler always peer back?

We meet. I try for a few bucks in hard cash. "There's not a lot I can do for you," Pico said. "We're sorta friends, right? But not the loaning-money kind of friends, you know what I mean? Guys who don't have collateral don't get money. Nothing personal."

"That's life," I said.

"Wait a minute," said Pico, moving closer until I could smell his staleness. "Why didn't you tell me you had one of those?"

"One of what?" I said. Pico had already grasped my left hand and was examining my pinky finger, pulling it up toward his face, his eye squinted as if it held a jeweller's glass.

"A World Series ring."

I snatched my hand from Pico, pulled the ring toward my own face. No question. It was an exquisite gold-and-diamond World Series ring.

"Where the fuck did I get this?" I rack my brain.

"You're one jump ahead of me, McCoy. I usually hear about something like this, some really valuable piece goes missing. You gone to B and E? A night creeper? Bet whoever owned this don't even know it's gone."

The ring looks familiar.

"Dangerous to fence in the USA," says Pico. "I know a guy could get $200,000 in Japan. They love baseball stuff over there, my guy tells me a Japanese collector paid $50,000 for Bob Gibson's jockstrap, not even signed, not even hot. Private collectors over there keep their mouths shut. Whatever they buy disappears forever. It'll take me a day or two, but I could give you, say, $50,000 for that ring."

Pico's greedy eyes are bulging and wet with avarice.

"See what you can do."

I can't sleep. Unusual. I value sleep. I enjoy sleep. But tonight I thrash like a fresh-caught fish. Francie groans, covers her head with a pillow. Little Joe babbles politely, his hands moving in front of his face as if he were engaged in knitting or crocheting.

I walk down the windy street, hunching my shoulders, pulling my jacket collar up. It is colder than I remember L.A. being, the street busier, the lights more garish. A car zippers alongside me, the back door opens and a hand reaches out for me.

"Joe, where the fuck have you been?" A meaty hand clasps my arm like a bear trap and gently but firmly pulls me into the car.

The hand belongs to John Kruk. I know him to see him from kicking around the Show for ten years.

"What's going on?"

"We're on our way to win the World Series," says the driver, who I recognize as Darren Daulton, the Philadelphia Phillies catcher.

"World Series," I say stupidly.

"They claim I operate on a single brain cell," says the man in the passenger seat, Lenny Dykstra. "What's the matter with you, Joe? When we came to leave the hotel you were nowhere to be found. Maureen said you went for a walk hours ago."

"Everybody else is at the ballpark," says Kruk.

"Maureen?"

"Your wife, dimwit," says Kruk. "You on something? Don't you dare fuck up. We're counting on you tonight."

Here I sit in a car with three giant baseball players. Why? I want to ask them where I am, but I can't let myself look more stupid than I already have. Philadelphia? World Series? These three players were on the 1993 Phillies, the team that lost the World Series to Toronto. That narrows it down. I'm on Yonge Street in Toronto, I recognize some of the garish restaurant signs, the Eaton's Centre flashes by on the right. I see a Queen Street sign. We're not far from the Sky Dome. Can I be pitching for the Phillies in the World Series? Can it be that I'm important to them?

As we walk into the hubbub of the clubhouse it's as though I've shaken my head after a sharp blow and suddenly everything is crystal clear. In August I had been languishing, a word that described most of my major-league career, as a long reliever for the Chicago White Sox, when I was called to the manager's office and told I'd been traded to the Phillies for a player to be named later. Whenever I hear that term I picture a ballplayer in a bedraggled uniform kneeling while a pastor dribbles water over his head and christens him something like Julio Esteban Pimental. The player protests, "Hey, I'm not from Courteguay or the Dominican, I'm Irish, I had a name," but no one pays any attention.

When I arrived in Philadelphia the manager and pitching coach said they had been analyzing my performance with the White Sox and noticed that for my first sixteen pitches I had an ERA of 1.06. After that my pitching went straight to hell. I had pitched 57 innings for the Sox, given up 68 hits, 35 walks, and had a 5.21 ERA.

The Phillies were desperate for a consistent closer. Mitch "Wild Thing" Williams would be a hero one night, a bum the next.

"We want you to close for us. Never more than an inning, less if we can manage it. Never more than sixteen pitches."

Those words changed my life. When I walked onto the field in Philadelphia for the first time, a one-run lead, one out, two on, I felt invincible. I made one pitch. Brett Butler, one of the fastest men in the league, hit a screamer to short stop, an easy double play. The adrenalin was pumping through my veins like gasoline. I had nine saves in September, only one blown save.

So far in the World Series I've saved game one in Toronto; coming in with a two-run lead I got out of the inning on six pitches. Game four was a different matter, a wild and woolly game, we were ahead 14-9 in the eighth when things began to fall apart. By the time I came in there was one out, four runs in, and runners on second and third. I felt like my arm was made of steel, in my elbow and shoulder joints well-lubricated ball bearings. I got Rickey Henderson to pop up, and struck out Devon White on three pitches. I used only nine pitches in the ninth to save the game and even the series at 2-2. Kurt Schilling pitched a shutout in game five.

With a 6-5 lead and the series on the line I came in in the last of the ninth in game six and immediately got into trouble by walking Rickey Henderson. White fouled out. Molitor singled, but Henderson had to stop at second. Big trouble.

Home-run hitter Joe Carter came to bat. The count went to 2-2, I struck him out on a change-up. Olerud then hit me a comebacker and we were World Champions.

Did I win the Series MVP? I can't remember. Did I receive a multi-year, multi-million-dollar contract? I can't remember.

I think of Francie waiting for me. Do I love Francie? It never occurred to me that I would. She is not the type of woman I'd choose. I'm attracted to her. I love the idea of Francie. "Francie Bly," I whisper. "What magic warms your heart? You never doubted, never hesitated, stepped across a line tenuous as stardust, dragged me after you, my feet of clay leaving long rope-like lines behind me."

*　　*　　*

I hurry out of the International House Of Pancakes toward my car, which is parked in the far corner. The top is down and my mother is sitting in the passenger seat. She is her wan self, wearing the white quilted bedjacket with the large purple angels. Our eyes meet.

"Hello, Joseph."

"Mom! Are you an angel?"

Mom ignores the question. "I'm here to talk about Maureen."

"My Maureen? You scarcely knew her. You never came out of your room."

"But I liked her very much. She was the kind of girl I wished I'd been."

"You?"

"If I only I hadn't been ill. I was such a disappointment as a wife and as a mother."

"You did your best, Mom."

"I don't think so, Joseph. That's why I'm here. Maureen was such a comfort after you went off to college."

"You only met Maureen twice. You sniffed disapprovingly both times. You hardly said a word."

"That may well be true. But I called her up after you left and she came for lunch. She came to visit me regularly right up to . . . the end."

"By that time we'd been broken up for a long time."

"That didn't make any difference to Maureen."

I stare around surreptitiously to see if anyone notices our conversation. I hate to be standing here in an International House Of Pancakes parking lot carrying on a conversation with myself. But several people walk by, give us desultory glances and carry on.

"Mom? Are you aware that I'm in a certain amount of trouble?"

"Of course."

"Well? Isn't there something you can do to help me?"

"You weren't listening, Joseph? I'm here to talk about Maureen."

"I haven't seen Maureen since your funeral." I wonder if I should have mentioned that.

"Maureen needs you."

"Maureen's been married for ten years, has a life of her own."

"I'm perfectly aware of Maureen's marital status. She needs you. I want you to come back to Iowa."

"I have other priorities at the moment, like staying one jump ahead of the FBI and several other organizations on both sides of the law."

"Maureen needs you."

What is it Yogi Berra is supposed to have said, '*Déjà vu* all over again'? This conversation could have taken place in my childhood home in Lone Tree, my mother making a request, like clean your room, or take out the garbage, and me offering excuses, other things I have to do. Nothing changes people, not even death.

Later that night I wake from a horrendous dream, find myself staring wildly into the darkness of another strange motel room. It is one of those dreams that ends with me falling helplessly, endlessly. Francie sleeps calmly beside me, her breathing even.

In the image that crowds into my mind I am falling toward water, my legs churning helplessly in air. Water holds as much terror for me as land, for I have never been able to swim. It takes me several moments to force the image to retreat. I think of Maureen.

In Iowa City there is a place called City Park.

"Such an original name," my father said, with great irony.

The park sits on several acres of low land in a crook of the Iowa River, below the imposing buildings of the University of Iowa Hospitals. The grounds of the hospitals are separated from the park only by paths, and visitors to the park sometimes wander onto the hospital grounds, while ambulatory patients and bored visitors sometimes cross into City Park.

There was once a zoo, but it was poorly tended and the animals either died or were sold off. When I was a child, all that was left of the zoo was one forlorn buffalo, ragged as a tramp, motheaten, perpetually dozing, near death. There were terrible arguments among city counselors, reported word for word in the *Iowa City Press Citizen*, as to what should be done with the buffalo, who was appropriately named Bill.

At one time there was also a merry-go-round in City Park. Like the buffalo, it had been abandoned. The operators crept away in the night, leaving a sad carousel with two dozen horses, their paint scarred and chipped by forty years of contact with truculent children. Some of the horses were eyeless, their foreheads and flaring nostrils scarred by cigarette burns.

The young are fascinated by death and abandonment. What else can explain why teenagers gravitate to deserted houses, dead-end roads, forsaken carousels in parks that are closed to the public after dark?

It wasn't just to be alone with Maureen that I went to City Park.

The smells of carnival still clung like lint to the carousel. The odors of burning grease, frying onions and cotton candy touched my face like ghostly cobwebs. The weathered, gray flooring creaked and groaned, our foolish laughter piercing the night like bird calls.

Maureen straddled one of the pock-marked horses, lit a cigarette. I imagined the air compressors banging away, the hoarse, crusty voices of the barkers . . .

Hopping off the carousel, I took hold of one of the poles that held up the roof and, pushing with all my strength, managed to advance the carousel about fifteen feet until, somewhere beneath the horse, in a dark mechanical labyrinth, a gear locked.

Maureen's horse had lowered on its pole as it advanced until its feet were even with the flooring. Maureen sat with her legs straight, her feet almost touching the floor.

I put an arm around her.

"That's as far as she'll go," I said, breathing heavily.

"You tried," said Maureen, laughing. She lowered her face and kissed me, her tongue fierce in my mouth, her taste sweet and smoky, her manner urgent. She climbed off the horse, leaned her back against it as we kissed, our pelvises grinding together, denim against denim making its own sweet song.

Maureen, her arms locked behind my neck, turned us slowly around until my back was against the horse. Without parting our mouths, Maureen forced my right arm away from her body, pushing it back until it was behind the horse's mane. She then posed me with my left hand holding onto the saddle horn. Maureen stepped back half a step.

"Geez, but you're pretty like that, McCoy."

"Pretty?"

"You know what I mean. A real tough dude. I'd call this pose 'Joe McCoy Says Fuck the World If It Doesn't Do as I Say.'"

"I'm all for that."

"Oh, baby, I'm gonna make you feel so good," she said, sliding down until she was kneeling, taking me in her mouth, her tongue as demanding as it had been in my mouth seconds before.

The faraway lights from the hospital on the hill, from the town across the Iowa River, made Maureen's hair glint like fire. Eyes closed, I imagined I could hear the tinkling music of the carousel, feel the flow as it rose and fell like water, wished that I could always love Maureen as I did at that moment.

How many times over the years have I thought of that night, with warmth, with love, with regret.

At least I know that that evening occurred. It is the other dreams that have me worried. The one, for instance, last night that took place in Iowa City, in our home, Maureen's and mine, that old house at the corner of Johnson and Ronalds that we have so lovingly restored. This is not a happy dream: Maureen, dark circles under her eyes, her hair limp, turned from the kitchen sink to face me. I have been complaining about something, though in that fragmented way dreams work I do not know what it is. Over her shoulder I can see the hummingbird feeder we have installed in the oak outside the window.

"Do you think you're the only one who ever lost someone they loved?" Maureen yells, her voice full of tears. She raises both fists in helpless rage, steps toward me, pounds on my chest and shoulders. I make no move to stop her. Dishwater and suds dampen my shirt, spatter my face.

In a half minute she becomes tired, collapses against me sobbing. I have never felt so helpless. I see flashing images of a tiny coffin, my heart wrenches as if slammed by a powerful fist. A girl of perhaps three lies in the coffin, banked by satin pillows. The child has Maureen's red hair, my nose, her cheeks are still baby-plump. I can almost say a name. A well-worn doll is cradled against the child's breast.

I wake sobbing uncontrollably. Francie is shaking me gently, asking what is wrong. "I don't think being a fugitive agrees with you," she says. "Maybe we'd better think about packing this all in."

"What city is this?" I ask.

"I don't know," says Francie. "But we were in Arkansas yesterday, weren't we?"

Just as Pico said, the credit cards are like gold, no one gives us a second glance. We are now dressed like wealthy tourists.

*   *   *

The red Lincoln hums along quiet as a baby snoring. On our second odyssey across the country I decided to reacquire my beautiful car. There is nothing like having your own key when it comes to stealing a car. If you have the name you may as well have the game. I just walked up to my car and drove out of the circular drive in front of the Armenian's white-pillared home in Beverly Hills, smooth as grease through a goose, as my dad often said. We take more than two weeks to make the long, leisurely drive east and north until we are in sparse, rugged rural Maine.

I'm feeling so invincible, I take off my baseball cap as we cruise down the highways, defying the odds, flaunting ourselves in my stolen scarlet Lincoln while the radio blasts out various versions of "The Kid's Last Fight." The song is now number three on the pop hit parade, and Frankie Laine, who has been playing obscure night clubs in Vegas and Reno for many years, gets a shot at prime time when "60 Minutes" does a story on the Kid McCoy phenomenon.

I suggest we dress Little Joe as a boy again instead of disguising him in pink overalls and a pink blanket.

I have to admit it is a curious thrill to walk into a post office and see my picture on the wall. KIDNAPPING AND FLIGHT TO AVOID PROSECUTION, reads the bold, black headline. Francie and I share a poster. The photo of Francie is very good. It was taken by Rosslyn during Adam and Francie's most recent visit.

"I like it," says Francie, after first staring around to be certain no one is within earshot. We are passing through Portland, Maine.

My likeness is copied from a Topps bubblegum card, the photograph taken at the beginning of my final season in the Bigs. I am wearing the square, bumble-bee-colored cap of the Pittsburgh Pirates; I look about twenty-two years old—my ears stick out like Alfred E. Neuman's.

"Who's he?" Francie says, laying a dainty index finger on one of my paper ears. "No woman in her right mind would kidnap a baby and run off with someone who looks like that. I'll use that as a defence if we get caught."

At this point I shut down the story for the day. I can see that Gideon is anxious to get away. He says he has to get Missy home to her "preferred environment." What surprises me is that Francie leaves with them. "I'm going to see Gideon's house," she says.

"Joe!" Francie throws herself into my arms later after she's come back from Gideon's. "By bringing me here you've set me free."

"Free at last! Free at last!" I say with as much irony as I can muster. Francie pays no attention.

"I'm going to spend mornings for the next fifty years staring out the windows of Gideon's wonderful old house in Onamata. I'm going to love and enjoy Missy for whatever time she has. We're going to have babies and Missy will live long enough for them to remember her bending over their cribs, cooing them asleep or awake. They'll remember her magical love. Do you know that in Gideon's kitchen the dishes wash themselves? The hollyhocks outside the windows sing 'We Shall Not be Moved.'"

"Oh, Francie Bly, what have I got you into?"

"I don't care what you've gotten me into. I don't remember much of anything before I walked into Annie and Ray's kitchen and met Gideon Clarke. Oh, I went to college in New York and had another life. But nothing was important until that moment."

Francie dances out of the room, her face, lit with love, young enough to be one of Ray's daughters.

Did I dream this? Or did it happen?

Loneliness rushes at me like a shaggy pet that has missed me while I've been away on a long road trip.

Have I done something horribly wrong for which I'm being punished? Am I doomed to travel America forever, forever on the run, forever evading capture or escaping captivity by the skin of my teeth? What am I? A Flying Dutchman? An Ancient Mariner? A Sisyphus?

FIFTEEN

JOE McCOY

THE TANGLEWOOD TRAILER PARK IS ON A GRAVEL ROAD a mile from what passes for a town—a Shell service station surrounded by dusty junkers parked three deep on three sides, Boyer's General Store, a wooden barber pole attached to the porch of a weathered frame house—a hand-painted sign in the window reading "Bev's Beauty Salon." Something called Min's Café is across the gravel road from the Ellis B. Trammell High School, which is built of dark brick and closed for the summer, tall dandelions brilliant on its lawns.

I picked up a weekly newspaper at a town outside Bangor and discovered the ad for room and board, giving directions to the Tanglewood Trailer Park.

"Well, I wasn't expectin' a couple, especially with a baby, and I wanted someone more permanent, but beggars can't be choosers, and cash is cash. You able to pay a week in advance?" asks the woman who answers my knock.

She is tall and rawboned, in her late thirties, wearing ill-fitting khaki work pants and a colorless sweater. She stands on the makeshift porch of the mobile home, arms wrapped around herself. She has a slight squint, in spite of granny glasses that do not enhance her long, reddish face.

"The big bedroom's the one for rent," she says. "It's the one off the living room and has its own toilet and sink, but the toilet gave up the ghost years ago. There's two bedrooms at the far end; me and the husband has one, the kids the other. You'll have to share the bathroom down to our end."

"That'll be fine," I say. "I'm planning to write a book set in this part of the country," I lie. "Me and the wife just want to get the feel of the land, if you know what I mean. I'm Lester Armbruster and this is my wife, Tammy-Jo."

"I'm Maggie Levesque."

On the porch, I count money into her hand and we move in.

I am not prepared for sharing space with the Levesques. As a reporter I encountered a fair amount of poverty. But there is something so permanent about the way these people live. The occupants are like the trailer they live in, trembling and held together by rust, sinking hopelessly into the spongy earth.

This is logging country, flat-deck trucks and front-end loaders are standard sights on the roads, in front yards and on the sorry streets of this hamlet. I expect that Maggie Levesque's husband is somehow connected with the logging industry. I am wrong.

We meet the children at the evening meal, two husky boys of nine and seven, dressed in green work pants, red-and-black checkered shirts, and green duck-hunter's vests, the uniform for all males in the area it seems.

"The husband's laid up," is Maggie Levesque's only explanation, as she carries a tray toward the bedroom at the rear of the trailer.

"Dad's an artist," says the oldest boy, and he points toward what I thought was a wall plaque. When I examine it I see it is handcarved, about 8"x 10", an intricately detailed street scene. In spite of having passed through the town only once, I recognize the store, the high school, the service station.

"This is beautiful," I say. "Your dad is very talented."

"Ma takes them into Portland once a month. There's a department store and an art gallery sells them. Dad didn't start carving until after his accident," he says. "He used to drive a logging truck, like I'm gonna do when I grow up."

"Even though the Levesques need the money and nobody would ever think of looking for us here, I don't think we'll stay long," I say to Francie that evening. "Everything is so depressing."

I go for a walk after supper; there is a derelict truck sinking into the mossy earth behind the mobile home. The home itself has translucent plastic flapping around its windows, and truck tires at intervals on the rusted roof.

Our room is immaculate. Our bed is a built-in one that came with the trailer, which must be twenty years old. Little Joe sleeps on the floor in his car-bed. It gnaws at me that Maggie Levesque is renting out the biggest bedroom while she and her husband are crammed into a very small room at the other end, the children in a room scarcely big as a closet.

"Make yourself at home in the living room," Maggie says, "there's a record player and a few records the kids haven't made sticky. We keep the TV in Jim's room, but we can bring it out if there's something you really want to watch. We ain't got the cable though, so it's only good for two channels."

It is late on our third day before I meet Jim Levesque. I am on my way to take a shower when, as I walk toward the bathroom, the door to Jim's room swings open slowly, probably dislodged by my stepping on some bulging floorboard. I see a figure lying on a bed, head against the outside wall, a small shaded lamp shining light onto his chest.

I change my course and walk toward the bedroom door. Though I try to control it, I know my face shows shock and surprise at what I see. I recall an assignment I was sent on by my newspaper. A neighborhood was trying to raise money for a little girl who had been horribly burned in an accident. I went to interview the child and her parents. I knocked on the door to a glass sunporch and, in spite of being prepared for the worst, still leapt back in horror when the child stood up from where she'd been playing on the floor of the porch: two deep-set eyes staring out of a mottled pink and purple face, two black holes where a nose had been. No hair, no ears. Her face appears in my thoughts frequently.

Jim Levesque's face is not mutilated, but it seems to be the only part of his body that is not. He is propped up on pillows, his left arm held at a grotesque angle by a wire sling of some kind. His body is twisted on its side, his legs, one in a metal brace, are bent at unnatural angles. As I get closer I see that the bed is tiered; he looks as though he is lying on a badly constructed set of stairs.

"You must be Joe," he says. "Maggie said we had new renters."

I can't see his eyes because of the lights and shadows, but I know he can see the surprise and avoidance registered on my face.

"You're a very good artist," I stammer. "I've been admiring your work, it's really excellent."

"I do what I can to help out."

"I wish I had some artistic talent. Unfortunately, I can't draw anything but stick figures. Have you been doing this long?" I nod to where he has a wooden rectangle fitted into a metal frame a few inches above his face. He is holding a stylus and carving at the picture with his right hand, which appears to be the only part of his body not misshapen. His face, though prematurely lined by pain, is younger than I would have guessed. I have to revise my estimate of Maggie's age; she is closer to thirty than forty.

"I used to whittle, just as a hobby; but after I got wracked up, well if I didn't have a talent before, I made myself develop one. I have a family to provide for."

"Surely there must be agencies?" I hear myself saying.

"We don't accept charity," he says, closing the subject for good.

"Jim was driving a logging truck with a full load, down the mountain to the sawmill," Maggie said later. The mountain, I discover, would be only a large hill in other parts of the country.

"It was snowing, and the truck jack-knifed. If it had stayed jack-knifed the load might have missed him, but he fought the truck, and straightened it out about the time he ran out of road. The load of logs crushed the cab with Jim inside it. Most men who have accidents like that die on the spot, but Jim's lasted eleven years."

I had assumed the accident to be quite recent.

"We weren't married yet when it happened," says Maggie, surprising me even more. "I was in nursing school up in Portland, had a year to go to graduate. We were gonna get married and, why, we might have moved all the way to Boston, or even Providence. Jim was fixin' to learn a trade, had his heart set on air conditioning.

"My family was horrified that I dropped out and came home to look after Jim, more horrified when I married him. The doctors said he couldn't last more than a year or two, but we've proven them wrong." And she smiles.

I want to ask why she didn't finish her nurse's training. But I guess I know. Maggie Levesque has done what her heart dictated, rather than what was expected of her. She's made no compromises. How I wish I had done the same.

When our week is up, after counting my money carefully, I pay Maggie Levesque for another seven days.

"We'll move on tonight," I say to Francie. "Bet we'll be the only people who ever sneaked out of a place in the dead of night when our rent is paid up for a full week."

I could see the questions in her eyes.

"How else can I help them out? I've considered letting them find out who we are—the most useful thing would be to let the Levesques collect the rewards."

What with various police organizations, the Airline Pilots' Association, organized baseball, Crimestoppers, to name a few, we're worth over four hundred thousand dollars. Pico says the word on the street is that the Mob will match anything the straight community posts. I tend to believe Pico, most of the time.

"They know," says Francie.

"Then why . . ?"

"The boys know. They've been sworn to secrecy by their mother. But they couldn't resist telling me."

Francie has become fast friends with the boys. They are fascinated by having a baby in the house. Francie can take a piece of newspaper and fashion a kind of spacecraft that actually takes off like a stringless kite on the slightest breeze. The folding process is very complicated but I think she has taught the boys.

Off and on during the day I surreptitiously pack the car. By evening all that is left is ourselves and a few of Little Joe's necessities. Deep in the night Francie carries the sleeping baby to the car. Little Joe's extra blanket tucked under my arm, I am about to exit when I decide to make a final trip to the washroom. I tiptoe the length of the rickety trailer house, trying to avoid the noisiest bulges in the floor.

As I turn toward the washroom door I somehow shift the balance of things so that the door to Maggie and Jim's bedroom swings silently open. I freeze in mid-step. The amber glow of a neighbor's yard light washes through parted curtains, spilling across the floor almost to my feet.

Maggie and Jim are not asleep, but they are as oblivious to my presence as they are to the door falling silently away from the wall. Their bodies, bathed in golden light, seem to have all the rough angles obliterated, making what they are doing tender and erotic and beautiful beyond description. Maggie, on top, barely moves her body; she has moulded herself to accommodate Jim's statue-like form; she is bent far forward, her face against his. Jim's good right hand clutches the curls at the back of Maggie's neck, caressing. The bed grumbles, the room is filled with soft moans, their eager breath, the lush sounds of love.

Holding my breath, I inch my way backward, farther and farther from the tines of molten light. Finally, I am able to turn and retreat to the back door and make my way outside. I no longer feel sorry for the Levesques. Whatever they may lack, they have each other.

I slip into the driver's seat, close the door gently, lean across and kiss Francie's cheek. For just an instant I feel an intolerable sadness, as if someone I love very much has died. I feel desperately lonely. As I start the car Francie smiles, cuddles Little Joe to her breast. A tear has overflowed onto her cheek and is poised there like a droplet of dew.

SIXTEEN

JOE McCOY

IT WAS WHILE STOPPING FOR LUNCH IN ASPEN on our way to Denver that I got the idea. The best ideas often come from overheard conversations.

There are no inexpensive restaurants in Aspen, where movie stars own hillside ski chalets, and store after store exists by providing only luxuries, nothing necessary to the continuance of human life. At lunch we were being served by a waiter in a white shirt and black vest whose name was Viktor. I could tell it was spelled that way because of his accent, which, though he may have grown up in the Bronx, was vaguely Swiss, as were the accents of many shop clerks and all hotel employees. It always puzzles me that the concierge and the maître d' at every high-class hotel I've ever stayed at, and I stayed at a few when I was in the Bigs, have foreign accents, preferably German but French will do, Italian is acceptable if all else fails.

The couple at the next table were television executives—they talked loudly enough to let everyone know their business.

"I interviewed Adam Quinn yesterday. A pompous son of a bitch if there ever was one," said the woman.

"The right place at the right time," replied the man. "Why couldn't my fiancée run off on a crime spree with some washed-up jock? I could do better than a cookbook. *She* keeps a diary."

"If I could just have interviewed Francie Bly," said the woman. "That would be a story. Big Harvey, the antiquarian book dealer, says he'd pay a thousand dollars for one of those books signed by Francie Bly."

I had taken my sandwich apart and was trying unsuccessfully to scrape off the alfalfa sprouts.

"How much money do we have left?" asked Francie.

"Enough for the check, and a tank of gas."

"Then I think we'd better find Big Harvey."

"What if we did an interview?" I suggested. "These guys would go for it. Probably pay well, too."

"Then we'd have to really run again. The pressure's been off the past few days. I enjoyed the Indian pueblos, Taos, Santa Fe, the Salt River Canyon."

"There's a wonderful bookstore in Denver," I said. "It's called The Tattered Cover. It's huge, five stories. If we told them we were desperate for cash, if we promised to sign only for them, they'd probably pay a couple of dollars a book. You could do a thousand."

"Let's see," said Francie. "I could do a thousand books at maybe two dollars each, or I could do a couple of books at a thousand dollars each. Which sounds better to you? Take your time before answering."

"Big Harvey," I said.

"Antiquarian book people are very strange," Francie said, "and book collectors even stranger. Adam used to collect Anne Tyler. 'She's very collectible,' he used to say, 'someday these volumes will be worth a lot of money.' I was always thrilled when he got a new book. I loved to read Anne Tyler. Adam, of course, never read a word except for her signature on the title page. He was always afraid I was going to break the binding or damage the dust jacket, or get lipstick on the pages."

Big Harvey wasn't difficult to find. The yellow pages had a half-inch ad for Harvey's Antiquarian Books and Collectibles, signed first editions, American Literature our specialty.

Francie dialed.

"Rumor has it you would pay a thousand dollars for a signed copy of *The Francie Bly Cookbook*."

Fifteen minutes later we were in his shop. He closed the door and flipped the closed sign outward. Big Harvey was a rough-hewn man who looked like a door with a hundred-pound sack of flour strapped to the front of it. He had a round face with a stiff salt-and-pepper beard. His eyes were probably blue behind large thick glasses.

"I sense that I can trust him," Francie said on the short drive to the bookstore. "He won't turn us in. I have something he wants very badly. It's nice to have something someone else wants very badly, the greed becomes palpable. I could feel it clogging the phone wires."

"I phoned over to a retail bookstore," Big Harvey says. "I ordered ten copies and they'll be delivered in a few minutes." He poured us coffee. He had only pale milk to doctor it. Why would a fat man deny himself cream in his coffee? The shop was small and every inch was books: shelves, stacks of books on the floor, boxes piled here and there. His desk was a rat's nest of papers and books.

"Why ten books?" asked Francie. "On the phone we agreed to one signature on one book for one thousand dollars."

The coffee tastes like rust, is probably left over from breakfast.

"I've made a couple of quick phone calls," says Big Harvey. "I'd like to get a couple more signatures."

"A thousand dollars each," says Francie. "Also, you wouldn't have bought ten books if you didn't want ten books signed."

"I can't afford ten thousand dollars," says Big Harvey.

"How much can you afford?"

"Maybe five thousand."

"Five thousand will get you five books."

Big Harvey sighed. The phone rang. Though he tried to keep the gist of the conversation from us it was obvious that a collector was ravenous for a signed copy of Francie's book.

"There's a little problem on this end," Big Harvey said. "The price I quoted on your answering machine was a little low. How do you feel about ten thousand?"

The collector didn't appear to feel very well about ten thousand.

Francie tapped Big Harvey on the arm. He excused himself, put a hand over the mouthpiece.

"What if I used your stamp pad there and autographed each book not only with my signature but with Little Joe's footprint?"

"I could sign the copies, too," I said. "I used to play major-league baseball."

Big Harvey repeated the offer to the caller. I think they settled for seventy-five hundred.

"So you'll clear seventy-five thousand and Little Joe and I will clear ten thousand," said Francie. There was a knock and the books arrived.

As Francie inks Little Joe's foot, he giggles and flings his arms about.

"I want one of them signed for me," said the bookseller, "to Big Harvey with love." Francie complied.

"You can't do this again in Denver or Albuquerque, or wherever you're headed," said Big Harvey. "It would destroy the value of what I have here."

"What do you think," Francie said, "that we're crooks or something?"

SEVENTEEN

JOE McCOY

THERE IS NO BETTER PLACE THAN HAWAII to be a fugitive. Francie has never been to Hawaii. The air is warm and loving, there are a hundred thousand tourists to blend in with, we have a delightful view of the ocean and Diamond Head from our window and we have made friends. On the floor below, here at the Yacht Harbor Towers, a couple from Iowa are wintering with their young son. I thought at first that the father might be a spy of some sort, for, strangely enough, he writes about baseball. He is a novelist who must be successful to live half the year in Yacht Harbor Towers, though I have never read him.

This does not surprise him. "Baseball players," he says laconically, "are not the great readers of America."

"I'm a reporter," I say in my defence, "I read, I just haven't read you."

Their baby, Tommy, is about the same age as Little Joe. The babies wiggle like slugs on the thick carpet in our suites while we visit. The women take the babies to the beach in the afternoon. In the evening Bill and I walk to the University of Hawaii's beautiful Rainbow Stadium, where we watch baseball. He is tall and secretive. Between innings he reads novels, usually by Southern writers, and watches the games as though they were chess matches. After checking his pockets for paper, he makes notes on the back of his left hand, which has a permanent bluish tinge.

The first night we were in Hawaii I phoned Pico.

"Wiser's dead," he said. "A car bomb. It's been kept hush-hush. Natural causes, for those not in the know. Private services. I'm told even his wife didn't attend. Nobody knows who to blame, though you're a prime suspect. He didn't appear to be working on anything dangerous except your case, though Tony the Pianist did send an elaborate floral tribute in the shape of a white picket fence."

"In which dimension," I am tempted to ask, but do not.

Four of them ooze from the shadows of the dwarf palm trees that line the alley, which is part of the grounds of one of the larger and more opulent hotels in Waikiki. They are wearing blue-and-white Hawaiian shirts and dark trousers: small, swarthy men with nationalistic moustaches and fervor-filled eyes. Each has a revolver that glints like moonlight on ocean. The guns are all pointed at me. The nearest one nuzzles non-erotically against my crotch.

"Why are you doing this?" I say to the crotch-nuzzler.

"Where would you least like to be shot, Señor?"

"You will lead us please to the child, Jose Joachin."

I deem it best to co-operate.

"May we inquire as to whose employ you are in?" the heftiest asks, during the short taxi ride to Yacht Harbor Towers.

"I am in no one's employ."

"We understand loyalties, Señor. This is unpleasant business we are involved in, is it not? That is why it will make us sad to kill you and your lovely traveling companion once we have recovered the child."

My captors nod sympathetically, their oiled hair shining with menace.

"My friends and I have different loyalties. Some of us favor El Presidente, some the Revolution. However, this assignment has brought us together: we all favor fathers and sons."

"I, too, favor fathers and sons," I say.

"Do I not know you?" the crotch-nuzzler asks, "beyond the fact that you have stolen the baby of our ambassador to America?"

"I spent a few months in Courteguay once."

"You are a pitcher," cries the small man, his voice rising. "You played for the Azaleas of San Barnabas."

"I played for the San Cristobel Anthurium Rapists."

"Of course. I am Hector Crucible, shortstop for the Camelias of El Presidente, three-time champions of the Courteguayan Senior Professional Baseball League. I was only fourteen the day I played against you. I went 2 for 3 with a sacrifice bunt. I threw you out from the left-field grass when you hit one in the hole. You did not exert yourself running to first."

"I prefer the designated hitter rule."

"El Presidente is a traditionalist. He does not allow designated hitters in Courteguay. I, Hector Crucible, have signed a contract with your California Angels. I am to be assigned to a team in Canada, where I am told there is ice in the outfield all year round."

Francie and Little Joe, or Jose Joachin, as my Courteguayan captors refer to him, are nowhere to be seen. I thought I caught a glimpse of them as we passed through the lobby, but didn't turn in their direction in case I was right.

"Where are the woman and child?" Hector demands.

"I have no idea," I say, which is true. "But, believe me, we are just a simple couple from Iowa vacationing with our son. We don't know anything about the baby you're looking for."

Two of the Courteguayans remain in the hall. Two enter with me and stand around, pistols drawn.

"This is all a mistake," I maintain. I try to recall how my movie heroes would handle a situation where they were held captive by armed men, who, though they bear no real grudge, are probably going to kill anyway, perhaps apologizing before they fire. My imagination is paralyzed.

A headline on USA Today is visible from the coffee table: THREE BILLION IN U.S. AID TO COURTEGUAY.

"Have you gentlemen seen this?" I ask, stalling for time.

"Paid out of guilt, Señor. The United States has been made to feel very guilty because one of its own kidnapped our ambassador's baby."

"What will you do with three billion dollars?"

"There are brokerage fees, perhaps one billion will find its way to El Presidente; it will stem the tide of revolution for a few months."

"And the other two billion?"

"We assumed you knew. We have encountered several emissaries of Don Bablioto, who are also seeking your whereabouts."

"Tony the Pianist got the other two billion?"

"Of course. He's Courteguayan, you know."

Hector Crucible produces a pad of white paper, a stamp pad, and photostats of Jose Joachin's footprints.

"As soon as your good lady reappears, we will conduct a simple test which will prove conclusively that the baby you possess is the missing child of our ambassador," says one of my captors.

"Juan here once led the league in triples while playing shortstop for the Butterflies of San Pedro," says Hector Crucible. He points at the smallest Courteguayan, a boyish-looking fellow with a pointed chin and a squint. "Unfortunately he did little else than hit triples. An average of .132 for the season, am I wrong?"

Juan smiles weakly.

"He could have used a few outings against you, Señor McCoy."

"There's a batting cage downtown. We could all go there after this business is completed," I say.

There is a light knock at the door. Hector Crucible opens it and there is Francie and the baby in the company of the two hall-bound Courteguayans. Francie looks perplexed and outraged.

"He's *my* baby," she repeats several times.

At their request, Francie unwraps the baby who gurgles and coos, happy at all the attention. He is pink as strawberry ice cream, with reddish-blond hair and green eyes.

"You will excuse the inconvenience of my dirtying the feet of the baby," says Hector, pressing a foot on the stamp pad then on the white paper.

There is a knock at the door. The Courteguayans, guns drawn, take elaborate precautions before opening it, only to find one of their own. A brief conference follows.

Hector Crucible studies the footprints for a long time. He holds a consultation with his compatriots. He shrugs and says, "We are greatly sorry. Science confirms this is not the baby we seek."

They start for the door.

"Perhaps the baby is truly the son of you and your charming lady."

"How about a little baseball?" I say to Hector. "I wouldn't mind throwing batting practise for you and your friends.

"Another time, Señor McCoy."

The last one out closes the door with compassion.

"What kind of magic is this?" I say to Francie.

She shrugs. "I saw you in the lobby. I stopped by and traded babies with Bill and his wife. Little Joe's having his nap downstairs."

This happened. I'm certain it happened. But, later, when I attempt to discuss the switching of babies, Francie only smiles dreamily.

"If you believe something happened, then it probably did," she says, which could mean almost anything.

Our plane drones toward Seattle, full of sunburned tourists clad in leis and muumuus. The Courteguayans, though I hardly noticed as I was so happy not to wind up air conditioned, confiscated my wallet with all my cash, credit cards and I.D. Fortunately, our return tickets to the mainland were in the bottom of Little Joe's diaper bag.

Being a fugitive is a very lonely business. There is no support group. *Feeling neglected? Tired of eating in bad restaurants, sleeping days, driving nights? Miss your family and friends, going outdoors without sunglasses? Then call 1-800-FUGITIVE.*

I've been thinking about friends. A person is lucky to have one friend in a lifetime. The test of true friendship goes something like this: you phone late at night to say that you have (a) held up a 7-Eleven store and murdered three people in the process, (b) wiped out your family and buried the bodies beneath the floor of your garage, (c) embezzled half a million dollars from your employer, which you have lost in Las Vegas.

If the person is truly your friend, he will say, "I'll mortgage my house to put up bail and pay a lawyer."

How many people other than relatives and current lovers would you go out on a limb for?

For me, there are only two people in the world: Maureen Renn, whom I haven't seen for over ten years, and Blind John Brimbacomb, who works at the Kingdome in Seattle.

Maureen, in spite of the way I've treated her, would help me. I'll put the second friendship to the test later today.

Blind John Brimbacomb played briefly in the Negro Leagues in the 1940s. He would have been a superstar, might have, instead of Jackie Robinson, been the first black in the Bigs, had he not been run over by a team bus outside the stadium in Omaha in 1942. The blindness came many years later and was unrelated to the bus accident.

At Sea-Tac Airport I approach a middle-aged couple bedecked with leis, mai tais oozing from their pores. As we wait for luggage a young woman waves at them, one with the same equine face and lank blond hair as the woman. They have a ride.

"Any chance that you're driving through downtown on the way home?" I ask. "There's no sign of our ride, and we're short of cash."

"Spent all our money on souvenirs," says Francie, flashing a winning smile and the sleeping face of Little Joe.

"My brother works at Elliott Bay Book Store," I say, naming a business close to the Kingdome. "You can drop us off there."

Blind John is taking the sun outside the Press Gate.

"How much you heard about my troubles, John?" I ask as we accompany him into the depths of the Kingdome. "And how did you know to be outside when we arrived?"

"Oh, I keep up on things pretty good."

"I didn't see your radio around."

"I don't rely on radio as much as I once did. Radio these days is mostly nasty music or Jesus freaks, sometimes both on the same station. I have me a young boy drops by every day, reads me the *Seattle Post-Intelligencer* cover to cover."

"Blind John adopts street kids," I say to Francie.

She smiles at John. Sensing what she has done he smiles back.

"You should see John take batting practice," I say. "He can hear the ball."

"Right. It's the whirr of the seams as it travels toward me. I can tell by the sound if it's a curve or a fastball."

"Only thing that kept him out of organized baseball after his accident was the noise of the crowds. If some night everyone in Seattle stays home to watch TV, Blind John could still pinch hit."

"Used to hit in the Negro Leagues long after I was blind. Coaches could holler me to first and third, but I had a hard time finding second base on my own." John grins until he resembles the grille of a Cadillac. "I'd hit a homer at dusk and the sun would be down, time I got around the bases."

"And he can umpire."

"Somehow that doesn't surprise me," says Francie.

"I still call intersquad games in spring training. I love it when a rookie turns around and says, 'Whassamatter, ump, you blind or somethin'?'"

"You could have been a great one," John says to me later, when we are alone. There is sadness in his voice.

"Sometimes, John, I feel like a traitor to the game. I could have been a star. I never had the desire. Just because someone's a mathematical whiz doesn't mean they want to be an accountant or a physicist. Maybe that mathematical whiz is happy building bird houses. I'm happiest writing a good news story. The story's the thing. In the bullpen I'd day-dream about writing up the game. I'd get called to warmup, I wouldn't know what the score was or who was coming to bat."

"You should have gotten out earlier."

"Hard to do. Do you believe in dreams, John?"

"You mean do they predict the future?"

"The past. I've been dreaming a past I've never lived."

"You dreaming of how your life might have been?"

"Should have been."

"Are the dreams about . . ?" and he nods toward the shower room where Francie sleeps on a blown-up air mattress.

I told Blind John the whole story. He put things in perspective. "You'll forgive me, Joe, but I don't figure you're smart enough to think up all these things on your own."

As always, he is right.

Blind John's beeper sounds.

"FBI to see you," says the voice of the gatekeeper.

"Stay around the corner with your lady. I'll give these lawmen my dumb darkie routine," and Blind John chuckles away down the hall. If only Little Joe doesn't cry. Sound carries for great distances in the passages and walkways of the Kingdome.

"Howdy, gentlemens," says Blind John. He is probably in his armchair, legs extended far in front of him.

"Good morning, sir, we're looking for . . ."

"Ah, I see you gentlemens is from de FBI."

"You see? The man upstairs said you were . . ."

"When de man way upstairs took my sight he heighten up my other senses. Don't need eyes to smell guns. Yours in a genuine leather holster. Yours ain't." I try to imagine the surprise on the faces of the agents.

"That's interesting, but we're looking for Joseph McCoy and one Frances Bly . . ."

"What they done?"

"Have you seen them?"

"Depends on what they done."

"What they've done is not your concern. Have you seen them?"

"This Francis Bly, he a tackle for the Seahawks?"

"No. Frances Bly is a woman . . ."

"Ain't no woman on the Seahawks, you boys should know that."

"We understand you're a friend of Joe McCoy's," says one.

"He's known as Kid McCoy," says the other.

"What he done?"

"Have you seen him?" the agent with the deepest voice fairly roars. "Has he contacted you? He was a ballplayer."

"Joe McCoy?" I can see Blind John scratching his long, bald head. "He a splayfooted basketballer, size sixteen feet, come from South Carolina, play six games for the Sonics, spend his sneaker money on co-caine?"

"No. This Joe McCoy played baseball. And he's white . . ."

"A white athlete name of McCoy? Lord, I didn't know they made any white McCoys no more . . ."

"He played for the Mariners for part of two seasons. He was average height, slight build, a relief pitcher with an ERA about the same as his age, which was about twenty-seven or twenty-eight when he was here."

I can hear Blind John scratching, considering.

"A medium-sized white relief pitcher with a Jell-O arm. Describes everybody ever come out of the Mariner bullpen since they began. Check out that splay-footed basketballer. Sonics moved to the other side of town, don't play in the Kingdome no more."

"You won't mind if we look around?" says the least talkative agent, his frustration showing.

"Suit yourselves."

They tour the locker and training rooms.

"They have a baby with them," I hear the deep-voiced agent say, as they come within earshot again.

"Why didn't you say so," says Blind John. "What you doin' lookin' for a baby in the Kingdome locker rooms?"

"Well . . ."

"I's just an old, blind darkie, but if I lost me a baby I don't go lookin' for him in the basement of the Kingdome."

The footsteps and voices draw closer.

"What's in there?" asks a voice right outside.

"Empty showers," says Blind John. That's where the Sonics used to shower. Nobody able to use that room no more. Baseball players ain't tall enough to reach the taps."

An agent sticks his head in, glances quickly around. They are not ten steps down the hall when Little Joe whimpers loudly. Francie cuddles him to her breast. The footsteps continue to retreat.

"They've left a man out front," says John. "It ain't safe here no more."

And Blind John, friend that he is, put us on a southbound bus that night, with a few dollars, a bag of food and a small cloth toy for Little Joe.

EIGHTEEN

JOE McCOY

PICO THE RAT, UNSHAVEN, BUG-EYED, as fetid as the street, seems to be the only one who even vaguely comprehends what I am going through. He, too, waits for the translucent light that blocks his vision to melt into crystal-clear water, through which he will see a fresh, welcoming world.

Pico has information he feels is newsworthy.

"Why don't you meet me at Amelia Earhart's?" I say.

I can hear the puzzled silence on the other end of the line. Why in the world would I say that to him? Amelia Earhart's is, was, a café just down the street from the *Iowa City Press Citizen*, and I can't even visualize Pico the Rat in Iowa City. Was it there before I left Iowa? I don't know. I don't think I've ever been to that café. My sister wrote me about it, that's it, a favorite hangout of hers. But, wasn't there a propeller above the front counter? I remember fresh-squeezed orange juice, scrambled eggs on a croissant, fresh-sliced strawberries like a row of bleeding hearts across the top of my plate. Do I know only what Agnes has written me? Imagine Pico the Rat in Iowa City. Talk about finding a cockroach in your Jell-O! No debris-filled doorways full of stale comfort; the sidewalks of Iowa City are freshly hosed in summer, freshly swept in winter. Business people would peer through their squeaky-clean windows at Pico, and call the police on general principle. In Iowa, we know what a criminal looks like.

"Sorry," I say to Pico. "I forgot you were downtown. Thinking of a place out in Glendora." I'll take odds that Pico has never been to Glendora. "My mind wanders a lot these days. I'll see you by your phone booth in an hour."

In the shadows behind Pico the Rat's favorite pay telephone:

"Kid?" says Pico. "What are you doing here?"

"We're about at the end of the line. The novelty of being a fugitive has worn off."

"Give yourselves up. No. Let me turn you in."

"If that time comes, you'll be first to know. We want to get back to the Midwest. There's someone in Iowa I've got to see."

"And you're broke."

"Stone cold."

"What's in it for me?"

"The reward when the time comes."

"I never work on credit."

"Sorry. I've come to think of you as a friend. I hoped you might feel the same toward me."

Pico studies me. His tiny receding chin seems to be trembling.

"I've told you secrets, McCoy. Things I haven't told another living soul. You know my dreams." He sniffs loudly. Clears his throat. "I'm gonna help you. I'll arrange five thousand up front on the movie deal. I'm this close." He holds his stained fingers a half-inch apart.

"The movie people are gonna advance you five grand?"

"Not exactly. Trust me, Kid. You'll have it by the end of the day. I got a scam all figured. You know how to hot-wire a car?"

"No."

Pico frowns. "I never like to do the preliminaries myself. It's a shame to get busted for something petty when you're on the verge of a big score. But, what the hell. You ever committed a 211?"

"Armed robbery? Of course not. What do you think I am?"

"The crook at the top of the FBI's 10 Most Wanted List. Listen, not to worry, this scam is foolproof. Here's a ten spot, go buy me two broom handles. I'm gonna phone a guy who'll rent a cop uniform from a costume shop and leave the package in his car so's it can be ripped off. I'll let you know where it's parked when you get back with the broom handles. By that time I'll have boosted a car. When the movie comes through we'll be millionaires, McCoy. I tell ya, I'm this fucking close."

I go to a supermarket and pick up food for Francie and the baby, and two broom handles from the hardware aisle.

"You know the McDonald's down the drag?" says Pico. "That's where we score." I have just handed over the costumer's box which I pilfered from the front seat of an unlocked Buick.

"You and me?"

"At closing time. We'll clear close to eight thousand. This is gonna be so easy. I already got us a car, a '79 slime-green Chevy. It's parked across from McDonald's. Later on you an' me are gonna sit in it for a while. Run along, McCoy. Take your little family to a movie or something. The car at midnight. Go before I change my mind. How many guys would I do this for?"

At midnight I walk past McDonald's. The car and Pico are just where he said they'd be.

"Try and look nonchalant," he says, as I slip in beside him. I notice the suit box on the back seat.

The restaurant blazes with light. There are about twenty cars lined up at the drive-thru window.

"I been casing this place," said Pico. "They close at 1:00 A.M. At about 1:10 three guys come out and head for the night depository on the corner. The manager carries a canvas sack, one of his assistants wears a shoulder holster."

"Then how do we . . ?"

"Not to worry. I make a phone call. All McDonald's have silent numbers," says Pico. "Had to slip one of the counter kids a twenty to get it."

At the phone booth, Pico dials. "Hello. Let me speak to the manager, please. Good evening, this is Sgt. Zefferilli, LAPD. Don't be alarmed, but we have reason to believe you're going to be held up at closing time. Here's how we want you to handle it . . ."

I shut my eyes and listen. Pico is so convincing I believe I am listening to a police officer.

"When you get off the phone, take a casual look across the street. The green Chevy is an unmarked police vehicle; there'll be a detective and a uniform in it. If you look up, and don't be too obvious about it, you'll see we've got snipers on the roof across the street. The guy's white, about 5'9", 160 lbs., long blondish hair, a real loser.

"When he comes in act scared and hand him the cash. We'll be waiting outside the door. Any questions? Good. My name's Zefferilli. We'll talk to you later. Thanks for your co-operation.

"Am I good, or am I good?" says Pico. "Let's head back. We want to be seen in that car. Here's a baseball cap. Cover up your hair."

"So that's what you did with the broom handles," I say, casting one quick glance at the roof.

"Look for all the world like rifles, don't they? I saw Hopalong Cassidy use that scam in *Girl of the Golden West*, Columbia Pictures, 1946."

We settle into the car.

The restaurant closes. The staff and lingering customers file out, the manager escorting each one to the door.

"Now he'll be in the back counting the cash. Slip out the passenger side, take one turn around the block, go in and hold him up."

"Do I get a weapon?"

"A hand in your windbreaker will do."

I walk into the restaurant and make my way to the office. I hope the manager hasn't decided to be a hero.

He is a plump young man with beady eyes, wearing a black tie and white shirt spotted with food stains.

"Give me all the money or I'll blow you away," I yell.

He looks up at me, his expression calm. What if he has called the real police? What if I am about to die in a hail of bullets? What if he has his own gun easily within reach? To my relief, he continues looking at peace with the world. I decide it is because he trusts Sgt. Pico Zefferilli implicitly.

"Don't make any trouble," he says. "It's only money." He pushes the canvas sack across the desk. I grab it and flee.

When I hit the street, there's Pico, looking like a reject from *Police Academy*, revolver pointed menacingly in my direction.

"Freeze Slimeball! Drop the loot! Hands over your head!"

I comply with each command.

"Down on the sidewalk," says Pico, relishing his role. While my cheek grinds into the filthy sidewalk, Pico produces handcuffs and roughly fastens my hands behind me.

"Good work!" he says to the wide-eyed manager. Pico pulls me to my feet, picks up the evidence, presses the gun to my back and points me toward the car across the street.

"Zefferilli," he says to the manager. "Sgt. Zefferilli. Call me tomorrow afternoon. I'll bring over the evidence and take your statement. You won't see this perp on the streets for at least ten years." We walked across the street, Pico intoning, "You have the right to remain silent, you have the right . . ."

Pico pushes me into the back seat. He drives away.

"Slick as grease through a goose," says Pico.

He stops on a quiet side street, changes his clothes, counts the money, puts five thousand in the glove compartment, pockets the rest.

"The car's a bonus," he says, as he stuffs the costume, prop gun, and handcuffs into a hedge. "Have a good trip to Iowa. Hey, remember, if you decide to give up you surrender to me. Deal?"

"Deal."

"Hey, when this is over, if you ever get out of jail, I'll hire you as a consultant on the movie. I tell ya, McCoy, I'm this fucking close."

"I'm sure you are."

"Hadn't we better have a talk?" I say to Francie as we head toward Vegas in that blue hour before dawn. I had traded the Chevy for my Lincoln.

"When we get to Iowa," she replies.

"How did you know I've decided to go there?"

"I know."

"Wasn't there a flying horse named Pegasus? It's gonna take four days to get to Iowa. I'm sure a flying horse would take less than that."

"I have no idea what you're talking about," says Francie.

Sometimes as we drive the endless highways of America I compose imaginary letters:

Dear Ann Landers,
Dear Larry King,
Dear Heloise, When traveling by car in the company of a
small child, as I have been doing lately . . .

We are on a Greyhound headed south. Francie sleeps, her head at an
odd angle, resting on the window ledge. Little Joe is asleep in the crook
of my arm. I feel him wiggle, glance down and find him awake. He stares
up at me with fathomless dark eyes. He looks wise, conspiratorial. I feel
the greatest love for him, the need to protect. And, strangely, this is not
the first time I have felt this way. The bus is three-quarters full, mainly
of old people who talk in their sleep. I watch the blackness slip by the
windows and recall a bizarre conversation I had with Maureen in the
back of my father's antique car.

I remember my body being jammed up like that of a magician's assistant, my feet braced against the passenger door, one knee on the seat,
one on the floor. Maureen had one leg resting on the back of the front
seat, while my tongue moved like a butterfly in the slick sweetness of
her. She crooned softly all the while, then her legs straightened and she
cried out, convulsing against my tongue.

A moment later, safely inside her, Maureen whimpering, ravenously
licking the taste of herself from my mouth, when suddenly . . . "There's
no name for what you just did to me," she says.

I had not spent many an evening with the carefully guarded sex
manual from the library for nothing.

"Textbooks call it . . ."

"I don't mean *that*, McCoy. You know what I mean. Love talk.
Fucking talk. There's a medical term for everything from hangnails up.
When I go down on you I give you a blow job. There's no equivalent.
It's unfair. I've got a cunt, a twat, a pussy. What have you got? There are
no sexy nicknames for your collective parts."

"Cock and balls are not exciting enough for you?"

"No. That's just one degree less formal than penis and testicles. Why
couldn't you have a twat? If I can have a pussy why can't you have a tom
cat? Why isn't it called a tiger or a boar? Or . . ."

"You act as if it's my fault."

"It is. You want to be a sportswriter, you're supposed to be creative, make up nicknames for players. Oh, Babe, when you go down on me I come like a fucking cannon. There's got to be a name for that. It's like the fucking Fourth of July."

Maureen was swirling her thighs as she spoke, like a whirlpool drawing me deeper, making me explode inside her.

"Fireworks," I said, breathing heavily into her shoulder. "Fireworks. We'll put up a poster in the post office, notify the people who put out *Webster's Unabridged*. It will become the third or fourth definition in every dictionary. 'Fireworks: When Joe McCoy goes down on his lady.'"

"Okay, but none of this *his lady* shit. I want my name there."

We revised the definition, and it became our private joke.

That was memory. What came next was not, but was just as vivid. It was winter and we were searching for a Christmas tree, we being Maureen and I and our Charlotte. I was carrying an ax with a red and white handle; we were somewhere east of Lone Tree, maybe on the Renn's farm, though the land did not look familiar. The weather was temperate for winter, the sun blindingly bright. Charlotte was about three, dressed in a pink snowsuit, a scarf wrapped round and round her until she was almost immobile. She tottered when she walked. We found the tree we wanted. I tried to cut it down but with little success.

"Come on, McCoy," said Maureen, "you're not trying to hit a triple. You cut a tree on an angle, the ax bounces when you hit it straight on."

"Paul Bunyan I'm not," I said.

"Easy to see you've never lived on a farm." Maureen was wearing tight jeans tucked in calf-high black boots. One cuff had worked its way out, snow lay in the denim creases. There was something so sexy about that. She took the ax and dispatched the small tree with three accurate chops. I carried the tree while Charlotte trudged behind us. In the car Maureen took off Charlotte's mittens, showed her how to pinch a few needles between her fingers in order to bring out the fresh pine scent.

"Smell, Daddy," said Charlotte, three pine needles that Maureen has squeezed held in her tiny fingers and thrust toward my nose.

The tang of the needles is so strong I know I couldn't have imagined it. I'm still sniffing as I struggle awake, the terrible knowledge within me that this was our last Christmas with Charlotte. Worse, I sense that I am going to lose Maureen, too.

Fantasy and reality, wakefulness and sleep swirl slowly about me. I am on a bus, but the baby I'm holding is not Charlotte. My head clears. I want more than anything to see Maureen again.

SECTION THREE

IF WISHES
WERE HORSES

There is no such thing as diligent fruit.

— Yukio Mishima

NINETEEN

JOE McCOY

BEING A FUGITIVE IS A GAME NO MORE. We are two days from Iowa. No longer do I watch the rearview mirror for police cars; I don't stick to the 55 MPH speed limit. I don't disguise my features under an oversized base-ball cap. We have given up all pretext of hiding, and by doing so have become even less conspicuous. We are a tired couple traveling across the country with a cranky baby. We look the part.

Except . . . who would have thought that the McDonald's on Sunset Strip would have a surveillance camera? We are back in the news. That poor sap of a manager must have found out when he called LAPD the next afternoon that he had been conned by Sgt. Zefferilli, a.k.a. Pico the Rat. The real police no doubt carried the film off to a developer, and, voila, there I am, my hand jammed in my windbreaker pocket, looking tense and threatening. Whatever radio station we tune in is playing "The Kid's Last Fight," the Lionel Ritchie version. A syrup-voiced announcer states that Eddie Murphy has been approached about playing me in the movie.

In the parking lot of a restaurant in Wyoming, a highway-patrol car pulled in next to the Lincoln. Francie barely glanced at the occupants, as she extracted a diaper from the oversized box. They, in turn, barely glanced at us.

I have to supply a little background for the next event that happened to us. Butler was the catcher on my first minor-league team. He was an extremely awkward catcher. I suspect he suffered from fetal alcohol syndrome. Butler was going to play in the low minors until a better prospect came along or the organization got tired of him.

He was huge, probably 6'4", with a flabby appearance that belied his superior strength. He could throw a baseball farther than anyone I've ever known.

He had limitless tolerance for pain. The manager had to be certain he was wearing all his protective gear—we all joked that Butler gave "the tools of ignorance" a whole new meaning. The umpire sometimes had to remind him that he wasn't wearing his mask. And I've watched him catch a fastballing pitcher barehanded, suffering no apparent damage.

It was assumed that Butler was illiterate, and he did nothing to change our minds. He ordered ham and eggs for every breakfast, and hamburger steak for all other occasions. He also appeared incapable of counting his money. We were all poorly paid, but someone always helped Butler settle his bill and stuffed the change into the side pocket of his baggy trousers.

We were in a small Montana saloon one night, a long bar with high stools and a few tables covered in oilcloth. A jukebox wailed country music and the place smelled like it hadn't been aired out this century. Eight or ten of us nursed beers, none of us having enough money to be serious drinkers. Butler drank Coke, or "Coke'n'ass," as the middle-aged barmaid pronounced it. There was our group and a table of cowboys and that was it. Unfortunately, there was a girl with the cowboys, dark-haired, wearing Levi's and a denim vest. The cowboys could afford to drink, the girl was drinking Wild Turkey, water back, and trying to convince the cowboys to dance with her, something none were inclined to do.

One of our pitchers, Everall Williams, who had never been outside New Jersey until that summer, decided to take up the challenge. While the cowboys didn't want to dance, they certainly didn't look kindly on a baseball player treading on their territory—particularly a black baseball player.

When the girl stood up to dance with Ev Williams, a sinewy hand clamped onto her wrist and pulled her back down on her chair. A few words were exchanged and all of a sudden Ev Williams found himself sitting on the sawdust-strewn floor looking puzzled, a trickle of blood at the corner of his mouth. We were generally a pretty law-abiding group, but we rose as one and soon a genuine free-for-all bar fight was in progress.

Baseball players are better at sitting on the bench needling than they are at brawling. Butler and I stood at our table hoping the altercation would burn itself out before it reached us, but there were about four more cowboys than ball players. Eventually a hatchet-faced cowboy about fifty approached me with a fist cocked for action. I raised my open hands in a gesture of goodwill. The cowboy punched right between my peaceful hands, and bent my nose to one side. As I stood stupefied, the cowboy was cocking his right arm to do me even more damage, when Butler grabbed him by the collar and slammed him into a chair so hard the chair collapsed like it was made of balsa.

Another cowboy, a very large one with a forty-pound beer gut, approached. I was still sitting on the floor, my T-shirt pulled up to sop up the blood spurting from my nose. As soon as Butler understood that the cowboy intended him harm, he buried a fist in the gut, then when the cowboy exhaled like a tropical storm, Butler unleashed an upper cut that lifted the cowboy off his feet, and when he did land it was like a pole-axed steer, and he relaxed into unconsciousness, sighing peacefully. The local police arrived and did their best to break up the brawl, collecting money from both groups to compensate the bar owner for broken glasses and damaged chairs. Ev Williams and the cowgirl were gone, apparently in her pick-up truck. Ev returned late the next afternoon, grinning happily and displaying three loose upper teeth.

Butler understood enough to be able to run the bases; he could pick up the third-base coach's signal to keep running, though he was a plodding runner. "Slightly slower than shit moving through a long dog," was how our manager put it, and Butler would grin, just as when the coach or manager praised him for slamming a three-run homer.

We were parked on the highway in front of a sleazy drive-in restaurant on the outskirts of some nameless burgh. It was approaching midnight and we'd just lost a 16-15 twelve-inning game with more walks than hits. The manager had decided we should send one person in to get a giant take-out order, and Epcott, the second baseman, was chosen. We shouted orders to him while he tried to keep track on a sheet of paper with a stubby pencil. After about fifteen orders he threw up his hands and said, "I can't keep track. You're all shouting at once."

"I can," said Butler, who as usual was sitting silently in the front seat staring dreamily at the road as if there was actually something out there to see. "So far, sixteen hamburgers, two cheeseburgers, three chicken strips, two with plum sauce one with barbecue, a BLT hold the mayo, a grilled cheese, seven chocolate shakes, three vanilla, four strawberry, six Cokes, three diet, a Seven-Up, and two root beers."

"Jesus Christ!" said Epcott.

Butler placed the order with the tired-looking woman in the drive-in window, someone else collected the money and made change.

Later that night, the bus driver recited a raunchy poem that must have gone on for twenty minutes. All I can remember are the opening lines. It was a juvenile, bawdy tale well suited to testosterone-spraying young males on a road trip where, regardless of the stories players told, any sexual experience was as rare as Ev Williams' liaison with the sexy cowgirl.

Near dawn in a musty-smelling motel room, four of us to a room, two to each double bed, a guy named Artemus Nenn, a weak-armed center-fielder, said "I sure wish I could remember that poem, my brothers back in Texas would go wild for that." Whereupon Butler began to recite the poem in the voice of the driver, a flat, nasal Nebraska twang.

Kansas. It is late evening, already dark. We are either running out of gas—the gauge is low but doesn't appear that low—or we're about to experience mechanical breakdown. My knowledge of mechanics is limited to turning the ignition off and on, kicking the tires and cursing my luck. The car is lurching like a determined drunk as an exit appears, offering a town. The car limps down a heavily treed street, I turn into the yard of a huge frame home built into an elderly grove of trees. It is a small mansion. The car stops and dies, pinging helplessly into the night. I try the starter. As expected, nothing happens.

The house has a wide wooden verandah, newly painted and swept. On the top half of the beveled glass door are painted the words, JOSIAH

F. MORRIS HOME. Is this the home of a Mr. Morris, or is it a Home? The elderly? Unwed mothers? (Do they still have homes for unwed mothers?) Juvenile delinquents?

I ring the old fashioned black-headed bell on the wall, three chimes emanate through the building. A light goes on. A tall, forbidding woman of sixty or so, short hair, long colorless dress, opens the door.

"Good evening, I was . . ."

"You must be Mr. McCoy," the woman says in a deep voice, her words clipped. A New England accent?

"Well . . ."

"We've been expecting you."

"I have my wife and baby with me," I say, playing along.

"Of course. Mr. Spragg will see you in the morning. Your room is ready, we've installed a crib for the baby, and the room has its own bath. You must be very tired."

"We are. And my car seems to have died."

"I'll have Gerald look at it first thing. He's a very good mechanic."

"I'm sure he is. Thank you."

"Oh, and Mr. McCoy, your identity is safe with us, so sleep well. Mr. Spragg and the board will meet with you immediately after breakfast."

Little Joe doesn't even wake up as we transport him from the car to the crib in the large, old-fashioned bedroom. The bed has a flowered canopy that matches the curtains. The floor is highly polished hardwood. I notice that outside our door is what appears to be a recreational area, a couple of easy chairs, a green leather couch, a TV in the corner. Two men in dressing gowns are watching the TV; they pay no attention to us.

"I think I'll check on the TV," I say to Francie. "I want to find out what we've been up to." Francie smiles her dazzling smile.

"Just don't take too long," she says.

I close the heavy oak door quietly. The late evening news is on. I sit on the green sofa, the leather is cool, the cushions uncomfortable. The news is local, delivered in an uninspired manner by a man and a woman, each with plastic hair. I keep glancing at the man closest to me. There is something familiar about him. His lower lip protrudes, his day-old beard is coal-colored, his hands are huge and scarred.

Butler! It is Butler. I realize that if I ever did know his first name I have forgotten it. I keep staring at him; he concentrates on the TV, but I have the feeling that nothing from the TV is penetrating his consciousness.

"Butler?" No response. "Butler, is that you?" I tug at the sleeve of his raggedy chenille dressing gown.

He looks at me, his eyelids at half-mast. His eyelids flutter as if his brain impulses are on a ten-second delay.

"Sixteen hamburgers, two cheeseburgers, three chicken strips, two with plum sauce one with barbecue, a BLT hold the mayo . . ." He recites the complete food order he took to the drive-in window that baseball evening so many years ago. "Joe. You still playing baseball?"

"I've been retired for a few years," I say.

"I seen you on TV, on the news."

"My life has been a little strange lately," I say with great understatement. "What brought you here? And where exactly is here? What kind of a place is this?"

"You didn't come to take me away?" Butler says after a long pause.

"My car broke down. I had no idea you were here."

"But we've been expecting you. I told Mr. Spragg you'd be here."

"Who's Mr. Spragg?"

"He's expecting you, too," Butler says maddeningly.

"What is this place?" I insist. "Who is Josiah F. Morris?"

Butler remains silent, his head slumps a few degrees forward. He's napping.

"Butler!" I say louder than I intended. He looks at me, his eyes stunned, I hope with medication.

He recites for me then, I assume from a newspaper article or book. "Josiah F. Morris, a star outfielder for the Kansas City Monarchs of the Negro Baseball Leagues in the 1940s, went on, after his baseball career, to found Morris Tire Stores Inc., which, by his death in 1970, numbered 168 stores in eleven states. Mr. Morris funded a number of charitable institutions throughout the Midwest, including one that bears his name in his hometown of Salina, Kansas, a home for indigent former baseball players." The voice Butler uses for this recitation is high and feminine, the voice, I assume, of whoever read the information to him, goodness knows how many years ago. Butler can't be more than ten years older than me but he looks fifty.

"As soon as Gerald repairs your car, and after you meet with Mr. Spragg in the morning, we'll be leaving for Iowa. I've tied up my clothes in a sheet and hidden them in a hall closet." He points down a darkened hall. The other occupant of the room shuts off the TV and disappears silently on slippered feet.

Why not? "Butler, do you remember a poem the bus driver recited one night out in Montana or Idaho?"

Time suddenly reverses. The nasal twang of the nondescript bus driver fills the quiet room.

"On the street of a thousand assholes," says the voice, "'neath the sign of the swinging tit . . ."

"Mr. McCoy, I hope your accommodations were satisfactory," says Mr. Spragg. "Mr. Butler has told us all about you. We're honored that you could stop with us, even if only for one night. I'm sure Mr. Butler will be in excellent hands."

What's going on? Have I agreed to take Butler with me? Why would they be expecting me? Did I call ahead?

"Mr. Butler is a very proud man. He wants us to think that he's running away with you, and we're willing to go along. He's been our guest here for several years, and what with new therapies and all, we feel he's ready to re-enter society."

I feel a little dizzy.

"The excess of Mr. Butler's disability pension has been held in trust by us, and we've taken the liberty of opening an account for him at Hills Bank in Iowa City," Spragg goes on.

Before I know it we are out on the highway. Gerald apparently did whatever repairs were needed, for the car burst into life. Butler and Butler's worldly goods are crammed into the back seat. Francie has become so accustomed to weird that she doesn't even ask about Butler.

We are stopped in some cookie-cutter prairie town in Nebraska. Francie has taken Little Joe while she shops for baby things. Butler and I finish our take-out order from the De Luxe Drive-in. We sit quietly sipping

Diet Cokes. What would I say to Maureen if she were here right now, if Maureen were sitting next to me instead of Butler.

I've pleaded statute of limitations before.

"Maureen, I love you. I've always loved you. I've never loved anyone else. I never will. I have no excuses to offer. I knew what I was doing when I left you. I was an adult. I suspected there was something better waiting for me out there. I had no idea how lucky I was to have you. It is only recently that I've realized how much I gave up. I should have stayed in Iowa, gone to work for the *Iowa City Press Citizen* after I graduated. We should have had children together. I have dreamed so often that we did, it sometimes seems like it was true, like I've lived two lives, one as the mediocre baseball player, the mediocre journalist I was after my baseball career ended, and another life with you, with our children. Though it's far too late, I want you to know that I realize my mistake, that you're loved, Maureen, that I'm sorry for the life with you that I've missed out on."

His brown eyes lusterless, Butler slurps up the last drops of his drink.

Last night, at a Holiday Inn in Omaha, I dreamed of something that had actually happened. We were in Des Moines, Maureen and I; my final year of high school, I was there for a tournament. We were wandering the streets downtown, a particularly seedy area of nine-'til-fistfight bars with winking cocktail glasses etched in pink neon on their windows, the sidewalks strewn with paper and last year's leaves. Maureen is wearing my team jacket, pale blue and white with MCCOY spelled out across a bar on the left sleeve in tufted material. We are laughing, arms about each other's waists, window-shopping in pawn shop and surplus store windows, when we are accosted by a wino.

He is sitting on his haunches in a debris-filled doorway, wearing an army jacket, ill-fitting pants and sneakers. He holds out a trembling hand. "All I need is a quarter," he rasps. A sourness emanates from him. I try to pull Maureen past him quickly, but she balks, her shoes skidding on the gritty sidewalk.

"Hang on, Joe," she says. "Didn't you hear what he said? *All* he needs is a quarter."

"Let's go."

"Joe, how many times do you think this is going to happen? Imagine it being within our power to give someone all they need? Give him a quarter."

Reluctantly, I dig in my pocket and deposit a quarter in the wino's conspicuously unwashed hand. His mumbled thanks is not nearly as articulate as his request.

"I love you, Joe," says Maureen, kissing me, hugging me happily.

Looking back, Maureen was right. I can't think of another time when I have been able to give someone all they need.

"Before we go to Maureen's, I want you to see City Park," I say to Francie. We have come off I-80 at the Dubuque Street Exit to Iowa City.

"Being your former home and all, shouldn't we be careful?"

"We're less conspicuous being reckless," I reply, making a right turn, crossing the Iowa River where it flows gray-green and placid in the late afternoon of a cloudy day. I turn into the park. "There's the carousel," I say.

There is something so American about City Park. It is like Main Street, or Maple Street, or *Our Town*. A purple thunderstorm hulks on the western horizon. I guess you have to have a bank of memories for City Park. Everything is smaller than I remember. Francie tries to act impressed, but cannot show any genuine enthusiasm. The abandoned carousel has suffered more attrition and vandalism, the horses look wild-eyed, desperate. The Iowa River must have flooded in the spring, the grass is silty, there is a water line on the carousel horses, the whole park smells like a wet basement.

From a pay phone in the air-conditioned lobby of the Holiday Inn in downtown Iowa City, I call Maureen. Iowa City used to be unique in that for a moderate-sized city it had no hotels and only one motel in its downtown—the Rebel Motel across from the post office—then, for several years after the Rebel was converted to apartments, there were none. Outside Iowa City, in a garish suburb called Coralville, there were nearly two thousand motel rooms, two miles of blinking neon offering AIR CONDITIONING, FREE TV, WATER BEDS, CABLE, SATELLITE, HBO, FREE SHUTTLE SERVICE TO HOSPITALS as inducements. But most of the quaint downtown of Iowa City has been replaced by shopping malls, a Holiday

Inn and a plethora of glass-and-concrete franchise food outlets and clothing stores. I might be in Los Angeles, except for one constant: Dubuque Street was cordoned off and dug up when I left Iowa City; more than ten years later it is still cordoned off and dug up.

I fidget at the telephone, dial half the number a couple of times before letting my finger miss a digit, or hit two at once, anything to buy time. What if, as Maureen is certainly entitled to do, she hangs up on me? What if her husband answers? If a man answers hang up. Maureen probably has kids old enough to answer the phone.

Maureen answers. She says hello twice before I can utter a word.

"It's Joe. Can you talk?"

"I answered the phone didn't I?" That's the kind of answer I'd expect from Maureen.

"You haven't changed."

"I've been expecting you."

"You have?"

"Well, Christ, McCoy, you've been sighted a thousand times a week, all over the country, all summer. The law of averages says you have to turn up here eventually. You've been everywhere else."

"I'd like to see you, Maureen."

"Do you know where I live?"

"Not exactly."

"Four miles south, one east of my folks' place. Big yellow house, three silos sitting behind like bowling pins . . ."

"Somebody named Vickery lived there years ago."

"You got it."

"But is it okay for me, us, to come? What about . . ?"

"Tucker and I aren't together any more. I live here alone. There's a machine shed about fifty yards behind the house. I'll open the door for you. I assume you don't want to be seen."

"You assume correctly." Let her enjoy the aspects of intrigue. Why tell her I'm not even capable of getting arrested?

There is a long silence.

"I just want to see you, Maureen, before things falls apart . . ."

"I'll put the coffee on," says Maureen brusquely, attempting to save me from babbling. I do anyway.

"No matter what the papers and TV say, there's nothing between me and Francie. We were just thrown together . . ."

"Why should that matter? It doesn't matter."

"Of course it matters. To me." There is a sharp edge to my voice. "Do you think I'm so self-absorbed that I'd bring a girlfriend, a lover, and expect your help?"

"It doesn't matter, McCoy. I've always been a sucker where you're concerned."

"Please, Maureen, it's important to me."

"Okay."

How I've missed Maureen's voice. How many times I used to sit in the dark hall in Lone Tree, after everyone else was asleep and talk on the phone with Maureen. She has what I've always thought of as a brown-eyed voice, husky, sultry, sexy, oh so sexy. "If you were here with me, McCoy, you know what I'd do to you?" And then she'd tell me, in detail. "I can tell by your breathing that I'm getting to you, McCoy. I love your excited breath, Joe."

Tucker Wegman gone. What had I imagined? Something insane, fighting a duel on white horses, lances and armor? I don't have to fight for Maureen, I thought. How little I knew.

We stop at an Eagle Supermarket and stock up on food and diapers. As we are leaving, at the side of the building we see a mechanical horse, the kind small children whine to be allowed to ride. "Thunder" is printed in yellow letters on the base of the machine. The horse is white with flaring nostrils and ears pinned back as if he is angry; he is stretching forward as if striving for an imaginary finish line. The machine, though unoccupied, is murmuring quietly, driving forward, rocking back, driving forward again. It is dusk, a pre-thunderstorm wind slices across the parking lot.

"Look!" I say to Francie.

We stand and watch for a minute or more. The first rain plops on the windshield as we leave the lot. In the rearview I can see Thunder, ears back, raging into the wind.

The storm passes to the south, the wind subsides. As we drive the secondary highway in the blue-blackness of the Iowa night, I realize I have almost forgotten the serenity of the cornfields on a summer evening.

The air is fragrant with growth, with life. The moon is a slice of peach floating in the inky sky, the silence broken only by the clang of the cattle guard as I turn into the long driveway leading to Maureen's farm.

I park the Lincoln in the machine shed, slide the door closed. As we approach the house I can see Maureen's form, the light behind her as she stands at the back door, the screen pushed open in welcome.

For Francie this is probably another totally new experience, the smells unfamiliar, the terrain dangerous. I'm struck by the thought of children knowing only the place where they are raised, and, having nothing to compare it with, accepting it as the way things are, so that extremes, like the bitter cold of a Minnesota winter, or the thick wetness of the air in a Louisiana July, are not considered abnormal. And no matter where that child goes as an adult, the extremes of childhood—climate, topography, isolation, poverty—remain acceptable, are even longed for as a sign of stability in the often tilting adult world. The odors of childhood remain with us always, invoke pleasant memories, for the brain has a wonderful way of putting unpleasantness aside, like a grandmother sweeping the house clean on the first sunny day of spring.

We are all awkward, full of urgent small talk, afraid of what will happen if we become silent. Maureen is immediately captivated by Little Joe; she unwraps him, holds him to her as she fusses with the coffee. He cuddles into her neck and I'm jealous, recalling how many hours I spent with my face buried there, recalling that in some ephemeral, inexplicable way Maureen smelled perfect.

"I don't have any kids," Maureen says, answering my unasked question. "Tucker wanted children, but I . . . well, we never . . ."

Maureen has slimmed, her cheeks are drawn, her eyes darker, more prominent. Little Joe blends into her neck and cheek as if he were her own.

There is some confusion about sleeping arrangements, until I point out emphatically that Francie and I are traveling felons only. Maureen assigns Francie and Little Joe a room upstairs, across the hall from her large bedroom. I carry up Little Joe's basket. The room is dominated by a large brass bed with many comforters, and is redolent of mothballs and emptiness. There is a small room at the end of the hall for Butler.

Francie tactfully shoos me away while she settles Little Joe. I go back downstairs to Maureen, we sit at the kitchen table. An orange cat with one cropped ear lies coiled like a cushion on a small rocking chair, a slit of green eye visible.

Maureen lights a cigarette.

There is so much I want to say; I want to tell Maureen of the dreams I've been having. I'm wondering, probably without cause, if she might not have been having similar dreams about me. I can find no starting point. I am about to reach across the table and cover Maureen's hand with mine when she speaks.

"You haven't noticed, have you?"

"Noticed what?"

"Look at me, Joe. For once in your fucking life look at me! My eyes look like I've put charcoal under them, the way ballplayers do when they're playing in bright sun."

"Are you sick?"

"Francie noticed right away. She stays clear of me, not because she's jealous but because she can smell Death on me. Oh, Joe . . ."

Maureen walks around the table and plops herself in my lap, flings her arms about me, burying her face in my neck. She is wearing a bulky green sweater, and I'm totally surprised by how light she is in my arms. She is right: her face is drawn, her color poor.

"I'm dying of the fucking cancer, Joe. It's inoperable, and I won't prolong my misery by any of this chemotherapy. A month ago the doctor gave me a big bottle of painkillers and sent me home to die."

"I'm sorry, Maureen. I'm sorry you're ill. I apologize for being so unobservant. This wouldn't have happened if I'd been here." I kiss her cheek. She turns her mouth to me and kisses me ravenously.

"I've always loved you, McCoy. Remember how I invited you to my wedding? I kept seeing that wonderful scene in *The Graduate* where Dustin Hoffman charges into the middle of the wedding and whisks his true love away. I dreamed that you'd do that, and I'd have gone with you in a second.

"But you know what my big regret is? That we never made love in a bed, that we never had our own damn bed, that we didn't pool our money one Saturday night and drive down the Coralville strip and rent one of those two thousand fucking motel rooms they advertise on billboards. 'Maureen,' I thought, 'if you'd just once got him into a real bed he'd have never run off to journalism school without taking you along.' I'm not so broken up about dying; I just wish I'd spent what life I've had with you."

"You don't pull any punches."

"What have I got to lose?"

"On one of the rare occasions I got on base, the next batter hit into a force play, but the shortstop mishandled the ball then threw high to second. As I slid, the second baseman went way up to grab the bad throw. He dropped on me with both knees, one on my chest, one on my midsection."

"And that's how you feel now? I know, because it's the way I've felt every time I've read or heard your name or thought of you. Poor old Tucker, he put up with a lot from me."

I kiss her again, breathe deeply of her familiar odor. "Maureen, if I had it to do over again . . . what is it they say—if wishes were horses? We'd have spent every minute of our lives together."

"If wishes were horses, beggars would ride. You don't see many beggars riding, do you?"

"Maureen? Have you had dreams, or premonitions, or . . . or, indications that we might actually have spent our lives together? There's a house in Iowa City on Johnson and Ronalds. I think we might have lived there, had a family . . ." she interrupts me with another kiss. I touch a breast through the bulky sweater. There is so little of her left.

"Joe, you're here now, I have all I need."

We were silent for a long time.

"How long have you and Tucker been apart?"

"When he found out I was sick he ran like a rabbit. Some people can't stand illness. I don't blame him."

She sees the look of surprise on my face, and smiles wistfully. "Oh, don't get me wrong. Tucker Wegman's a good man. He's lived all these years with a woman who didn't love him and wasn't very good at hiding the fact, a woman who wouldn't have his children because she didn't want any permanent ties to him. But you know what galled Tucker more than anything else? That I kept my own name. Refusing to take his name showed independence, but it was more. As long as I was Maureen Renn I was the same person you left behind . . ."

"Maureen, I wish you wouldn't . . ."

". . . we were always Tucker Wegman and Maureen Renn."

She smiles up at me, her eyes clouded with tears. When she smiles the dimple in her left cheek still winks.

"I don't have any excuses, Maureen, except maybe no one should be held responsible for things they do when they're eighteen. I think there should be a statute of limitations on stupidity."

"I'm sorry, Joe, I don't have any pride left these days . . . but do one thing for me Joe?"

"Anything."

"Help me put up a front for my family. I don't want them to know how sick I am until it's too late. I don't want to go to the hospital. I want to die here, in my own house."

"I'll do whatever I can."

"There's enough driveway out there that we have a good view of anyone coming, plenty of time for you and Francie to get upstairs. The cattle guard clangs like a burglar alarm whenever a car crosses it, so no one can sneak up on us in the middle of the night. Oh, and one other thing . . ."

"Name it."

"Make love to me, Joe."

Making love with Maureen is what I've been missing ever since I left Iowa. I carry her upstairs to her room. Under the covers our passion knows no bounds but all I can feel is terrible loss as I taste the sweetness of Maureen's body, rise above her as she pulls me into her. "I love you. I love you. I love you," I repeat, the heat of her drawing me toward ecstasy, the thought of losing her causing hot tears to flow.

Our second week in Iowa. I held Maureen in my arms for a long time this evening. She clings to me like I am life itself. We make love whenever she feels strong enough. Mostly she is content to be encircled by my arms. After she is asleep I tiptoe out of her room. She put on a brave front while her parents visited this afternoon. She hasn't been able to get out of bed without help for several days, but there was no way they could know, for she was able to point to the spotless house, the food cooking in the oven as her accomplishments.

Yesterday evening, Maureen and I at the kitchen table holding hands, Butler sitting quietly, dreaming whatever he dreams, staring out the window at the green fields of corn and the skyline. I am my usual inarticulate self, though at least I try to tell Maureen how I feel about her. She accepts my closeness for what it is, a declaration of love. But I want more.

"Maureen, I want you to know . . ."

I make more than one attempt, but my throat constricts, allowing a few stuttering compliments to deteriorate into silence. Suddenly, I hear my own voice emanating from the corner of the room. We both turn toward Butler, who stares dreamily out the window at the sunset over the cornfield, while, his lips barely moving, he speaks in my voice, repeating the words I spoke in his presence days ago in Nebraska.

"Maureen, I love you. I've always loved you. I've never loved anyone else . . ."

Francie is sitting in one of the easy chairs in the living room reading a newspaper. She looks up as I enter.

"I have something extremely important to tell you, Joe. Something that's going to take a while to explain."

I stare at her with curiosity. Since we have been here at the farm, and especially since Francie's met Gideon, my situation with Francie has been nothing short of eerie. Francie is not jealous of Maureen. "I understand," she has said several times. "You're making Maureen very happy," she has also said.

"What is it?"

"I'll tell you in the morning. I want us both to be fresh, and I want you to have time to prepare yourself. It's the talk you wanted to have when we were leaving Los Angeles. What I have to say may be very difficult to accept, but I've made a decision."

"Do you think you should keep me in suspense?"

"Yes." Francie smiles disarmingly. "Trust me. It can wait until morning, but not much longer."

TWENTY

GIDEON CLARKE

I CAN'T BELIEVE WHAT I JUST DID. I bought a copy of *The Francie Bly Cookbook*. I left Missy in the truck parked on South Dubuque Street, crossed the road in the middle of the block and walked into Prairie Lights Bookstore. The slim volume was on display both in the window and at the front of the store, $22.95 in hardcover.

"It's for Missy," I told the proprietor, Jim Harris, a tall, red-bearded man, a die-hard St. Louis Cardinals fan. Sympathies in Iowa City are about evenly divided between Cardinal fans like Jim Harris and Cub fans like myself. On hot summer evenings, he and I occasionally go around the corner from Prairie Lights to an intimate place on Iowa Avenue called Joe's Bar (no kidding, that's really its name) to watch baseball in air-conditioned comfort on a big-screen TV. I drink Diet Coke with lime, while Jim enjoys a beer. Some evenings there'll be fifteen or twenty of us sitting around watching, cheering, grousing about how baseball isn't as pure as it once was.

"Missy's been following the Joe McCoy business on TV," I lie.

Why should I care what Jim thinks of my buying a faddish cookbook?

"Francie Bly's boyfriend was on 'Good Morning, America' promoting his book, and there was this recipe for quesedillas that Missy wants to try . . ." I babble on for no good reason.

Jim raises his eyebrows as he tosses a Prairie Lights bookmark into the sack with my purchases. To show that buying the cookbook is an aberration, I've also bought Lee Smith's latest novel, a book of critical writing about Flannery O'Connor and paperbacks by Ellen Gilchrist, Louise Shivers, Tim Sandlin and Cynthia Applewhite. Jim is making a ninety-some-dollar sale, he couldn't care less if Missy wants to make quesedillas, or whether I want to sit at my kitchen table and moon over the dust-jacket photo of Francie Bly's smiling face.

Francie's green eyes crinkle with suppressed laughter, her fawn-colored curls are perfectly complemented by a frilly, high-necked mauve blouse. I run an index finger down the slick paper, touch her chin, her cheeks, imagine kissing her parted lips. I never thought I would feel this way again.

The weight of grief seems to be slipping from my shoulders like a chain-mail cloak. I have spent my life being abandoned, first by my mother and sister, then by my father who gave up on life on a spring afternoon in Milwaukee, the first suicide by foul ball in history, then repeatedly by my wife Sunny. And by Sarah.

I was the prime motivator in convincing Joe that he should chance bringing Francie and the baby from the safety of his friend's farm to meet the rest of us at Ray Kinsella's. I fell in love with the Francie Bly of the photo that appeared on TV and in newspapers, the one with the large disembodied hand still clamped on her right upper arm. I become sexually excited reading her recipe for Illegal Pineapple Upside Down Cake or Assassin's Beef Stew. I don't imagine the recipes were labeled in that cutesy way in her computer; the names that so excite me were likely supplied by her stockbroker fiancé, Adam Quinn.

I fantasize about Francie standing at the stove in my big kitchen. I walk up behind her, put my arms around her, turn her toward me. As I bend to kiss her I see a bit of gravy on the corner of her mouth from sampling the simmering Assassin's Beef Stew. I lick it off.

"What's for dinner?" I ask.

"The usual," says Francie. Then, "though I've thought of a wonderful appetizer. But we have to go upstairs for that."

Wishful thinking. What would a beautiful young woman like Francie Bly want with an aging, rudderless hulk like me? If wealth impressed her she would have married Adam Quinn. No, she obviously enjoys adventure, bizarre adventure from what Joe tells us. I have had my adventure.

When I first saw her, in person unstrapping the baby from its car seat, I almost ran to her. I stopped a few feet away, stood wringing my hands like someone's slightly strange uncle. My knees were quaking as I took her small, cool hand when Joe introduced us. Francie was wearing a vest and fatigue-like pants with a thousand pockets. She wore a squashed hat of crushed black velvet with maroon cloth roses. Her eyes were hidden by small, round sunglasses that had slipped to the end of her nose. She looked like a tiny Janis Joplin, a woman whose façade of belligerence made her, in my opinion, the sexiest woman of her—my—generation. I wanted to praise the book, but she probably hated even the idea of the book, considered it opportunistic and hateful of Adam Quinn to take advantage. I considered telling her I thought I was in love with her. She must be conditioned to weird situations.

Being in love does not become me. I am at my best being totally responsible, caring for Missy, wandering around my massive old home in Onamata. I love Missy dearly, but I am not in love. I was in love with Sunny, who deserted me repeatedly, and, I assume forever, since it has been years since I've heard even a rumor of her. I was in love with Sarah when I traveled back in time to prove the existence of the Iowa Baseball Confederacy. Sarah died in an accident in 1908. I have, ever since my return to present-day Iowa, held out a forlorn hope that I might one day cross the barriers of time and somehow, armed with foreknowledge, save Sarah's life and settle in to live with her in 1908. As time passes each possibility becomes more and more of a dream.

Joe McCoy was driving a scarlet 1956 Lincoln Continental. While he himself is nice enough looking—though of a slight build he has a fresh complexion, long sandy hair, intense blue eyes—in spite of what I'd been told about Francie Bly, I'd even seen photographs of her in the newspapers, I was completely unprepared for her when she did exit the passenger door of Joe's car. My heart flipped about like a jumping bean and I'm sure I blushed to the color of a stop sign. One of the disadvantages of being almost albino (I have some pigment in my eyes, which are the palest of blues) is that when I blush, no one can ever mistake it for anything else.

Fortunately no one was paying any attention to me as I lurked inconspicuously in the background. When I was eventually introduced to Francie Bly I stuttered helplessly and must have looked like a total fool. However, by that time Francie had met Missy and saved the day by asking about her, letting me know that she was acquainted with several adults with Down's.

That conversation only confirmed my instant fascination with Francie. I hate to even think "love at first sight," it sounds so impossible. There is the age difference, too. I can't bring myself to ask, but I'm sure Francie is in her late twenties. I passed forty quite some time ago. What could a Vassar graduate, a sophisticated young woman, ever see in a reclusive Iowa baseball researcher? The only thing I feel I have going is that because of an almost inconvenient inheritance, I have enough money to buy Johnson County, Iowa, if I really wanted to. My accountants tell me I may be the richest man in the Midwest. Then I think that Francie has given up a secure situation to go on the run with an unemployed ex-baseball player, so she can't care about money. What, then, have I got to offer?

I miss bits of Joe's story as I keep going off to the kitchen, supposedly to check on Missy's well-being, but really to glimpse Francie, hoping she will direct a kind word in my direction, a glance, anything but indifference.

TWENTY-ONE

JOE McCOY

SOMETIME AFTER MIDNIGHT TWO CARS come barreling down the driveway. The clang of the cattle guard wakes me and I barely have time to escape from Maureen's room, where I have been sleeping in an overstuffed chair next to the bed. My first guess, of course, is that it is the police coming for me and Francie. Getting caught isn't terribly important any longer, all I regret is that I won't be able to spend Maureen's last few days with her.

But it is not the police. The visitors turn out to be the Renns: the whole family, the sad old father wearing a green-and-black checkered mackinaw over baggy bib-overalls, the frazzled mother, the three hulking sons. The oldest, Timothy, was apparently between sojourns at the crowbar motel. They are accompanied by a young, nervous priest. Only the mother and possibly the priest haven't been drinking.

The Renns, as ignorant people often do, have turned, in a nonsensical way, to religion in their time of grief. In spite of the good front Maureen put on yesterday, the mother had sensed the imminence of death. She had contacted Maureen's doctor, she explained, who had admitted that he was following Maureen's wishes by allowing her to die peacefully at home.

To my knowledge none of the Renns have ever attended church, although in their background there was some vague connection with Catholicism. These fools have decided that Maureen should be denied the right to die with dignity in her own home. They don't even have the sense to call an ambulance; one of the beefy brothers wraps a blanket around Maureen and carries her in his arms.

Francie and I huddle in the bedroom across the hall, hoping all the stomping up and down the stairs won't waken Little Joe. I search the part of the house available to me, hoping that Tucker Wegman may have left a gun behind, it would be such a pleasure to put a glimmer of fear into the murky eyes of Maureen's brutish brothers, but, as I should have known, Tucker left no guns. I'm sure his rifles were stacked stiff as phalluses in their rack in the back window of his truck when he left the farm for good. I am no match for the Renn brothers physically, and talking common sense to grief-stricken religious fanatics accomplishes nothing.

I make coffee and spend the rest of the night pacing the kitchen floor. Francie, swaddled in one of Maureen's woolly housecoats, sits at the table staring at me wistfully.

"It's time we had that talk, Joe," she says to me.

"Not now," I say. "Get the baby. We're going to the hospital."

"I think we should talk about . . ." but I don't give Francie a chance, I'm out the door to retrieve my red Lincoln from the machine shed.

TWENTY-TWO

JOE McCOY

"I KNOW WHY I CONTACTED YOU," I say to Ray.

Ray looks at me quizzically. We are drinking coffee in his kitchen.

"I mean other than needing a friend, an audience, a sympathetic ear."

"The field?"

I nod. "I don't know how all this works." I wave toward the emerald of the outfield, the corner of the bleacher and backstop visible over Ray's shoulder. "But I'm lucky enough, or unlucky enough, to recognize a major turning point in my life."

"The state championship?"

"What do you think? What would I have to do?"

"There's not a lot I can tell you. I don't understand any more about the source of the magic than I did years ago. The positive thing is that you *see* what's happening, you enjoy the games. Not everyone sees, you know. That was why I took you out there early on: if you were able to see the games, I reasoned you had a solid connection with baseball and with magic."

"The pure of heart?"

"I wouldn't go quite so far."

"Could you arrange . . ?"

190 / W.P. KINSELLA

"I have nothing to do with it. My stadium is always dark on Tuesday night," he adds innocently.

"Give or take a few days, it's almost fourteen years since the night I refused to pitch."

"What is it the police look for in a criminal case? Motive. Opportunity. Something else? All you can do is try. You have need of what the field can offer."

"I'll never forget the night of the semi-final game in Cedar Rapids. We were playing a school from Sioux City, which is a long way off, so the full house of fans were nearly all from our area. I had won our first game, three nights before, a three-hit, complete game. What more did the fans want from me? That was on Wednesday. Here it was Saturday and they expected me to pitch again. I'd already let the press know I wouldn't. I thought I'd explained so everybody would understand. I had prospects as a pro. More than that, I'd been scouted by sixteen teams. There was every possibility that I'd become a major-league pitcher. Could I be expected to put that on the line for a state championship?"

Apparently the fans thought so. When I was introduced, they booed and booed and booed.

I was angry. Confused.

TWENTY-THREE

JOE McCOY

"HERE I GO," I SAY TO RAY. We have been sitting on the porch swing, drinking iced tea from perspiring glasses. The children are in bed. Annie is reading in the living room.

"No." Ray puts a hand on my shoulder as I walk toward the wall-switch that activates the scar of floodlights beyond the outfield. "Walk down to the field," he continues. "Stand there and absorb the night. What will happen will happen."

I look back at him from the bottom of the stairs. He looks pale, his features distorted by the light from the single yellow bulb above the door.

A frog croaks. Behind me the porch swing creaks as Ray returns to his seat. My eyes begin to adjust to the humid darkness, like black velvet. A sprinkle of fireflies rises from the dewy grass.

Is it possible to be in two places at once? I am eighteen years old, a senior at Lone Tree High School, pitching in the state championship; and I am thirty-one years old, a fugitive from justice, watching my younger self perform. But I am somehow inside both bodies at the same time.

We are in the third game of the the tournament. I pitched and we won the first. Karl Schootman pitched the second game. He pitched well and we should have won, but we could score only two runs and eventually lost 3-2.

Now I'm going to pitch as long as I can lift my arm. In the back of my eighteen-year-old brain lies my history, my future, my uninspiring years as a marginal big-league pitcher. Lone Tree High School is going to win the state championship, or some team is going to have to beat me.

Early in the semi-final game it looks as if this may be the day and Sioux City might be the team. Bottom of the third, no score, the first batter pops up, the second singles, the third whacks a double off the right-field wall. The Sioux City clean-up hitter is next. The guy's batting about .750; today he's still in the Bigs earning five million a year.

Our manager ambles out to the mound to confer with me and the catcher, Dusty Blenheim. The manager never talks to the pitcher. He thinks pitchers don't have brains, can't make decisions.

"How's he throwin'?" he says to Dusty.

"I'm doing fine," I reply.

He ignores me.

"Good stuff," says Dusty. "The double was off a good pitch."

"I think we should walk this guy. The number five hitter tends to get in front of the ball," I say.

Manager and catcher both ignore me. Manager puts an arm around catcher's shoulders and they walk toward the plate. Manager heads to the dugout. Catcher crouches, give me the fastball sign, outside part of the plate.

I deliver a fastball, very high and outside, that makes Dusty stand up to catch it. He glares at me, fires it back.

The clean-up hitter digs in. Dusty calls for a fastball inside.

I plunk him in the ribs. He trots to first. Nobody figures I'd intentionally plunk a guy with two runners on.

Dusty suspects. Walks half-way to the mound. Snaps, "Throw the fucking ball over the plate."

I keep shaking off signs until Dusty reluctantly flashes the change-up. I throw. The batter nearly breaks his back; he's a foot in front of it.

I insist on throwing the change-up again. Dusty scowls. The manager is pacing. I throw. The batter's way in front again, hits a weak one-hopper right into my glove. I throw to Dusty for the force out at home, he relays to first. Inning over. They never even come close again. We score eight in the seventh. Our relievers finish up. We have a day off before the state championship.

When I come out of the ballpark a few girlfriends and relatives of players are hanging around. Dougie Glenville's mother is there.

"You pitched so brilliantly," she gushes. "I'm so proud of all of you." She hugs me. She smells of lavender. Dougie appears at that moment, expertly ducks her hug. "See ya later, Ma," he says, as he disappears around the corner.

Maureen leans against a power pole smoking a cigarette.

"Hey, sailor, you lookin' for a good time?"

"I'm here for a good time, not a long time," I reply. She throws herself into my arms for a long kiss. We walk away, arms around waists. There is something about the way Maureen's hand feels in the small of my back. So perfect. I am in love with Maureen. Yet I remember the way I felt in my other life, where I refused to pitch on less than four days' rest, where I was tiring of Maureen, where I was anxious to leave Lone Tree, to leave Iowa, to meet the world head-on, to find all the sweeter, sexier Maureens waiting for me as I made my climb toward the major leagues.

"I got a surprise," says Maureen. As we walk, she has directed me, with light pressure of her hand on my back, like she directs her horse with a light squeeze of her denimed knees.

"What?"

"Egg money," she says. Maureen has a dozen or so hens she has raised from chicks. She sells the eggs to the Blue Parrot Co-Op in Iowa City. It keeps her in spending money. With baseball and studying I only have time to make a few bucks helping my dad. I'm always terminally short of cash.

"I faked a dental appointment," she goes on. She is leading me into the parking lot of Ace Auto Court, a row of a dozen or so white stuccoed units, each about as big as a good-sized truck box.

"Our own damn bed, McCoy. For the whole fucking night. And it's going to be one long, fucking night." She turned and wrapped her arms around me again, her tongue tracking my teeth, probing my throat. I had my hands up under her T-shirt under her denim jacket. Maureen likes her nipples squeezed.

"I called your Mom and said the team was putting you up in a motel so you'd get a good night's rest. Ha! My family doesn't give a fuck where I am. I've paid for two nights. I'm gonna wear out everything but your good right arm, McCoy."

And she did. Our bodies so wet, I lay on top of her and tried to melt into her, to truly make us one. One of the reasons I pitched the championship game was that I knew I could never leave Maureen for the minor leagues or a distant university. I'd accept the scholarship to the University of Iowa, and I'd marry Maureen and we'd live in married student housing over by the Finkbine Golf Course. Even if I did ruin my arm, between us both working part time and with a little help from my father, we could manage to pay in-state tuition.

The next morning when Maureen set out for a nearby donut shop to get coffee and chocolate-coconut donuts, the manager of the motel stopped her in the parking lot and asked, "Are you the girl the police are looking for?"

She came back into the dusky motel room, laughing, tossing a bag of donuts at me, uncapping the coffees on the cigarette-burned chest of drawers. "Do you think I'm the girl the police are looking for?"

"What did you tell him?"

"I said, 'I hope not.' But I wonder why they're looking for someone who looks like me? Drugs, prostitution? Maybe she's a forger. Or she's conned some eighty-year-old man out of his life savings by giving him a blow job every day for ten days until he thinks he can't live without her. His children have called the police because they're afraid he's going to give away the house next, and they're counting on it as their inheritance."

"Only thinking of themselves. Not one of them worried that the blow jobs will stop when the cash runs out."

"Selfish children. How sharper than a serpent's tooth . . ."

"*Hamlet?*"

"No," said Maureen, feigning crossness. "*King Lear.*"

I ate the donuts and drank the coffee without tasting either. The idea of a fugitive nearby, who looked at least somewhat like Maureen, sent my imagination into spasms.

I could see myself, the situation reversed, coming back to the motel with donuts and coffee, my ever-watchful eye picking up a slight movement way down by the manager's office, my sense of danger telling me it was police, and they were after me. Just as two blue-suited types began walking rapidly down the row of dismal motel fronts, not wanting to alarm me yet, but wanting to get within striking distance quickly. I dropped the coffee, the cups bouncing, spewing creamed coffee over the asphalt like they were vomiting. Still clutching the sack of donuts I ran full speed toward the back fence, a mass of warped boards that had once been painted white, and dove head first into the unknown.

And then I was sitting on the bleacher on the first-base side of Ray Kinsella's magical ballpark, and then I wasn't, I was leaning on the railing of the dugout in Cedar Rapids, Iowa, fourteen years ago, trading barbs with my teammates, staying loose as we prepared for the championship game. I was warmed up, waiting nervously for the introductions. We were playing a team from West Des Moines. They had new uniforms, they looked bigger and older than us. They looked like professionals, we looked like amateurs.

"Pitching for Lone Tree, starting his third game this week, Senior, Joe McCoy."

The fans, who were about two-thirds in our favor, cheered wildly, gave me a standing-O as I trotted to the mound. Maureen was seated behind the dugout, looking tough and sexy in jeans and a denim jacket, a row in front of the players' girlfriends, looking older, more worldly. The other girlfriends with their taffy-colored hair, pastel slacks and skirts, giggled, twisted coquettishly, held pink hands over pink mouths when there was action on the field. They came from solid, conformist, religious homes. Maureen came from a family of boozers and thieves.

My dad and Billy and Agnes arrived to claim the seats I'd arranged for them next to Maureen. Billy had driven down from Des Moines. My mother, of course, was not well enough to venture out even for the state championship. As I was taking my warm-up pitches, Maureen lit a cigarette.

"Just be sure she's the one," my dad had said of Maureen, a few weeks earlier, trying to give advice without giving advice. "You've got a long life ahead of you."

I wondered about his choice, my breathless mother in her beautiful bed jackets. Were my parents happy? Was there passion between them, had there ever been? What had my mother been like when she was young? Had she ever been adventurous, wanton? Did my choice of Maureen Renn have anything to do with her being an absolute opposite of my mother?

I watched that championship game, I participated in that championship game. I broke apart, then reassembled. We grabbed an early two-run lead. In the top of the fourth my arm began to ache like nothing I'd ever experienced. I was lucky to get out of the inning. They had men on second and third with two out. I was trying for a low strike on the black at the knees. My arm shrieked as I delivered, the ball went eye-high right down the middle, but the batter was so surprised that he swung, looking really bad. The fans cheered, few knew I'd gotten away with a mistake.

If my teammates could just score some runs for me, I could let the other guys mop up. But I'd want a five-run lead, probably more. Des Moines has a strong left-hander on the mound, he's deceptive. Everyone is swinging at pitches out of the strike zone, and about the time a batter decides to take he delivers a side-arm curve that looks like it will be a foot outside, then swoops in, popping to the catcher's mitt like a bursting balloon, getting a strike call from the umpire.

In the fifth, our second baseman, one of our weakest hitters, launches one to the right that looks like an easy out, then like a long fly, then carries over the fence above their leaping right fielder.

They score two in the top of the seventh inning. My shoulder is so painful that tears roll down my cheeks every time I deliver. I'm being crafty now, using my fastball just out of the strike zone because it's so ineffectual, to set up some junk pitch that doesn't make my shoulder feel like its being gored by a hot poker. The hitters don't seem aware that I'm suffering, they are too anxious to tie the game with one swat. They get out in front of the junk, test my third baseman repeatedly, pop up or hit lazy flies to left field.

"You're hurtin' too much, Joe," my catcher says to me between innings. "You're gonna ruin your arm."

"I'm fine," I reply, between pain-gritted teeth. He ignores me and confers with the manager, who walks down and stands in front of me, his shadow falling across me like winter.

"I can do it," I say, before he has a chance to speak.

"You've done more than we had a right to expect," he says. "I know your feelings, and I appreciate it. You're a gutsy kid, but I think it's time to make a change."

"No! Let me stay until I start to get in trouble. I won't whine about coming out then." I lowered my voice. "We both know there's no one we can trust to hold such a shaky lead."

His shadow continues to cast a pall over me.

"Okay," he says finally. "You've earned a shot at a complete game." Dusty Blenheim kicks a spray of sunflower seeds as he clumps to his seat at the end of the bench.

I'm running on pure adrenalin. There are speed skaters slashing through my veins. I rock back and forth on the bench like an autistic, my cap low over my eyes, my right leg tapping non-stop. Every inning as I head to the field I catch Maureen's eye, the wind is whipping her plum-colored hair about her face. She gives me a thumbs up.

My dad, brother and sister, usually as mild-mannered as they look, have become a cheering section, seem to have involved all the Lone Tree fans in the stadium. Usually fan noise is like the hum from a giant beehive, like the compressors at a carnival, it all blends together, cheers and boos.

But this is different. Each time I go into my wind-up a couple of thousand people are shouting, "Pour it on 'em, Joe." I can hear each word. I work to the rhythm of it. I swear it adds a few miles per hour to my ever-weakening fastball.

I survive the eighth with a walk and an infield hit. I go 3-2 on several batters, they foul off my best pitches again and again. I throw twenty-seven pitches in the eighth. My arm feels like a slab of cement, eels of fire wriggle through my elbow, travel up to my shoulder, pierce my back.

I am sweating rivers in the humid Iowa twilight. I must have lost five pounds from a frame that carries no excess weight.

Once again, my team fails to score in the bottom of the eighth. They go down one-two-three, in about ninety seconds, two grounders and a fly to center. My knees, as I head for the mound, feel like I've just had sex. I can feel them trembling like jelly.

*   *   *

Ball one. Ball two. I am so tired. The pitches are missing by fractions. I want to lie down in total collapse. I want the manager to make his way toward the mound, touching his left arm to indicate my replacement. Yet I have this terrible energy that supersedes my exhaustion.

One more pitch. Like a member of some ethereal twelve-step program, I force myself to complete one more play. If the twelve-step member can forgo drugs or drink or food for another minute, I can play baseball for one more minute.

I take a deep, ragged breath, exhale, accept the sign: fastball on the outside half. Every fibre of my body hurts. I hurl the ball. Whack! Easy grounder, a two-hopper to the shortstop. I relax for a tenth of a second until the ball skips between the shortstop's legs. The runner, who had probably hit against a take sign on 3-0, scoots around first, forcing the center fielder to be quick about getting the ball in to second base.

I glance at my shortstop Dan Durenberger. My instinct is to cover the few strides between us, leap on him, drag him to the ground, pummel him. Instead, I attempt not to show any annoyance. I know he is trying just as hard as I am, he's just as nervous as I am.

Keep control, I tell myself. Out of the corner of my eye I see the manager lumbering from the dugout. Maybe it's all over. I don't know if I have another pitch left in me. I walk toward the shortstop. He stands dejectedly, hands on knees, cap very low over his eyes. I force myself to think of how many times he has dived or leapt in the air like a greyhound after a Frisbee to turn sure base hits into outs. I pat his shoulder.

"Hang in there, Danny," I say. "We'll take two."

I feel my catcher's arm about my shoulder.

"You okay, Joe?"

"No. I'm not okay. But I've got enough left to get the last three outs."

The manager, who was closing in on us, heard those words and clapped his arm around my shoulder, almost causing my knees to buckle.

"Don't let a miscue get you down," he said. He actually gave me a hug, slapped the shortstop's ass, gave the first baseman a knock on the bicep.

I must have looked like a rag doll out there on the mound. The Des Moines players were ravenous for hits; they had me treed and cornered; they couldn't wait to kill me.

I delivered a ball way outside. I couldn't get ahead of a batter if my life depended on it. My curve broke six inches inside. Trying to get out of the way the batter managed to take the ball about six inches from his hands, a weak hopper to short. Danny charged it, fielded it, the second baseman was on the bag waiting, bracing his feet for the throw to first to complete the double play when Danny tossed the ball three feet wide of the base. The second baseman lunged and caught the ball but his momentum took him far off the bag. First and second, nobody out.

We go through the whole ritual of forgiveness and encouragement again, except the manager is not allowed another visit to the mound. They are certainly going to sacrifice the runners into scoring position. High and tight, my catcher signals. There is so much sweat in my eyes I can barely see him; the fans behind the dugout are a blur, I can't pick out Maureen or my family.

The batter squares. High and tight, ball one. He squares again, ball two. He knows I can't go 3-0. I know I can't go 3-0. I throw a strike at the letters, he gets under it, pops it straight up behind the plate, it settles into the catcher's mitt. He squeezes it gently as an egg. On my first pitch the next batter smashes a scorcher to the right of second base. If it goes through, the score is tied. But out of nowhere comes Danny Durenberger, scooping the ball on the run, crossing second base for the force, firing to first for the game-ending double play.

Joy, ecstasy, adrenalin. My catcher leaps into my arms as if he were a small child. I hold onto him, stagger about the infield while teammates pound our backs, reach for my hands, eventually pull me down on the soft grass of the infield, where we all writhe about like a litter of puppies.

We are all for a few instants invincible. In the aftermath, the mayor and town council appropriated money for a sign at both entrances to Lone Tree, had a company from Iowa City paint the signs in bright reds, whites, blues and yellows: a baseball player with an uncanny resemblance to me, in full wind-up, the cleats of one shoe sparkling like diamonds. STATE HIGH SCHOOL CHAMPIONS, followed by the year.

I know that when I drive back to Maureen's tonight the signs will still be there, but the paint will be faded and weathered by a dozen Iowa winters, some sections of the sign will be sprung slightly, the underpinnings rotting into the earth, the signs sagging like aging skin. My moment of glory was a long time ago.

Then I'm eighteen again and Maureen is in my arms, my father, brother and sister patting me on the back, hugging me, telling me how proud they are of me. My face is streaked with sweat and dirt. There will be a photo in all the Iowa daily papers, it will even be picked up by some national newspapers, my grime-streaked, All-American face grinning uncontrollably.

"Norman Rockwell should be alive to paint you," my father says delightedly.

And I'm Joe McCoy, fugitive, sitting on the bleacher beneath a paper moon the sunflower color of a happy face. The air is soft as flower petals, the sweet perfume of the grass rises into the night air. I have seen what should have happened. My right shoulder aches as if I've had a tooth transplanted there, a new ache to Joe McCoy, fugitive; something Joe McCoy, sportswriter for the *Iowa City Press Citizen* has long ago learned to live with.

I'm somewhere in between two lifetimes.

There is a snap like a breaking twig and the lights of the stadium dim, the bulbs taking a few seconds to darken totally. I stand up. The silence is so total I can hear my own breath, hear my heart, hear my blood circulating.

I walk slowly back to Ray's house. He's lying on the porch swing, a flowered pillow under his head, lit from the back by a few tines of light escaping through the window blinds, he looks like some prairie godfather.

"So, what did you learn?" He motions to a sweating beer can on a small, white table.

"Did I derive a moral imperative? Other people's feelings are more important than my own, that's what I learned. But I should have known that since childhood." I pop the beer, take a long drink.

"Some of us are slow learners," says Ray. "I was."

"I saw one version of the past. Reminds me of all that bit about the road not taken. When I was eighteen I turned one way, and have been going that way ever since. Now I know at least partially what would have happened if I'd taken the other fork."

"Is it helpful? Are you glad you know?"

"I think I'm more confused than ever. I know I should have stayed with Maureen. I'm back here sort of trying to pick up where I left off, but I'm a fugitive tagging along with a strange girl and a baby, and Maureen's dying. What the hell am I supposed to do? Do you think you could put in a word for me?" I ask.

"The trouble is," he replies, "I'm not sure where to direct the word. A number of things have happened, but I've never been able to determine how or why. You're a newspaperman, you're supposed to use all those Ws—who, what, where, when, why, how, whatever. Well, I know what they are, but I don't know what propels them. Mystery. I've just rolled with the mystery, so has Annie, Karin, the twins, everyone who sees my ballfield. I'd be afraid to ask too many questions. I'd be afraid to know."

"But our, my, situation is different."

What can I do to defend myself? Did my temptation in the desert have something to do with my present situation? I could stare him right in the eye and say "Look! When I was eighteen, I was kidnapped by a bad fairy who made me live my life in a secondary dimension where bizarre events routinely happen to me. On rare occasions I scratch and claw my way through the thick gauze of time and space and see, for seconds, or moments, or hours, what might have been. Or, perhaps I obtain a glimpse of what is, and I am living in what might have been. One or the other is always right around the corner, across the park, at the end of an elevator ride, in the next room, or the next, or the next. Like my mysterious little friend, Pico the Rat, who knows with a certainty I can barely tolerate, that he is about to crash through the walls of dimension, that soon, soon, soon, he will wake up in Hollywood, a garrulous little street hustler no longer, but a renowned movie producer. I feel myself getting closer to my real life, whatever that may be. This is why I gravitate back toward Iowa."

I decide silence is the better part of valor.

Then, "I want to know."

"Mystery is mystery, best left alone."

"But aren't you curious why you were chosen? I want to know why someone's been messing with my life since I was a teenager."

"What would you do if you found out?"

That stumps me for a moment.

"Probably not much except I'd feel more secure."

"We're all curious about the exact day and hour of our death. If someone offered you that information would you accept it?"

"No," I answer quickly. "It would take all the mystery out of life, without mystery there's nothing to live for."

"I rest my case," says Ray.

"Still . . ."

The other afternoon I walked over to the house at the corner of Johnson and Ronalds, the house I've dreamed about. It has been restored, the beautiful verandahs, the wooden siding painted a virginal white. There are green shutters on the upstairs windows, a gala of hollyhocks rise, reflect, bump gently against the ground-floor windows. A woman standing on the porch seems to be studying her reflection in the front-room window. My breath tightens as I see the plum-colored hair spilling down her back. She wears a bulky, rose-hued sweater, faded jeans. I am so sure it is Maureen that I am about to call out, when the woman, perhaps startled by my reflection in the window glass, suddenly turns toward the door, opens it and disappears, wraith-like, into the interior.

TWENTY-FOUR

JOE McCOY

"THERE AREN'T ANY VISITING HOURS UNTIL AFTER NOON," a nurse tells us. "Are you relatives?"

"I'm her husband," I say. "My wife's dying and I'm going to see her, now."

"Oh," the nurse says, eyeing us suspiciously as we quickly leave the nursing station, searching for Maureen's room. I glance over my shoulder to see the nurse holding a phone, barking something into it. As we pass a small alcove-waiting-room furnished in blue, chrome-trimmed furniture, I spot Maureen's father slouched in a chair, staring at the floor, smoking. A three-day growth of spiky white whiskers covers his face. He stares up at me from the frigid blue chair. He does not recognize me.

"Where is Maureen's room?" I ask.

"Who are you wants to know?" he says, the Irish edge to his voice more prominent than I recalled.

"I'm the specialist your wife called," I snap.

"End of the hall, Number 411," he replies.

The door to Room 411 is closed. I am about to turn the handle when two large orderlies burst through a stairwell door and head for us. Francie, carrying Little Joe, is several steps behind me. I get the door open, try to pull Francie inside, but one them has her by the arm. We engage in a brief tug-of-war, which I win, but not before the orderly has ripped Little Joe from her grasp. I lock the door.

"I've got a gun," I shout, hoping the idea will keep them from breaking down the door.

The baby shrieks in the hall, Francie is clutching my arm and crying. There are surprised voices behind us. The room is lit by one tiny bulb, a pimple of subdued light high on the wall above the bed. Maureen lies on her back, arms at her sides, still as a corpse. There is a tube in her nose, various long, evil needles inserted in her arms. To the right of her bed there is a bank of electronic medical machinery that blinks and murmurs like a video game.

A hulking brother occupies each of the two chairs in the room. The form sitting closest to the bed I recognize as Harley. He, unfortunately, recognizes me.

Suddenly I remember Maureen, sweet and moist in my arms all those years ago. "You know what an Iowa virgin is, McCoy? A girl who can outrun her brothers."

"You!" Harley Renn spits out the word.

In the dismal light the ends of Maureen's hair still glow like campfire coals.

"Hello, Harley."

"What the fuck are you doing here, McCoy?"

"I care about Maureen . . ."

"You fucking jerk, McCoy." He stands up, towering over me. "You asshole baseball player. You . . . you . . . never cared about Maureen. You only cared about Joe McCoy, big-shot sports hero. You son of a bitch! If it wasn't for you, Maureen wouldn't be lying here dying. You broke her fucking heart, you no-good—"

"Jeez, it's the crook," says the other brother, whose name escapes me.

"Get out," I say to the brothers, as I move to the corner of the room.

"I shoulda cleaned your clock fifteen years ago, McCoy," growls Harley, advancing. "But I'm sure as fuck gonna do a good job now."

"Yeah," echoes the other brother, whose name I recall is Magnus.

"I'm armed," I say, reaching a hand inside my jacket, where I feel nothing but my heart trying to escape from my chest. "Do you want me to kill you right in front of Maureen? I will. I have nothing to lose. You've seen the TV, I'm armed and dangerous," and I push two fingers against the front pocket of my windbreaker hoping they resemble the muzzle of a gun.

The brothers stop in mid-lurch, as the possibility of injury reaches the part of their brain that processes death threats.

"Get out!" I repeat, indicating the door with both my head and my hidden hand.

Harley unleashes another rumble of curses, but he and Magnus grind slowly toward the door, where Francie, looking pale and wraith-like, presses herself against the cream-colored wall.

"We'll get the cops," snarls Harley.

"Yeah," says Magnus.

"Do whatever you have to do," I reply.

When they open the door, just enough to squeeze out, I see there is already a crowd in the hall, some of them in uniform. As soon as the door closes I lock it, for surprisingly it is equipped with a deadbolt.

I scrape one of the chairs back and forth on the floor.

"I've placed the medical monitors against the door," I yell. I'm sure that's what they expect from the notorious Kid McCoy.

"I'm going to turn this equipment off," I say to Francie. "I've never done what I should have for Maureen in life, the least I can do is see that her wishes about death are carried out."

"No!" cries Francie. There is a terrible urgency in her voice.

"Don't tell me you've gone religious on me too."

"Joe, listen to me!"

"No. I love Maureen. I'm going to do what's best for her."

I start across the room, but Francie's voice stops me cold. Or, rather, *a* voice stops me.

"I've got something to tell you." The voice is deep and sandy, reverberating.

"What?" I stare at Francie. She is sitting on a scum-green chair, head bowed, hands clasped in her lap.

"Joe, listen to me carefully." I cross to her. Her lips are not moving. I stare into her face. The voice seems to be coming from everywhere in the room.

"This is not Francie."

"Then who . . ?" I glance again at Francie, who sits silent, drawn into herself, so small and fragile looking. "I knew it. In the desert, that pink fuzz rubbing about like a solicitous cat. It wasn't my imagination."

"If that's what you want to think."

"And I suppose you touched Francie, too, in LAX?"

"If believing that will make you feel better."

"What have you done to Francie?"

"Francie is sleeping. Like a fish at the bottom of a cool stream."

Pico says I'm a stumblefuck. I guess Pico is right.

"Who have I been with these past weeks?"

"You live in a multidimensional world, a world full of delightful and bizarre mysteries of which so little is understood."

"What's going to happen?"

"There have been misunderstandings," the voice says enigmatically.

I get to hold a conversation with my voice. Ray never did that. Wait until I tell him.

"Misunderstandings about wishes and horses?" I ask.

"Among others."

"And Maureen? Is there any way to help Maureen? Take me in her place," I cry, my adrenalin level rising dramatically. "I'll die if Maureen can live . . ."

"I'm going to take your hand, and like stepping over a baseline onto a ballfield, I'm going to try to lead you across a dimension to the life you were always meant to live."

"I want to see *you*."

"Your eyes aren't conditioned . . ."

"Why have you put me through so much these past weeks?"

"Put you through? Your fondest wish has been fulfilled."

"To be on the run?"

"What else?"

"My dreams . . . the horses . . . but the baby. What about the baby?"

"The baby is your son . . ."

"I don't have . . ."

"Borrowed from the life you would have lived if you'd done what your heart told you to do."

"Then everything that's happened since we accepted the baby in the airport has not really happened. And everything that I've dreamed has been the truth?"

"More or less."

"Where is the baby? Where is . . . my son?"

"Out there," the voice says vaguely. A pinkish shadow passes briefly across the closed curtains of the hospital room. "Being cared for . . ."

"Are you an angel?"

"While Maureen is in the hospital your son is being cared for by your friend Gideon Clarke and a girl named Francie Bly, who, on the other side of that ephemeral line, have fallen in love. If events progress well, in a few months you'll be best man at their wedding."

"Gideon and Francie?"

But how did Francie get to Iowa? Oh, I don't care, it's all so . . . impossible, so extraordinary.

I look to where Francie was sitting. She is gone. This is not as much of a shock as I might have expected.

I glance at Maureen.

"Can you help Maureen?"

"Take her hand." I cross the room quickly, reach down and take Maureen's cool, dry hand in mine. "Now, take my hand."

"But I can't see . . ." I'm alone with Maureen and . . . and . . . whatever.

"Do it!"

I extend my free hand. My arm tingles and I want to close my eyes, to dream.

"Follow me! I am leading you."

"And if Maureen dies?"

"There will be silence."

My heart lurches. I try to will my energy into Maureen.

"Why put yourself at risk for Maureen?" I ask the vibrating air.

"Who loves whom and for what reason makes no more sense in my dimension."

There is a terrible commotion in the hall, someone is wailing on a bullhorn for me to give myself up. A shadow crosses the window. There is perhaps a scraping sound. Is someone rappelling about on the outer wall of the hospital?

I can't even find a pulse in Maureen's wrist.

"What happens to me if we . . . you, fail?"

"For you everything will be exactly as it was before you made your journey into the desert."

"None of the last few weeks will have happened?"

"Your life with Rosslyn will resume. You'll continue at that newspaper, exposing bait-and-switch advertisers, another colloquialism I don't fully understand."

"Is the word *hell* in your vocabulary?"

Maureen alone, dying. My heart swells with love for her, my indignation at her situation rises in my throat.

"Concentrate on Maureen."

"Might I be on my own? The most wanted man in America barricaded in a hospital room with his dead sweetheart. And if I'm taken alive, Little Joe will belong to the Courteguayan Ambassador, and there will be a trial, and . . ."

"Concentrate on Maureen . . ." the voice repeats.

"I feel like . . . sleeping."

"We are traveling . . . if all goes well, you're going to be swamped with memories. It will be like a two-way conduit. You will forget virtually everything since high school, you will remember what has really happened to you. The wishes buried deep in your heart, so deep you barely know they exist, are going to come true. You never left home, and I understand why. Iowa is the best of all the places we've been. You married Maureen, just as you've dreamed so often, and you'll remember every sweet moment and every sad moment with her. Your mouth will water as you recall the sweet tastes and scents of her, as your memories rise up like drawing sparkling water from a deep well."

"How can you know? If I try very hard I can taste Maureen on my lips, the salty sweetness, the musky smell of her skin . . ."

"I know. You work as a sportswriter for the *Iowa City Press Citizen*, have done ever since you graduated from the University of Iowa. Remember the big, old house at the corner of Johnson and Ronalds that was abandoned for so many years? Well, it's yours and Maureen's now. Its turrets and three-sided verandah are all restored. You live on the top floors, rent the basement. Two Japanese students with short-wave radios are living down there this year. You and Maureen joke that they belong to something called the Japanese Victory Society, that they believe the Japanese are still going to win the Second World War."

I can barely distinguish whether the voice is *a voice*, or whether it is my own thoughts.

"I never left Iowa?"

"Not even for college. You never played professional baseball. You realized early on that you didn't have the stamina, the mental toughness, the dedication necessary to get by on your rather limited talent. You play two evenings a week in a slo-pitch softball league. Maureen and Little Joe come out to watch every game."

I try to assimilate what I'm being told. I can see a scene from thirteen years ago as clearly as if it is taking place right now: Maureen cuddled in my arms in my father's old car, "With you, baby, things are twice as good but only half as bad."

"If Maureen lives . . ?"

"You'll simply be a concerned husband sitting at the bedside of his critically ill wife. Incidentally—as you stayed in Iowa, you and your sister have become very close. She's a registered nurse, her life partner is an endocrinologist. They've adopted a baby girl."

"Thank you. Whatever happens I'll know everything possible has been done for Maureen."

I sound so formal. How does one speak to a concept?

I remove my hand from Maureen's and gently place it on her chest; the tingling sensation up my arms intensifies.

"Count off a minute," the voice commands. "Keep your hand on Maureen's heart. This could take a very long time."

The beneficent stardust that speaks to me seems to be settling into the bed sheets, into Maureen's hospital gown.

I am being kissed in the sweetest, most romantic, most loving way, though no one is standing next to me. I keep my eyes tightly closed. "One, one-thousand," I say, when the lingering kiss ends. "Two, one-thousand . . ."

Until I bought the plane ticket and decided to accompany Francie and the baby to Boston I had seldom been able to walk away from people's expectations. If I had had the maturity and the fortitude to turn my back completely on baseball, I might have been a pretty fair journalist, not the kind I ended up as. That character, that caricature in shades, a beeper chirping at his waist, was a person I didn't like very much, a person who spent his time turning over rocks and writing about what came slithering out, frightened by the light.

If I had concentrated on being a journalist I might have been one I could be proud of, not necessarily a successful one, a likeable sportswriter for a laid-back Midwestern daily, who took my wife and baby along on a summer evening when I drove a few miles into the country to cover a high-school baseball game; the kind of journalist who, though never having more than a local following, would not feel like an impostor.

On the other hand, what if I had had the determination to be a big-league baseball pitcher? As a kid I used to fantasize about the possibility. I would be in a science class, or sitting at the kitchen table eating supper, but actually I'd be on the mound, sneaking a strike on the outside corner past Frank Robinson, or Brooks Robinson, Mickey Mantle or Joe Morgan. As I poured gravy on my potatoes or watched my teacher move the planets on his orrery, Pete Rose was bouncing helplessly into a game-ending or World Series-ending double play.

But I didn't devote myself to either life. The terrible dichotomy between my interests made me fail at everything, business and personal.

If I could live to watch Little Joe grow up, if he were really my son, that's what I'd tell him. That's what I've learned in thirty-one years of trial and error. Do what you have to do.

There is a whirring sound, as if they are drilling the door hinges.

"Leave us absolutely alone or I'll turn off the life-support system," I call. I may as well be the heartless villain they expect me to be.

"We're monitoring the machinery. You touch the equipment, we attack," the voice on the bullhorn bellows from the corridor. I'm almost certain they are bluffing. My only concern is to keep them at bay for as long as necessary.

I peek across at the TV on the wall, oh, but the sound barely audible. A media circus is how the scene is described. The local stations, which usually go off the air at midnight, a color guard marching to the national anthem into the oblivion of a TV snowstorm, offer continuous coverage, their cameras, at various angles on the grounds and in helicopters hovering sometimes as far as a mile away, zero in on the window. I occasionally see my own shadow behind the half-closed blinds, as spotlights like shells exploding, light the night.

I glance at the window and see the upside-down face of a gray-capped SWAT team member. I reach inside my jacket in the most threatening possible way. The SWAT person screams something, tries frantically to pull himself out of my view; he looks like a turkey curling its neck upward while being carried by the feet. Unfortunately for the SWAT person, whoever is manning the rope is having some difficulty. He hangs there helpless for perhaps twenty seconds. I could have killed him several times. I suspect he is seriously considering a desk job.

Negotiation takes place by shouting back and forth through the door. I refuse to leave Maureen to answer the phone, which rings like a car alarm. They offer me drugs, cigarettes, food, liquor. I kill an hour by ordering a chocolate malt. They dispatch a police cruiser to some all-night greasy spoon. The malt that arrives has been made with sand-like soft ice cream from a machine.

The nurse who brings the milkshake wears a name tag, Corazon. Besides the milkshake she carries a small brown tray with pills and syringes on it, medication for Maureen. She is very slim with short black hair. I do not have to search her, a weapon would stand out like a T-bone steak in a jockey's stomach. I send the shake back, insist that I will only indulge in a malt from Pearson's Drug Store. They point out that Pearson's is closed.

"Get them to open up."

I picture them waking the owner of Pearson's, who phones Doreen or one of the other counter staff, offering double overtime to drive in to the store and prepare a chocolate malt for the waiting SWAT team member.

When the Pearson's malt arrives, I make Corazon take a healthy drink. We wait. When she appears normal after fifteen minutes I drink off the rest of the shake, discovering in the process that I was murderously hungry. I let the nurse examine the equipment, take Maureen's pulse, adjust the IV lines, but I refuse to let her administer any medication.

"You're not a nurse," I finally say to the young woman.

She gives me a level black stare for several seconds, her brain calculating odds.

"No. What gave me away?"

"A real nurse would have been scared of me. You were wary, but never scared. What were you supposed to do?"

I eye her closely considering whether, under the short white skirt, she might be clasping a gun between her thighs. No way, I decide.

"I'm a martial arts expert. If you'd turned off any of the life-support equipment I was to take you out. The hypos are tranquillizers, we thought I might be able to pitch them at you like darts."

"I assure you I'll never do anything to harm Ms. Renn. The threats are simply to keep everyone away from this room. I'm not crazy. There is a logical reason for everything I'm doing."

"Like keeping your hand on her heart?"

"Just give me a little time."

The nurse/cop seems mildly sympathetic. After she retreats, the hallway remains remarkably quiet. Perhaps she put in a good word for me.

For a while the TV was full of stories about Francie. Cameras followed her, circled by various law-enforcement types, as she made her way down the steps of the hospital. Officials let it be known that Francie Bly was in custody, that she appeared to have no memory of what had transpired in the past few weeks. In one sequence I'm sure I saw Gideon Clarke loping along just a few feet away from the officers surrounding her, his long, white aura glowing religiously in the bright lights.

Television coverage during the wee hours became quite boring, and to spice things up they ran interviews completed or attempted the previous evening. There was a shot of the house Rosslyn and I shared in Yorba Linda, camera zeroing in on the front door, a Mike Wallace-type, in hat and trench coat knocking, being told that Ms. Quinn is in seclusion and has no further interest in the activities of Kid McCoy.

Then the scene cut live to the Los Angeles Police Station where Nathan Wiser, cigar protruding from his mouth like a piece of broom handle, is being interviewed about my current predicament. If Nathan Wiser is not dead, does that mean time is already beginning to alter, that the cosmos are beginning the necessary repairs?

And here is an Entertainment Minute, a blonde with too many teeth excitedly announces that movie producer Giancarlo Piccolino has acquired the rights to the Kid McCoy saga. The camera cuts to Pico the Rat, in an expensive black suit, a gray ascot muffling his protruding Adam's apple. He is sitting on a director's chair, a tall, beautiful clipboard-clutching assistant beside him. "High concept," he is saying. "We are thinking John Travolta as McCoy, Meryl Streep as Miss Bly. Probably we'll make the Bly character foreign, exotic, Meryl's best when she's doing an accent . . ." The screen goes blank.

Minutes pass. Hours? Yes, hours. I sit in that gritty part of the morning when there is just enough light to make buildings and objects distinguishable, gray and depressing. The room is cold. The world is cold. Have I dozed? I hold Maureen's hand. My other hand is on her heart.

And then it is like . . . like the end of the world. A silence like predawn in a forest, when everything is totally hushed, before the first explosions of bird song announces a new day.

And a new day *is* about to break.

Looking down across the long, sloping lawn toward the Iowa River, which runs pale and calm in the dew-laden morning, I observe the long rows of police vehicles that have crowded the hospital's circular driveway. One by one, the local police, highway patrol, the neutral-colored vehicles that belong to various nameless government agencies, slide away. The swivelling blue-and-red lights of the vehicles are turned off, the portable flashers tucked away like guns under a pillow. The cars pull off into the bluey morning, tires seemingly making no sound on the pavement.

A SWAT team member who has been on the roof above me rappels down the face of the hospital, then pulls his tangle of rope and iron after him. Inside of ten minutes everything is gone. Even a stubby little cannon that had been trained on my window has been loaded into the back of a truck and blanketed with camouflage-colored canvas.

On the bed Maureen sleeps, her breathing even. The life-support equipment purrs quietly as a sleeping cat.

I remain beside the bed holding Maureen's hand, which is large, heavy-boned. Her fingers are larger than mine. I let my fingers creep up her wrist. I try to find my own pulse in the first finger of my right hand. I can't feel it. I press the finger to my teeth, my lips, the palm of my hand, my own wrist. Nothing. With my middle finger I grope for Maureen's pulse. I find it eventually; it is fluttery, but I imagine it to be stronger. My shoulder aches from keeping one hand on Maureen's heart all these hours.

I lean over and kiss Maureen's cheek; the scent of her is almost as I remember it, that erotic, earthy, sexual smell that was hers alone. An odor that cannot be destroyed by antiseptic or the imminent presence of death, an odor that complements my own, that makes my mouth water.

Maureen's body convulses slightly; she frowns in her sleep. She attempts to bend her right arm, lifting the tubes and wires leading to her arm from the machines. I stare at the machines, hoping for some message. They hum quietly. Has that red light been flashing all along? Maureen twitches again. What if she *is* dying?

I place my cheek against hers, feel her breath against my face, shallow and cool. I think with great fondness of whatever it is that has led us through the night, I smile when I think of this universal force misunderstanding, "if wishes were horses."

I turn back toward Maureen. Is her color better or is it just that the streaky silver light of dawn makes her seem less pale?

My head aches, as if something is trying to beat its way in, or out.

"Excuse me," I say, addressing the invisible source. I wonder if whoever is in the hall has microphones pressed against the door. "If you can hear me, if everything is going well, I wonder if you could do one thing for me? Kind of a sign. Not a neon sign, a signal. I'm sorry. I don't want you to misunderstand. But, the horses, all the horses. I wonder if you could let them go? If this works out I won't be needing them anymore . . ."

Maureen adjusts the position of her head slightly.

"Well, thank you, I . . ."

How stupid of me, I think.

I stare down across the expansive, silver-brushed lawn toward the river, the park, the abandoned carnival rides, the empty zoo.

I remember our wedding, Maureen's and mine. The stifling heat, the yellow-waxed floor of the Johnson County Clerk's office in the old stone court house across from the new post office in downtown Iowa City.

Maureen, uncharacteristically shy in a green skirt and jacket, me in a brown suit and tie, my new shoes squeaking.

Suddenly, from both sides of the hospital appear, some seemingly emerging from the building itself—horses! Dozens and dozens of horses: a palomino colt dancing sideways, tail arched like a question mark, a Clydesdale, a Percheron, Thoroughbreds, pinto ponies, wild-eyed, snorting.

There is a pony no bigger than a husky dog, a snow-white stallion, his movements graceful as a swan's, bays and chestnuts, blacks and grays, sorrels and dapples and silvers. They frolic across the lawn, their hoof-prints dark coins on the moist grass. The earth seems to tremble under the thudding hooves.

I unlock the window and push it up, just as the horses cross the now-deserted driveway and head down the hill toward City Park. As I open the window the edge of the sky turns from silver to what my father calls sky-blue-pink.

Somewhere a bird flutters out of foliage, disturbed by the riot of hoof-beats. Far down, near the foot of the hill the carousel begins to turn. The tinny music in the breathless dawn is one of the sweetest sounds I have ever heard. In the parking lot, blooming like a tropical flower, is my red Lincoln.

My body is stuffed to overflowing with memories of the life I was sup-posed to live. My remembered past is all with me, like boxes stored for years in a basement, out of sight. What I find, that life I am going to catch up to, traveling down years in the blink of an eye, is mercifully like blankets, not explosives. Other memories, ones of the life I am choosing to abandon, fly out of me like music and are gone. If I could consult the baseball record books, I'm sure I'd find that a lot of hitters who fattened their averages on the offerings of a mediocre relief pitcher named Joseph Armbruster "Kid" McCoy have had their batting averages lowered a point or two.

Since college, my only connection with baseball is a slo-pitch softball league. I play for the Noozmen, most of whom work for the *Iowa City Press Citizen*. Maureen and Charlotte used to come out to watch me play, before we . . . lost Charlotte.

The sound of the carousel seems to be reaching Maureen. She stirs. I am so full of bittersweet memories. We did lose our baby girl. We have Joe Jr.

I take her hand in mine again. The hospital tag on her wrist reads Maureen McCoy. The door is no longer barricaded. Was it ever?

Yes. The lights on the life-support equipment are almost all green. I have to go home and change my clothes. Gideon and Francie have been sitting Little Joe while I've been living at the hospital. Whoa! Is that right? Yes.

The hoofbeats are fading away. The door is opening. Maureen's eyelids flutter.